Bury Me A G 4

Tranay Adams

**Lock Down Publications
Presents
Bury Me A G 4
A Novel by Tranay Adams**

Tranay Adams

Lock Down Publications

P.O. Box 870494

Mesquite, Tx 75149

Copyright 2015 by Tranay Adams Bury Me A G 4

First Edition September 2015
Printed in the United States of America

This is a work of fiction. Names, characters, places, and incidents either are products of the author's imagination or are used fictitiously. Any similarity to actual events or locales or persons, living or dead, is entirely coincidental.

Lock Down Publications
Email: tranayadams@gmail.com
Facebook: Tranay Adams
Like our page on Facebook: Lock Down Publications
@www.facebook.com/lockdownpublications.ldp
Cover design and layout by: Dynasty's Cover Me
Book interior design by: Shawn Walker

ACKNOWLEDGEMENTS

Jasmine Devonish, Randy Coxton, Dorothea Creamer, Kim Leblanc, Tamara Greene, Roneisha Cooper, Lashawn Green, Monique Williams, Christine Ms. Gemini, Sharon Bell, Jane Pennella, Viola King, Eliza Tellis, Standifur aka Fee, Michelle Harvey, Joan Brooks, Milly Ann, Jeannette Frazier, Delores Miles, Denise Moore, Erica Jackson, Quanisha Goss, Tracy Spicer, Genova Rhodes, Tanya Gary, Judy Richburg, Adaryl Fisher, Alesha Kream, Nikki Hamilton, Larry L-Boogie Deadmon, Melissa Nicholson, Cyndy Twin, JS Queen, Diane Wilson, LaTasha Williams, Pamela Johnston Ward, Stephanie McL The Beast Reader, Michelle Chatman, Audreina.

Tranay Adams

Prologue
2015

Tiaz was bussed from the courthouse to the County jail. After going through all of the bullshit they put a person through when he first came through that shithole, he made his way to the telephone, slapping hands with the cats he knew and mad dogging others. He was surprised at how his name was ringing off behind the walls. Dudes were talking about how he was putting it down and giving it up in the streets. Although he got some love, he knew he'd also feel the hate. The two coincided with one another. It wouldn't be long before he had to set a mothafucka straight so they'd know that he wasn't one for the bullshit.

Tiaz pushed the thought of having to check a nigga to the back of his mental. Right now, he was focused on getting in touch with someone on the outside so they could get his money and hire him a decent lawyer.

Tiaz stepped to the payphone and reached for the receiver. Before his hand could grasp it, a bony one grabbed it. His eyes followed the bony hand, up its arm and over to the face of the body it belonged to. It was in the possession of a dark-skinned man with nappy hair and some serious acne. His face looked like plastic bubble wrap and his eyes were as yellow as lemons. His uniform was two sizes too small so his limbs looked like tree branches coming out of his sleeves and pants. He sized the thug up, studying him as if he was the tallest stack of shit he'd ever laid eyes on.

"My man, now I know you aren't tryna use my phone without asking?" Dark-skinned asked.

"Your phone?" Tiaz frowned. "I don't see your name on the mothafucka."

"The hell you don't." Dark-skinned pointed to the name on the phone.

"Your name is Pacific Bell?" He raised an eyebrow.

"Ya damn skippy, now pay up." Dark-skinned rubbed his thumb and index finger together. "What chu got, money? Commissary?"

"*How about an ass whopping?*" *Tiaz punched him in the mouth with all of his might. The force behind the punch was so great that it caused him to bump the back of his head on the wall and slide down to the floor. The dark-skinned man's bottom jaw split straight down the middle and his grill quickly filled with blood as he tried to push the separated halves back together. The pain was so intense that it brought tears to his eyes. Tiaz went to work on him, kicking and stomping him as he held his arms up trying to shield his face.*

Tiaz was so occupied with giving the man the business that he neglected to watch his back. A look of surprise came over him when he felt sharp metal puncturing his back and ribcage. He swung around with his full strength, bringing his balled fist across the jaw of a stockier, muscular cat. The blow caught the man off guard and caused him to stagger to the side, but he held tight to his shank. He righted himself before he could fall and wiped his bleeding mouth with the back of his hand.

His eyes took on a frightening glint and a satanic grin emerged on his face. The sight of blood seemed to entice him. He charged at Tiaz. The thug sidestepped him, grabbed the back on his neck and gripped his wrist. He twisted his wrist so hard and fast that a sharp pain shot through it. It was the equivalent of piercing the skin with a hot needle and it made the man drop his shank. The man's mind was quickly taken off of his wrist when his face smashed into the wall and his forehead split open like a coconut. The man fell to the floor in a heap, groaning in pain. He slowly made to get up when the cats Tiaz knew from the hood finally rushed in and mopped him and the dark-skinned man up. All he could do was watch before collapsing to the floor from blood loss. An alarm blared inside of his ears. The last thing he saw were the C.O.s suited and booted in riot gear rushing in to restore order.

A couple days later

Tiaz' eyelids fluttered open. His vision was blurry, but it came back into focus after a while. He sat up in bed and looked around. The room he was inside was dimly lit. There were hospital beds lined up on both sides of him. Some of them were occupied by inmates. A nurse was checking one of the inmates' vitals. He also saw a doctor standing in an open door jotting something down on a clipboard. That's when it dawned on him that he was in the infirmary. He looked down at his torso and saw that it was wrapped in a bandage.

Tiaz brought both his hands down his face and blew hard. He realized that he passed out from loss of blood, but he didn't know how long he had been out. The nurse walked inside of the room that the doctor was in. As soon as she went through the door, two inmates arose from their beds, slammed the door closed behind her and pushed a file cabinet down in front of it. A C.O. came running towards the two inmates. He radioed for help through his walkie-talkie and suddenly an inmate pulled a pillowcase over his head tightly and rammed his head into the wall until blood smeared the inside of it and he passed out. As soon as the C.O. hit the floor, the inmate along with a few others, barricaded the rest of the entrances into the infirmary.

They then moved in on Tiaz. The dim light in the room bounced off the metal of their shanks and caused them to glint.

Danger! Danger! Danger! The alarm inside of Tiaz' head blared like the dismissal bell for after school detention.

"Arrr!" He grabbed his side, his moving too fast caused pain to shoot through his ribcage like bolts of lightning. He shuddered, feeling groggy and weakened from his wounds, but forced his eyelids back open. These niggaz wanted blood, his blood. And he wasn't giving up a drop of it without a fight.

Swiftly, he pulled the IV from his arm and hopped out of bed. He wrapped his left hand up in a sheet and unscrewed the top half of the IV pole beside his bed. He held tightly to the lower half of the IV pole, planning to use it as a spear. He then backed himself up against the wall. His head was on a swivel as he surveyed his surroundings, searching for the first man looking to claim his life.

The shank wielding inmates formed a circle around him. He looked around at all of their ice grills wondering why they hadn't attacked. That's when the circle parted and a man came waltzing through. His face was partially hidden by the darkness of the room, so he had to peer closely to I.D. him. When recognition ripped through his brain, he had to blink a few times to make sure who he was seeing was actually standing before him.

"Sa...Sa..." Tiaz stammered.

"Savon, alive and in the mothafucking flesh," the man spoke.

Tiaz was speechless, he couldn't believe it. Chevy's brother was standing right before his eyes.

"You done my niggaz up real nasty, but they were throwaways. I got plenty more hittas where they came from." He swept a hand around to all of the men surrounding them. "Are you ready to die, nigga?" He pulled a sharp metal shank from the small of his back. It was about seven inches in length and had fabric wrapped around its lower half for grip. Tiaz readied himself for the fight for his life once he saw the weapon come into play. "You set me up, pussy. Left me to rot in this shithole, put cho mothafucking hands on my sister, got my nephew out here pushing poison in the streets! Ah, nigga, you gots ta go off of GP! What chu did was a violation punishable by death! And yo' sentencing has come, bitch-nigga!"

"You ain't saying shit, let's dance!" Tiaz shot back with a hard face. His heart was beating fast, but it didn't pump Kool-Aid, it pumped Gangsta Juice.

A flicker of movement at his left brought his eyes around. One of the inmates was tossing him a metal shank identical to Savon's. He threw the IV pole down and pulled the blade down from the air. As the alarm blared in their ears and the inmates cheered them on, the two men circled one another, looking for flaws in the other's defense. The thug's eyes were trained on his opposition's left side. He knew vital organs were on this side and attacking the right spot could kill a man.

With movements that looked like blurs, Savon thrust his hand forth trying to stab him in the heart. Tiaz knocked his hand aside with the hand that was wrapped in the sheet and stabbed him in the cheek, drawing a howl of pain out of him. Savon backed up and touched his cheek, fingertips coming away with blood. He avoided his rival's next few attempts at assaulting him, moving *with the agility and grace of a ballroom dancer. He was good on his feet until a slip-up cost him a bleeding shoulder.*

The fight went on to the point where both men were bleeding something awful. Their faces were coated in sweat and their hearts were slamming up against the interior of their chests. Their uniforms looked like they had been hit with splashes of red wine. Droplets of blood and sweat covered the floor of the infirmary. The doors of the entrances to the infirmary rattled as the riot squad of the County jail facility tried to force their way in.

One of the men moved in for the kill, thrusting his shank forward. The other man smacked his hand away with such a force that it sent his shank flying across the room. He then delivered an upper cut that lifted him off his feet and dropped him on his back. The man bumped his head and was nearly knocked unconscious. He lay on his back looking through narrowed slits and groaning in pain. The other man straddled him and gripped his throat, squeezing it and lessening the oxygen flowing into his lungs. The man beneath him squirmed and punched at his torso, but his opponent clenched his jaws and took the blows without complaint. He then slammed his seven inch metal blade into the man's armpit down to its handle. The blade pierced the man's heart, killing him instantly.

His eyes bugged and his mouth dropped open. He took his last breath and his arms dropped limply beside him. At that moment the infirmary went deathly quiet as the inmates stared at the man that was victorious. All that could be heard was the blaring alarm and the rattling of the entrance doors. The victorious man lay over his dead opponent, breathing heavily and bleeding from everywhere. He felt relieved having been the one that came out on top. No one could tell him that he wasn't completely justified. He did what he had to do to survive, so whatever punishment came for his actions, he was willing to face. It was survival of the fittest.

Boom! Boom! Boom!

The doors came flying open and the riot squad came pouring inside of the infirmary.

Years later

The C.O. opened the cell's door and he came waltzing out. He moved down the hallway toward his death as confidently as he could with his wrists and ankles in shackles. A host of correctional officers and a priest crowded around him walking with him as he moved down the mustard yellow corridor.

"Dead man walking! Dead man walking!"

He flinched hearing the officer's voice sting his eardrums. He glanced over his shoulder with a scowl and twisted lips.

"Damn, homie, you all in my ear and shit," he complained, heatedly.

Continuing on his way, he threw his head back at the other inmates on Death Row like 'What's up?' Never breaking his stride. His face was one chiseled out of stone, void of expression and emotion. It was like he was taking an evening stroll through his neighborhood, taking in the sunshine and mingling with the people of his community.

"Alright now, hold yo' head, bro!" A prisoner called out from his left.

"No doubt!" he responded.

"That's the realest nigga to have ever walked the earth right there!" Another prisoner called out from his right.

"Balls of steel." A third prisoner called out.

He locked eyes with him and said, "You mothafucking right."

He knew the life he led would lead to either death or the penitentiary and it led to both. Cold world. But what the fuck could the nigga do? The streets were all that he knew. He played the hand he was dealt and came up short. He wasn't about to bawl and cry about the shit though. He had a reputation to keep. He knew the streets would keep his legacy alive. Once he finally closed his eyes his name would be mentioned with some of the most gangster niggaz in history, he was sure of it. No one could tell him otherwise.

He was led to the room where his life was to end. He stared at the dark green leather cushioned gurney with all of the straps on it as one of the correctional officer's unlocked the shackles around his wrists, waist, and ankles. After the C.O. removed the *chains and shackles, he passed them off to the other officer who hoisted them over his shoulder. The officer then told the prisoner to lay down on the gurney. He obliged.*

His head snapped to all of the areas of his body that the correctional officers strapped down. They made sure that the thick leather brown belts were pulled good and tight to ensure that their prisoner wouldn't escape. Once the officers finished strapping him down to the gurney, they stepped back to allow the doctor through. He was a tall, white man with thinning hair. He wore glasses and a lab coat. He tied a tourniquet around the thug's arm, cleaned it with a swab moistened in alcohol and tapped it until a ripe, juicy vein was visible. Once he did this, he inserted the IV then removed the length of rubber. He repeated this same routine with the other arm, as well. He then opened his patient's shirt and attached the patches that would monitor his heart. This was done so that the time of his death could be recorded and confirmed.

When the doctor turned around walking off and pushing his specs back upon his face, he noticed a machine that housed three large syringes containing three concoctions. The first one was sodium thiopental, an anesthetic agent that would be used to render him unconscious. The second one was pancuronium bromide, a non-depolarizing muscle relaxant that would cause sustained paralysis to the skeletal striated muscles. The last one was called potassium chloride which would stop his heart, thus causing death by cardiac arrest.

Thump! Thump! Thump! Thump!

His heart was beating fast now because he knew that death was looming around him like a foul stench. But he wasn't afraid of dying. Hell mothafucking nah, he embraced it, welcomed it even. The next thing he knew the curtains were pulled open from over the large windows surrounding the diagnostics room, leaving a host of people looking in on him. They sort of resembled the audience at a talk show like Jerry Springer or Wendy Williams.

One face stood out among them all though. He'd come to love it like he loved breathing. She was beautiful, but at that time her appearance was less than flattering. Chevy's eyes were red webbed and pink. Her cheeks were slickened wet, making her face shiny. She swallowed the lump of hurt that had formed in her throat, her nostrils expanding and shrinking as she breathed angrily. He didn't know if she was mad at him for what had happened or not. One thing for sure was that he didn't care. Nah, he had other matters that had his attention, like all of the hoes he was going to get at once he got to heaven or wherever he was going.

He looked from her and took in all of the faces behind the thick glass. He figured that this was what an animal caged up at the zoo must have felt like. Most of the people in the audience wore solemn expressions. Some looked like they felt sorry for him, while others were crying. Not crying because they felt for him, but because they were happy that justice was being served for the murder of their loved ones. He cracked a wicked smile at them and they went ham, jumping to their feet and hurling chairs which deflected off of the glass. They talked shit and some of them even tried to rush out of the room to get to him. He chuckled and threw up his hood the best way he could with his arms being in restraints. It was his last fuck you to them.

After a couple of armed guards ushered the unruly guests out, kicking and screaming, the priest approached the prisoner with an opened Bible. He began reading off a passage when he shouted at him.

"Father, I don't wanna hear that shit, God gave up on niggaz like me a long time ago!"

The priest closed the Holy Book and cleared his throat with a fist to his mouth. "Very well, may the Lord bless your soul, my son."

"Yeah, whatever, nigga." His head whipped around to the warden, looking him up and down like 'Fuck you doing here?'
"Can I help you?"

"Any last words, Savon?" he asked. The room had a PA system, so everyone outside of the glass could hear what he had to say.

"Once y'all done killing me, and it's time to lay me to rest, y'all just make sure they bury me a G!" He said aloud, taking in all of the faces of the people in the audience, making sure he had

everyone's attention. "You hear me? Bury me a G, bury me a mothafucking G!"

With Savon's last words having been said, the doctor went on to start the procedure that would eventually relieve him of his life. One by one, the large syringes containing the concoctions emptied. The last one, potassium chloride, was the last of the syringes to be released into Savon's veins, its concoction coursing throughout his blood stream.

By this time, Savon's raging heart had begun beating slower and slower. His eyelids narrowed into slits and he looked around at all of the faces of the audience. The one that stood out to him was the one that belonged to his sister, Chevy. She stared right at him with tears sliding down her cheeks. Savon read her lips as she said 'I love you' and he mouthed it back. Right after he laid his head back, his eyelids shut and he expelled his last breath. At that moment, the curtains swept around the windows that allowed the audience to see inside of the diagnostics room.

Chevy had met who she thought was the love of her life, Tiaz, through a website called, Penpals.com. Tiaz was a handsome, smooth talking, charming thug that romanced his way into Chevy's heart and swept her off her feet. She agreed to let him parole to her house. At first things were rocky between Tiaz and her son, Te'Qui, but they eventually got tight. It wasn't until Chevy found out her boo was fucking her best friend, Kantrell, that things fell apart. On top of that, Tiaz had given Te'Qui and his little homeboy, Baby Wicked, crack to sell. Baby Wicked ended up getting smoked by the niggaz whose corner he was slinging on. When Chevy confronted Tiaz about him given her son and his friend drugs, the mothafucka flipped out. He was about to harm Chevy, but Te'Qui shot at his ass, backing him down.

Tiaz had a beef with some of the most feared niggaz to have ever laid their claim to the streets. He was on their heads because they'd killed his road dawg, Threat, over a robbery they'd commited against one of their own. He laid a couple of them down, but there were two of them left that had yet to pay him in blood. He ran one of them down into a store. The nigga thought he was in a safe zone because he was surrounded by patrons and the police had just arrived on the scene. Little did he know, Tiaz was a reckless and ruthless type of nigga that didn't give a mad ass fuck. Needless to say, Tiaz gunned the man down and earned himself a trip to the county jail where he'd await trial for murder. In the county he bumped heads with Savon whom he'd planted drugs and a gun on. At that time Savon was in the county fighting the drug charges and the murders on the gun.

Savon and Tiaz had a bloody shank fight that resulted in Tiaz' tragic death. This was what led to Savon being sentenced to death by lethal injection.

Having seen her brother expire, Chevy broke down sobbing and shaking. Hearing someone applaud higher in the stands, she whipped around with a creased forehead, sniffling. She saw a woman with her hair braided back in thick cornrows clapping her hands loud as fuck, making a mockery of her brother's death.

"Good! I'm glad that mothafucka is dead! May he rest in shit! I'ma make sho' my black ass is there to piss on his grave!" *the woman hollered out, moving her neck like hood rats do when they're on one.*

Instantly, Chevy's eyebrows arched and she squared her jaws, top lip trembling. She jetted up the steps, leaping them two and three at a time. Her fists were clenched tight at her sides and she was ready to whop off in the bitch's ass that was popping that shit.

"Bitch, you got me fucked up! You gon' show up here today and disrespect me and my brother? Oh, that's yo' mothafucking ass hoe!"

"I knew yo' ass was gon' want some! Come on, trick!" *the woman, Scrappy, threw up her fists and prepared to throw hands with a heated Chevy. Chevy reached Scrappy throwing Haymakers at her head. Scrappy ducked the wild swings. She came back up; slamming her fists into either side of her opponent's ribcage and then uppercutting her. Chevy's chin went upward as she fell backwards, tumbling down the steps and sliding down them on her stomach. She looked up at Scrappy wincing and aching. Scrappy broke loose from the people that*

were trying to hold her back from whipping off in Chevy's ass some more. As soon as she did, she charged down the steps in long strides toward Chevy. Chevy shook off her dizzy spell and got to her feet. Once Scrappy reached her, she swung at her head but she ducked before her fist could connect. Chevy came back up and punched homegirl in the face, and followed that up with a left hand punch. As Scrappy was blinking her eyelids dizzily, Chevy kicked her in the stomach and tackled her to the steps, causing her to howl out in pain.

Chevy straddled her and started raining blow after blow down on her face. Scrappy grabbed her by both of her wrists and wrapped her legs around her neck, forcing her to the steps. She then grabbed the wrist of her right arm and twisted it as she choked her out, locking her legs around her neck. Chevy's eyes filled with tears and she gagged violently. Scrappy looked down at her, eyebrows arched and jaws clenched.

"You stupid, high yellow bitch, I'ma send yo' ass to join yo' punk-ass brotha!" Scrappy frowned and clenched her jaws harder, causing the veins on her forehead and temples to pulsate. "Ahhhhhh, get off me! Get the fuck off of me!" Scrappy hollered out over and over again, as she and Chevy were pulled apart by correctional officers, kicking and swinging at one another.

"You fucking skeeza!" Chevy kicked Scrappy square in the face, launching her head backwards. "I'ma find you and fuck yo' ass up, bitch! Mark my goddamn words!" Chevy struggled to break loose from the piles of arms that she was wrapped up in.

"Oh, this ain't over! This shit far from over, hoe!" Scrappy swore as blood oozed out of her nostrils and over her lips. She was trying to pull free from the piles of arms wrapped around her too, but they were too strong for her. "Yo' ass is dead! You hear me? Dead, bitch!"

Scrappy sat low behind the wheel of her car, peering up at the rearview mirror as she dabbed her bloody nose with balled up Kleenex tissues. Looking at her reflection, she could already see that she was swelling from her fight with Chevy, and vowed to make her ass pay for her injuries.

That's okay, bitch! You gon' get cho' issue, I ain't letting shit slide. I put that shit on my nigga. You and that bitch-ass nigga Faison gon' get y'alls. That's on my daddy, rest in peace.

Scrappy wiped away the little blood she saw left, which was peeking out of her left nostril and then snorted back. Afterwards, she balled up the tissues and threw them out of the window. As she rolled the window up, she clocked Chevy walking through the parking lot, touching her lip to see if it was bleeding and holding an ice pack to her head. She was frowned up and talking shit about how she was going to whip off in Scrappy's ass should she ever run into her again.

Scrappy slumped down low in the driver's seat when she saw Chevy. She watched her like a lioness watched her prey, a sneaky smile spreading across her lips. The police had held her and Chevy at the prison for a while after their brawl, and agreed to let them go home once they'd calm down. They reasoned that the women were emotional and tensions were high during Savon's execution since they'd both lost loved ones and they didn't want to lock them up. The law allowed Scrappy to leave first. They then waited thirty minutes before letting Chevy make her departure. Scrappy knew she was supposed to take her fiesty ass home, but she refused to slide to the house without getting some get-back. Fuck that! That bitch Chevy earned what was coming to her.

Scrappy watched as Chevy hopped into her whip and pulled out of her parking space. She waited until Chevy was out of the parking lot before cranking up her ride and pulling off behind her. Once she was out on the street, she followed behind her from what she deemed was a safe distance. Without Chevy having noticed her, Scrappy had followed her all of the way to her house. Once she was there, she parked where she wouldn't be seen. Still slumped behind the wheel of her whip, Scrappy observed Chevy pull into her driveway and hop out of her vehicle. She then saw Faison pull into the driveway in a Benz truck and hop out. As soon as he did, Chevy rushed into his arms and broke down, sobbing loud and hard. He held her firmly and kissed her on top of her head, rubbing her back soothingly. Having seen enough, Scrappy pulled out from where she'd *parked and busted a U-turn in the street. Driving off, she stared back and forth between the windshield and the rearview mirror, watching Chevy and Faison grow smaller and smaller, until they disappeared before her eyes.*

Scrappy picked up her cell phone and looked at the time. It was two o'clock.

"It's almost time for my babies to get outta school," Scrappy said to no one in particular, sitting her cellular on the passenger seat and then turning on the radio. Surprisingly, P-Diddy's Missing You was playing. Instantly, her eyes watered and tears flooded her cheeks, thinking about the loved one she'd lost to violence. She found herself wiping her dripping eyes with her fingers and thumb, as she continued to drive. She was going to make sure Chevy felt all of the pain that she felt inside after the tragic death of her nigga. If she thought losing her brother hurt, she hadn't felt anything yet.

Tranay Adams

CHAPTER ONE
Ten Years later

T.J. walked out of the halfway house dressed in a white T-shirt, tan Dickies and black Nike Cortez. A pair of black sunglasses called Locs sat at the top of his head. T.J. was a fat nigga that stood a solid five-foot-nine. He sported a fade that spun with waves and had bushy chin hairs you could braid into a ponytail.

T.J. made his way across the grounds of the halfway house, crossing the shade of a tree. As soon as he did, his eyelids narrowed into slits having met the beaming rays of the sun. He pulled the sunglasses over his eyes to shield them from the rays of sunlight and continued to G-walk toward the Honda Civic idling at the curb.

T.J opened the front passenger door and jumped into the seat, slamming the door shut behind him. He tossed his duffle bag into the backseat and turned to his baby momma, Boo. She was a light-skinned chick with mad ghetto sex appeal. She rocked her hair in long cornrows which extended down her back. A butterfly was tattooed on the side of her right eye. She had her son's name, Cordary, inked on her tit and T.J.'s government name on the inside of her wrist. Inked on the side of her neck were red roses; Rest in Paradise Sophia which was her mother's name was below the flowers. Boo was dressed in a dark blue jean jacket and matching jeans that hugged her ample ass.

One hand on the steering wheel, Sophia turned to T.J. sucking on a cherry Tootsie Roll pop. She sucked on the delicious red orb and then licked her full lips, seductively. The way she eyed T.J. made his dick as hard as a brick of coke. At that moment, he wanted to fuck the shit out of her.

"Heyyyy, baby zzzaddy." Boo smiled at T.J. She then leaned forward and kissed him hard and sloppily. When she pulled away she had spit glistening at the corner of her mouth, which she wiped with her fingers and thumb.

"Damn, it's like that?" T.J. said as he looked her up and down, biting down on his bottom lip. He grasped the bulge in his Dickies, dying to run his dick up in her.

"It's like that, and then some." she stuck the Tootsie Roll pop inside of his mouth and looked around to make sure there wasn't anyone watching her.

Seeing that the coast was clear, she smiled devilishly and pulled down his zipper. His rock hard dick sprung forward and Boo stroked it. Looking up at his face, she watched as he leaned his head back and shut his eyelids. He moaned and groaned as she pumped his dick up and down causing a clear fluid to run from out of its pee hole. His dick seemed to have doubled in size while she was doing this, and he twitched from the sensation. Boo pulled off her shades and sat them down on the dashboard. After she licked her shiny, lip glossed lips, she dipped her head below his waistline and sucked him into her mouth. T.J. groaned aloud when he felt the warmth and wetness of her mouth. She hummed as she brought her lips up and down his dick, spilling her hot juices down his shaft. T.J. popped the sucker out of his mouth and looked down at her handle her business, placing his chubby hand at the back of her head. Quickly, he glanced around to see if there was anyone watching what was going down in the Honda. There were some people out and about, but neither of them was paying any attention to them.

"Yeah, that's right, suck that dick! Suck that mothafucking dick, girl!" T.J. egged Boo on as he stared down at the back of her bobbing head. Once she brought her head halfway up his shit and gurgled on it, he told her, "Spit on 'em, ma! Spit on that big mothafucka!"

Boo took her lips away from T.J.'s dick. She wiped her mouth with the back of her hand as she stroked his dick up and down. She spit on his shit twice and kept on stroking it before she threw her mouth back on it, sucking him off and massaging his slightly hairy nut sack, concurrently. Eyes still on her, T.J.'s face balled up and he pressed his sneakers against the floor, feeling himself about to explode inside of her mouth.

"Ah, yeah! That's it, that's it! I'm 'bouta nut, I'm 'bouta nut all up in yo' shit!" T.J. made promises of what was to come. As Boo sucked him harder and harder and massaged his sack, he stuck the sucker back inside of his mouth. He then gripped her head with both hands and started humping her mouth. The bitch didn't gag at all. In fact, she could take a yard of dick in her grill with no problem. "Unh, unh, that's it! Don't stop, I'm 'bouta cum! I'm 'bouta mothafucking cum!"

T.J.'s forehead shined with perspiration being that it was pretty hot outside and he was fucking old girl's mouth. Before he knew it, his toes were curling inside of his sneakers as he was releasing his warm, creamy jizz inside of Boo's mouth. Relief crossed his face. He humped her mouth two more times and ground into it, before falling limp on the passenger seat. Having finished him off, Boo popped the glove box and grabbed the napkins from out of it. She spat T.J.'s semen inside of the napkin, folded it and then wiped her mouth with it. She then balled the napkin up and threw it out of the window.

"Yo' finda park somewhere, I'm tryna get some pussy." T.J. told his baby momma as he rubbed her fat twat through her jeans.

"Alright," Boo responded and fired up her whip. She pulled away from the curb and drove down the block until she found an alley. She drove halfway down the path and cut the car off.

Boo and T.J. hurriedly unbuckled their belts and pulled their pants down. Boo crawled halfway into the backseat and pulled her jeans down around her thighs, leaving that fat ass monkey of hers bulging from between her legs. Her shit looked like a slightly hairy, balled, baby fist. T.J. couldn't pull his Dickies down fast enough as he came up behind her. His dick was sticking straight out and covered with veins. Its head pulsated and semen oozed out of its peehole. T.J. lifted Boo's shirt all the way up and spat in the palm of his hand twice, using his saliva to lube up his dick. Holding Boo's hip firmly, he pushed his dick inside of her pussy. They both gasped when they felt one another, enjoying sensation that taintilized their southern regions. T.J. held Boo's buttocks roughly and spread them apart, sliding himself in and out of her fuck-hole slowly. His throat moved up and down as he formed a pool of saliva inside of his mouth. Looking down, he released a steady stream of hot saliva, soaking his manhood as he continued to pump Boo's gooey center. Her eyelids were forming slits and her mouth was hanging open, feeling her insides being massaged by her nigga.

He was pulling his dick out to the tip and then pushing it all the way inside of her to his nut sack. Hearing Boo moaning and groaning, T.J. knew she was pleased with his thrusts so he sped up, going faster and faster. It wasn't long before Boo was hollering aloud and the smell of sex was filling the air. The sound of damp fleshing slapping against one another consumed the atmosphere. The car started rocking back and forth.

"Ah, fuck! I'm finna bust!" T.J. snatched his dick out of Boo and jacked it, shooting strings of warm semen onto her back. He then rubbed his dick-head on her left ass cheek as his chest swelled up and down as he breathed.

Tiaz wiped the perspiration from off his forehead and popped the glove box open, grabbing a handful of napkins. He wiped off his semi limp dick and wiped off Boo's back. Afterwards, he balled up the napkins and threw them shits out of the window. Falling back down on the passenger seat, he zipped up his Dickies and buckled up his belt. Once Boo had pulled up her jeans and buttoned them, she climbed back into the front and sat down in the driver seat.

"Yo', where my lil' man at?" T.J. inquired as he buckled his safety belt.

"He's at my motha's," Boo answered as she fixed her hair. She flipped down the sun visor and looked into the rectangle shaped mirror, checking out her makeup. She then flipped the sun visor shut, buckled her safety belt and started up the car.

"I wanna see my lil' nigga. We gotta scoop 'em up once we hit this lick."

"You got it, big daddy," Boo said as she looked over her shoulder and backed out of the alley.

That night

Boo pulled up a couple of houses down from the spot T.J. was going to hit. She pressed a button that opened a stash box which inhabited her baby daddy's twin .9mm handguns and a ski-mask. A broad smile spread across T.J.'s face when he saw the bangaz. It had been a long while since he'd held his babies in his hands and he missed those beautiful mothafuckaz. As soon as he took them shits out of the stash spot, he looked to each one kissing them how he'd kiss his woman, lovingly.

T.J. checked the magazines of his guns to see if they were fully loaded. Once he'd made sure, he slammed the clips back inside the butts of the handguns and *click clacked* them shits. He then sat them on his lap and removed the ski-mask from out of the box, tucking it into his back pocket.

T.J. lost his parents at a very young age; his father to the system and his mother to the streets. The death of his mother would stick with him forever. He'd never forget the night he'd lost her. She was shot down like a god damn dog right before his innocent eyes. He couldn't believe what he was seeing. It all played out like a movie, but it was real. A real life nightmare that he had never awoke from. He'd never forget her killa's eyes. They were merciless and hateful, like he had a vendetta against his mother. But he didn't know what his mother could have done for her to be murdered in cold blood in front of him. That shit was so heartless. That mothafucka that slept his mother didn't give a mad ass fuck about her or him seeing what he'd done.

Once his mother was killed, T.J. went to stay with his grandmother. She took good care of him, providing everything he could want and need. But that didn't stop him from lashing out. Nah, the death of his mother left the wolf howling at the moon. He acted out every chance he got. The little nigga stayed in some shit. His name was always connected to something that went down in the hood. It wasn't long before the OGs came around looking for him. They'd heard of his reputation and wanted to induct him into their ranks. They made T.J. feel like one of them, showing him the love and adoration that he'd lost due to the loss of his parents. He felt like he belonged among them and yearned to be apart of them, which is why he joined up with the same gang that embraced his mother.

T.J. became one of his gang's infamous shooters when it was war time. There wasn't anyone that he was afraid to get at or go up against. No matter how big or small the mothafucka was. If the nigga bucked then he was on that ass like stink on shit. T.J.'s ruthlessness and fearlessness got him christened one of the most revered savages of his set. His enemies and comrades alike spoke about him like he was the mothafucking Boogey Man. And rightfully so.

"Come on. Let's do this." T.J. told Boo as he hopped out of the car. Boo got out behind him and they entered the yard of the nigga she'd set up for the lick. T.J. used the butt of one of his bangaz to shatter the light bulb on the porch. He wanted to make sure that if someone turned on the porch light that his shadow wouldn't be cast on the floor which would blow his cover.

Once T.J. had taken care of the porch light, Boo walked up to the front door. T.J. posted up beside the door and pulled his ski-mask out of his back pocket, pulling it down over his head. He adjusted the mask over his face so he could see out of the eye holes in it properly. After he'd done this, he nodded to Boo which let her know to ring the doorbell. Boo nodded, took a deep breath and rung the doorbell. A moment later, they heard the wooden door behind the black iron door coming unlocked and then a chain being removed. Right after, the wooden door was pulled open, Boo found herself standing before the homeboy that had hollered at her when he saw her at Tam's burgers in Compton. She could tell by what he said next and his movements that he was flipping the light switch *on* and *off*, but the light wouldn't come on.

"Damn, that mothafucking light bulb must have gon' out, Slim!" Cutty proclaimed looking over his shoulder at his homeboy who was standing somewhere behind him, busy putting something back inside of the refrigerator.

"Again? I just put that bitch up in there. Well, shit, we got some more up in the cabinet above the stove. I'll put one up in there once I finished eating this bowl of cereal." Slim said as he closed the door of the refrigerator.

"Well, damn, Cutty, I drove this far, you gon' keep a bitch out in the cold waiting?" Boo fixed her face with a frown and placed her hand on her hip, switching her weight from one foot to the other. She'd gotten tired of standing outside on the front porch.

"Oh, my bad, lil' momma. Where the fuck are my manners?" Cutty switched hands with a big ass roll of duct tape before unlocking the black iron door. As soon as he opened the door,

T.J. barged in past Boo and kicked that mothafucka in his stomach. Cutty made a pained groan as he doubled over and dropped the roll of duct tape. Following up, T.J. whacked him upside the head with one of his .9mms. The nigga fell over inside of the house; T.J. stepped over him into the living room, waving his twin handguns around. Boo was right behind him, pulling the door shut behind them and pulling out .22. She swayed the lethal weapon around the room at any possible threats.

"Alright, bet notta mothafucka up in here move, or I'ma stank ya asses!" T.J. warned with his twin 9 Double M's, looking to see if there was anyone stupid enough to test his gangsta. His eyes landed on an old lady who was standing beside a coffee table which had an empty duffle bag on it. T.J.'s brows creased as he assumed the elderly woman was Cutty's grandmother. He couldn't help wondering why the fuck niggaz would be slinging out of the house with his granny living there. The old lady was scared. Her heart thudded. She swallowed the lump of fear in her throat as her palms became sweaty. She wondered if tonight would be her last night alive.

T.J. focused his attention on Slim who was standing inside of the kitchen with a big ass bowl of Apple Jacks. "You niggaz better let me know you understand where I'm coming from before I start nodding heads in here!" T.J. warned all the occupants of the house.

"Y-yeah, man, we understand!" Cutty said as he got on his knees, holding the side of his bleeding head as he winced.

"Good. Well, that's one busta-ass nigga that knows what time it is. Now, how 'bout chu?" T.J. asked Slim. He could tell that the nigga was shook. He wanted to wipe the milk from off his chin, but his fear of being shot stayed his hand. The hand he held the bowl with was trembling and so were his skinny-ass legs. "My nigga, you hear me talking to you?" T.J. inquired as he stuck his gun underneath old boy's chin and tilted it upwards, making him look up at him. Slim's throat rolled up and down his neck as he swallowed the lump of nervousness that had formed in it.

T.J. leaned forward and sniffed him. He could literally smell the fear seeping from out of his pores. He was wearing that shit like it was cologne. "I knew I smelled something. That's pussy! Nigga, you smell like straight padussy out this bitch! You ain't got the heart for this game, homie! You shoulda never jumped in the water with these sharks, 'cause when mothafuckaz like me smell bitch onna nigga, it drives us crazy."

"Please..." tears formed in the Slim's eyes.

"Please what? Please what, nigga?" T.J. asked him. "Dawg, you sicken me! I bet chu if I whipped out my dick you'd get on yo' knees and suck it to save yo' pathetic ass life! Now, wouldn't chu? Wouldn't chu, you bitch-made-ass punk?" he scowled at him so hard that his teeth gritted, causing the vein at his temple to bulge.

"Y-yeah." Slim answered timidly.

"Just like I thought, a wet pussy; dying to be fucked!" T.J. looked Slim up and down like he was a pitiful piece of shit. Suddenly, Slim gained some heart. He smacked T.J.'s gun from below his chin and slammed the bowl of cereal against his head. The ceramic bowl exploded upon impact, drenching T.J.'s ski-mask with milk and Apple Jacks. T.J. folded and grabbed the side of his throbbing head with the hand he held his gun in. Fighting back the pain in his dome, T.J. peeled his eyelids open to see Slim reaching inside of the cupboard for something. As T.J. ran toward him, he saw him taking something from out of the cupboard compact and black. As Slim turned around he could see the side of it. It was a mothafucking Uzi!

"Bitch-ass nigga, fuck you think you doing, huh?" T.J. asked as he cocked one of his guns back and whacked his ass upside the head, sending him stumbling backward fast. Slim dropped the Uzi and fell slumped against the bottom cabinets, where T.J. beat his face with both of his guns until they were both stained burgundy. By the time T.J. pulled back from whipping that ass out, Slim was breathing huskily and his chest was swelling and shrinking. The blood stains on his T-shirt looked like cherry Kool-Aid stains and the butts of his bangaz were dripping blood.

Slim's face was bloody and swelling. He moaned in agony and spat out a bloody tooth, which tumbled across the floor. T.J. tucked one of his guns at the small of his back. He then picked up the Uzi and walked back inside of the living room, stopping at Cutty's feet. The defeated man stared up at him with terrified eyes, holding his head and silently praying that he didn't open his chest up with some hot shit.

"What up, G? Whateva I got you can have! Take a look around, it's all yours!" Cutty swore as he put his hands in the air. He realized he was at T.J.'s mercy. And by the way he'd handled Slim, he knew he wouldn't hesitate to unload that Uzi in his face. In fact, he glanced at the Uzi he had clutched in his gloved hand and could tell that his trigger finger was itching from the way it was twitching.

"Nigga, I don't want any of this ol' bullshit you got up in here! Where the money and drugs at? And don't try lying either, or I'ma shoot the fuck outta cho black ass. That's onna gang!" T.J. swore as he stared him dead in his eyes, wishing he'd try him just so he could see what the Uzi would do to him.

"Okay, okay," Cutty said panicky. He was trying his best to keep cool and calm, but he was failing miserably. "I'ma keep it one-hunnit witchu. I don't stash no yay in here, but I gotta 'bout sixty gee's inside of an old Adidas shoe box at the back of the top shelf inside of the bedroom closet." his bitch-ass pointed to his bedroom with his shaking finger.

"Alright. Well, yo' ass is gon' get it for me. So, come on," T.J. shouted down at him and kicked him in his ass, hurrying him along. Cutty had grabbed the arm of the couch and pulled himself halfway up, when an impatient T.J. smacked him across the back of the head with the Uzi. He then kicked him in his back as he staggered down the hallway, slightly dizzy from getting knocked upside the head the first time T.J. stormed inside of the house. The kick to his back caused Cutty to nearly fall, but luckily he recovered his equilibrium. "Hurry yo' punk-ass up, nigga! I'm tryna collect and I don't have all day."

Still holding the .9mm and the Uzi, T.J. followed Cutty inside of his bedroom taunting him with the thought of killing him. Cutty grabbed the doorway and looked up wincing. He felt around on the wall until he discovered a light switch and flipped it *on*. Blood ran down the side of his face and dripped down to his shirt, as he staggered over to the closet. He opened the closet door and pulled the drawstring, restoring light to the small space.

Next, he pulled a bunch of shit down from off the top shelf and let it all fall to the floor, in a chaotic clatter of sorts. He then moved some boxes of stuff aside until he was face to face with a blue Adidas sneaker box Cutty had told him about. He took the sneaker box down and removed the lid, showing T.J. what was inside. The blue box was loaded with bank rolls of dead faces wrapped in beige rubber bands. T.J. glanced inside of the box and nodded his head, an evil smile spread across his face. There wasn't anything like new money to him.

"My man, dump the pillow out of one of those pillowcases on the bed and dump that loot from that sneaker box inside of the pillowcase. And hurry that ass up!" T.J. kicked the bitch-nigga in his ass again, causing him to stumble forward and nearly fall flat on his face. Cutty gathered himself and did exactly like T.J. had ordered him to. Once he was done, he tied the pillow case of drug money into a knot and passed it to T.J. T.J. tucked his other .9mm in his waistline and took the pillowcase. He looked at the floor at Cutty's feet and his brows furrowed once he saw something. "You dropped a stack over there." he pointed with the pillowcase. As soon as Cutty turned around to see where he'd dropped the stack, T.J. struck him in the back of the head with the pillowcase and knocked him out cold. Cutty's limp body fell across the bed and he snored aloud. Seeing him at his mercy, T.J. sat the pillowcase on the nightstand and picked the other pillow up from the bed. He laid the pillow on the back of a snoring Cutty's dome and switched hands with his Uzi. Pressing the Uzi in behind the pillow, he squeezed its trigger and splashed Cutty's shit all over the bedspread, silencing his snores forever.

Once the deed was done, T.J. made his way back up to the living room. As he strolled down the hallway, the grandmother's teeth chattered and she lifted her shaky hands in the air. T.J.'s forehead crinkled as he studied the clothing she was wearing. It was something off about their appearance. In fact, her appearance was so off it had him narrowing his eyelids into slits and tilting his head to the side, trying to figure out what it was. A light bulb came on inside of his head and he waved Boo over with his gun. Once she approached, he whispered something in her ear and she stripped the old hag's down. When she was done, the grandmother was in her tan bra and panties with kilos of cocaine duct taped to her body. It dawned on T.J. then that Cutty had been strapping her old ass down with yayo so she could fly them bitchez to whoever was looking to buy them. They knew that the authorities would be less likely to suspect a senior citizen transporting them thangz from state to state. This explained the roll of duct tape that Cutty had when he opened the door and the empty duffle bag on the coffee table. The keys must have been stored inside of there.

Clever, mothafuckaz, T.J. thought as a devilish smile spread across his face. He sat the Uzi down on the arm of the couch and untied the pillowcase. Holding it open, he ordered Boo to remove the kilos from the old lady's body and dump them shits inside of the pillowcase. Once she did, he tied the pillowcase back up and dropped it on the last cushion of the couch. Turning toward the old lady, he cracked the knuckles on both his hands and stalked toward her, menacingly. Right then, she dropped to her knees and stared up at him like he was God Almighty. There were tears in her eyes and her bottom lip quivered, as she wondered what he planned to do to her.

"Oh, Lord, please, please, don't kill me, son! I beg of you, have mercy! Have mercy on me. I'm just an old woman." she pleaded with her fingers interlocked, begging to have her life spared.

"Shhhh!" T.J. hushed her as he approached, holding his finger to his lips. The old woman shut up, but she continued to shake, staring up at him. As his shadow loomed over her, she shut her eyelids and more tears jetted down her wrinkled cheeks. She then crossed herself in the sign of the holy crucifix and accepted her impending doom. Head tilted upward, arms down at her sides; she chose to go out courageously at that moment. "That's it. Don't fight this shit, just let it happen. It will alllll be over soon." T.J. placed his hands on either side of her head, and twisted it to the right, hard as fuck. There was a sickening snap sound and the old lady's body went limp as he held her head in his hands. A second later, he let her dead body drop to the floor.

Staring down at the old lady, Boo shook her head pitifully and crossed herself in the sign of the holy crucifix. Looking back up, she saw T.J. grab the Uzi from off the arm of the couch and then one of its pillows. He casually strolled inside of the kitchen where he'd left Slim on the floor.

"Please, please, man, don't-don't kill me, please..." Slim pleaded as he tried to lift his hand to stop the inevitable.

The man's pleas fell on deaf ears as T.J. mashed his sneaker against his hand and pinned it against the floor. Helpless, the nigga watched as T.J. mashed the couch pillow over his face and pressed the Uzi in behind it. T.J. squeezed the trigger and blew his Slim's brains out. Afterwards, he tossed the compact machine gun and the couch pillow on the floor. He then made his way back towards the living room, where he recovered the pillowcase and motioned for Boo to follow him out of the house.

CHAPTER TWO

Kesha was in her bra and jeans as she got ready for the night's mission, strapping on her Kevlar bulletproof vest and loading up them thangz. While she was busy handling the mentioned tasks, Te'Qui observed his reflection through the mirror attached to the nightstand. Te'Qui was far from the skinny brown-skinned, ten-year-old kid that he used to be, running the streets with his deceased homeboy, Baby Wicked. He now stood a full six-foot-one and had a body covered in muscles and veins. There wasn't an area on his form that didn't have ink on it.

Te'Qui had a small Uzi .9mm tattooed on his forehead between his eyes, seven red teardrops going on either side of his cheeks and an image of Baby Wicked on his back along with his birth date and death date. He had X's on his thumbs which added up to the number 20, symbolizing his allegiance to the notorious Outlaw 20s Bloods Gang. Te'Qui wore his mother name, Chevy, on his neck, his father's name, Faizon, on left peck, Glocks on the lower half of his stomach with RTBG in the middle of it, dripping blood. There were also a host of other tattoos on his body, but these were the ones that stood out.

Since Te'Qui's best friend and road dawg, Baby Wicked, had gotten smoked over dealing, he vowed not to fuck with the crack game ever again. Instead, he became a jack boy, robbing the same mothafuckaz that were slinging poison in the streets. Sometimes when he'd hit a dope boy, he'd drive through the streets tossing cash out of his whip, putting the slums in a frenzy. The way he saw it since he was bringing death and destruction to the hood, this would be his way of giving back. Sure he could have done more for the communities of the niggaz he'd hit, but he wasn't trying to draw police attention to himself. The mothafucka wasn't stupid.

After the deaths of his parents, Te'Qui went to stay with his grand parents. At home, he was the good little choir boy who got straight A's in school and attended church with his grand parents. But when night fell on the city, he fled to the streets where he was the gangsta his environment groomed him to be. After his grand parents passed away from natural causes, Te'Qui made the streets his permanent home.

"You ready to go, baby?" Te'Qui asked Kesha with a smirk on his lips, staring down into her eyes as he held her in his arms.

"Yes, bae," Kesha flashed him an even bigger smirk. She was a slim-thick chick that stood a full five-foot-seven. She had rich chocolate skin, dimples and an easy smile. She also had thick eyebrows and thin dreads that spilled down her back. She was hood to the bone, and just as dangerous as the nigga she claimed to love more than life it self.

Te'Qui and Kesha broke their embrace and tucked their red ski-masks. They made their way toward the door, but Kesha suddenly stopped. Te'Qui turned around to her with a frown fixed on his face, holding on to one of her hands.

"What's wrong, momma?" he asked concerned.

"Oh, baby, I gotta throw up." Kesha's cheeks ballooned and she held her hand over her mouth, with her eyes bulging.

"You sho'?" Te'Qui asked, placing his hand on her shoulder.

Kesha nodded and sprinted off to the bathroom, slamming the door shut behind her. Te'Qui listened as she lifted the lid on the commode and threw up into the bowl. She threw up over and over again, sounding like she was going to hurl up her insides. Te'Qui heard her breathing hard. Looking underneath the slight opening of the door, he could see her shadow. She was on her knees hunched over the commode.

Concerned with his lady, Te'Qui approached the bathroom and knocked on it. His forehead was creased as he leaned up against the bathroom door.

"Y-Yeah," Kesha called out.

"You okay in there, ma?" Te'Qui asked her.

"I-I'll be fine, baby. Gimme a sec' and we on 'em niggaz. You heard?"

"My baby always on her shit, I ain't worried about that."

"Okay."

"Take yo' time, ain't no rush."

Te'Qui leaned his back against the wall on the side of the bathroom door. He then folded his arms across his chest, tapping his foot as he waited for his lady. A moment later the door clicked unlock and Kesha flipped the light switch *off*, walking out of the bathroom.

"You good, lil' momma?" Te'Qui asked her.

"Yeah." Kesha smiled.

Te'Qui studied her for a while and then said, "Yo', I think you might be pregnant. We gon' get chu a test from CVS once we finish this mission, alright?"

"Alright," she nodded. "I think you might be right. I have been feeling nauseated lately."

"Okay. I got chu faded once we handle this shit." He pulled her close, kissing her on the forehead and lips. He then took her by her hand and walked out of the bedroom.

***

"Hold up." Te'Qui told Kesha as he stared out of the passenger window at the house they were looking for.

"This the house?" Kesha asked as she brought the car to a stop and looked at the same crib that Te'Qui was looking at.

"Yep, there's the truck. It's parked in front of that old-ass Buick Lasabre." he informed her as he looked down at the picture of the vehicle they were hired to obtain. It was a white 2000 Chevrolet Tahoe. Besides its smoke black tinted windows and twenty-four chrome inch rims, Te'Qui didn't see what the big fuss was about the truck. For the amount of money he was getting paid to snatch it, the nigga that hired him could have copped ten of them mothafuckaz. Te'Qui didn't know his employer's reasoning behind wanting the Tahoe nor did he care. The nigga was paying him thirty stacks to bring him the truck, and that's exact what the fuck he was going to do.

"Babe, park around the corner from this mothafucka. We gon' go through the backyard of that house." Te'Qui commanded his lady.

Kesha did like she'd been told. She and Te'Qui had already done their homework on the thirty something Mexican couple that lived in the house they were going to hit. The woman went to night school while her man worked a third shift at a packaging company and slung a little coke on the side. The couple had two Doberman Pinschers in their backyard, but Te'Qui was positive they'd could get pass them. Once they'd taken care of the hounds, he was sure they'd be leaving with the truck that night.

Kesha and Te'Qui pulled out their red ski-masks. They pulled the masks over their faces and jumped out of the car. They threw their hoods over their heads and made hurried steps up the block, looking around to make sure that there weren't any eyes on them. Once they didn't see anyone, they continued towards the house they'd staked out. They made their way through the yard of the house, creeping on the side of the house and eventually making it into the backyard. Once they made it to the end of the yard, they came before a gate, which divided the alley and Armon's house. Hunched down from where they were they could see a couple of mean-ass Doberman Pinschers partroling Armon's backyard. One was brown and the other was black. They both had clipped tails.

Te'Qui tapped Kesha and said, "Do yo' thang, lil' momma."

"I got cha, lil' daddy," Kesha responded and pulled a small, slender bamboo branch from out of the confines of her hoodie. She loaded two darts stained with a sedative into it and brought the bamboo to her full lips. She blew into the end of the bamboo branch twice, hard. The darts flew out of the hollow branch so fast that they appeared invisible. The dogs yelped and looked around for who had shot them, but they didn't see anyone because Te'Qui and Kesha was ducked down and cloaked in the darkness.

"How long you say before those darts take effect?" Te'Qui whispered to Kesha.

"A minute or two," Kesha answered.

"Alright."

A total of two minutes had passed with Te'Qui and Kesha watching the dogs. The hounds were walking around the backyard like they hadn't been shot with anything. Te'Qui's forehead creased as he wondered why the dogs hadn't fallen asleep yet. Right then, he pulled back the sleeve of his sweatshirt and looked at his watch. Three minutes had passed since the dogs had been shot. He then looked back up to see the Doberman Pinschers staggering around on wobbly legs, before they eventually collapsed in the grass.

"There they go, come on," Te'Qui tapped Kesha and they scaled the gate, jumping down onto the gravelly ground inside of the alley. They then hopped the fence into Armon's backyard and made their way up the steps of the back porch where the back door was. Te'Qui stood beside Kesha as she kneeled and picked the locks of the back door. Once she finished, she stood erect and pulled the door open. She then handled the lock of the last door standing between them and their assignment.

"Alright, baby, she's wide open." Kesha stood up and told him, smiling.

"I see. Good job, lil' momma." Te'Qui dapped her up. He then pulled her into him and kissed her hard and romantically. When he pulled back from her, they were both smiling. "You ready to do this?"

"Fa sho'." she responded.

"Watch my back."

"Watch my front."

With that having been said, Te'Qui and Kesha pulled out their guns. Te'Qui took the led and pushed the door open, gently. As he and Kesha made their way inside of the kitchen, they clocked Armon, his wife, daughter and their grandfather eating dinner at the dining room table. Before they could make their move, the wife had spotted Te'Qui. Her eyes got as big as saucers and she shrieked.

"Aaaahhhhhh!" she screamed hysterically and threw her hands to her face, trembling uncontrollably.

At that moment, Te'Qui and Kesha rushed the dining room. When Armon saw them coming, he jumped to his feet and snatched the butcher's knife out of the pot roast. He threw the knife at Te'Qui's head and he moved to the side, dodging it. The shiny metal knife spun around in circles, gleaming as it flew passed his ear.

Thock!

The butcher's knife stabbed into the wall and Armon took off running. Te'Qui aimed his gun at Armon's calf as he ran. At this time, the man's wife was pulling her terrified daughter into her arms. Te'Qui pulled the trigger of the gun and a bullet ripped through Armon's calf, splattering blood everywhere. Armon threw his head back wincing and hollering aloud. He fell to the carpeted floor and turned over, face balling as he held his calf with both hands. His blood seeped between his fingers and spilled onto the carpet.

"Aaaah, fuck! Shiiiit!" Armon clenched his teeth as he tried to combat the pain in his wounded leg.

"Thought that ass was gon' get away, huh? Not on my watch, pussy!" Te'Qui said to Armon as he hastily approached him, gun pointed at him. He was going to pop that ass in the collarbone if he tried to get away again. The last thing on his mind was killing him because he needed the keys to the Tahoe if he was going to get paid.

"Everything is going to be okay. Y'all just stay calm. You hear?" Kesha asked the wife and grandfather, gun rose in case anyone tried to jump fool in that mothafucka. The wife nodded her understanding, while the grandfather just stared at her. "How 'bout chu, pops? You picking up what I'm sitting down?"

The grandfather still didn't respond.

"This yo' father?" Kesha asked the wife.

"Y-yes," the wife nodded rapidly.

"Fuck is his problem?" Kesha held both of her hands on the gun as she held the grandfather at gunpoint.

"I-I don't know. Check-check his hearing aid, it may be down."

"Nah, fuck that! You check his hearing aid." Kesha demanded.

The wife said something to her now crying daughter to comfort her before kissing her on the forehead. She then got up from the chair and walked over to her father, turning the volume up on his hearing aid. While the wife was doing this, Kesha clocked the old man hard. She could tell that he was an old school Chicano gangster from his tattooed arms and shit. The tattoo teardrops on both of his cheeks and the prayer hands on his neck stood out the most to her. Kesha couldn't help thinking about how many people he'd probably smoked. She was sure he'd put in a hell of a lot of work for his hood.

"You turn them bitchez up?" Kesha asked about the volume on the old man's hearing aids.

"Yes." the wife responded as she sat back down and pulled her daughter into her arms.

"What's his name?" Kesha asked the wife.

"Sylvester." she answered.

"Okay," Kesha said and then turned to the grandfather who was just staring at her. "Sylvester, I want chu to stay calm in this mothafucka. All of this will be over as soon as we get what we came here for. No one has to die. Is that understood?"

Sylvester nodded.

"Good."

"Alright," Te'Qui said to Armon as he stood over him with his gun pointed down at his head. "Gimme the keys to that Tahoe parked in the driveway, and you and yo' family will be left be. That's my right hand to God."

"Fuck you! My dead brother left me that car!" Armon winced continuously as he held his bleeding leg.

Te'Qui scowled and pressed his gun to the back of homeboy's skull and said, "My nigga, you gon' either come off that, or you gon' make me do somethin' I really don't wanna do to yo' family. You feel me? Don't take it there, homes! I don't need that kinda shit on my conscience."

While Te'Qui was going back and forth with Armon, the grandfather was pulling something out of his waistline. The wife, who was still holding her daughter, peeped what he was doing but she didn't say a word. At this time, Kesha was staring at Te'Qui and not paying the grandfather any attention. Seeing the grandfather pulling a gun in the reflection of the pitcher of ice tea at the center of the table, Kesha brought her gun around in time to see him pointing his gun at her.

Blowl! Blowl! Blowl! Blowl!

The grandfather dropped the gun and he danced in the chair as he took several shots, eventually topping over in his chair. He crashed to the floor wearing bug eyes and an open mouth.

"Grandpaaaaaa!" the daughter called out to her grandfather with her hand outstretched. Tears cascaded down her cheeks and her bottom lip quivered.

"Noooooooo!" the wife hollered out in tears, seeing the grandfather gunned down.

"I told you! I warned you both, but he wouldn't listen."

Te'Qui looked over his shoulder at Kesha wondering what the fuck happened. They exchanged nods. They had already agreed they wouldn't kill anyone there unless they tried something, so Te'Qui already knew that the old man had tested his lady's gangsta.

"Ahhhhh! Ahhhhh! Ahhhhh!" the daughter screamed over and over again, hysterically. Her mother pressed her face against her bosom and rocked her as she cried her eyes out.

"Mi padre!" Armon frowned up and tears spilled down his cheeks. Seeing his father lying there dead fucked him up.

Te'Qui nudged the back of Armon's head and said, "You see that? Huh? You see that shit? Now, gimme the keys to that truck out there, or yo' wife's next."

"Fuck you, puto! I'm not finna give you shit! Suck my cock!" Armon spat heatedly, looking up at Te'Qui.

"Alright, my nigga, you remember you did this to yo' self!" Te'Qui told him. He then looked at Kesha and said, "Put one in his wife's thankin' cap!"

"Please, no! Ahhhhhh!" the wife shrilled as Kesha grabbed her by her hair and slung her to the floor. Her daughter fell beside her on the floor, still crying from seeing her grandfather murdered in cold blood.

Kesha then pressed her sneaker down against the wife's chest and pointed her gun at her forehead.

"Sorry," Kesha said to the wife before she acted on her man's command.

"No! Stop! Wait, I'll give you the keys!" Armon told Te'Qui over his shoulder.

"Good boy." Te'Qui smiled and ruffled his head. "Now, where them keys at?"

Armon took one of his bloody hands from off his wounded leg and removed the necklace from around his neck which held the key to the Chevy Tahoe parked in the driveway.

Te'Qui snatched the keys and stashed them in his pocket. He then threw a pair of zip-cuffs down beside Armon and ordered him to put them on. Afterwards, he told Kesha to put zip-cuffs on Armon's wife and daughter. Kesha tucked her gun and pulled out the zips, restraining the mother and daughter's wrists with them. Once she finished, she stood upright and walked over to her man.

"What about the keys to the Blazer?" Kesha asked. She'd just recalled seeing the Blazer parked behind the Chevy Tahoe they were hired to steal.

Te'Qui turned to Armon. "Where the keys to that piece of shit parked behind the Tahoe?"

"It's in my right pocket," Armon nodded to his right pocket, and Te'Qui pulled the keys out of it. He handed the keys to both vehicles to Kesha and told her to pull the car out while he held down the house.

"Once you pull out the Tahoe, take that bitch to the location. You know where I'm talkin' 'bout, right?" Te'Qui asked her.

"Yeah, bae, I got chu."

"Good."

Kesha kissed her man goodbye and went off to handle her business. Once he heard her toot the horn of the Tahoe and drive off, Te'Qui knew that she'd carried out the assignment he'd given her. Once this signal was given, Te'Qui kicked Armon across the chin and knocked him out cold. He then ran out of the house and hopped the backyard fence, jumping down onto the graveled ground of the alley. Next, he scaled the gate of the house who's owners weren't home and darted to the front of the house where he procured the car he'd came there in. Jumping behind the wheel, he fired up the car and sped off to his next destination.

***

Calhoun, the nigga that had hired Te'Qui to steal the Chevy Tahoe, stood out on his porch taking pulls from a Black & Mild and blowing smoke into the air. He glanced at the time on his cell phone and then looked back up, wondering what was keeping Te'Qui and his girl. The young thug had called him half an hour ago and told him that they were on the way.

"Where this mothafucka at?" Calhoun asked no one in particular.

"They still haven't come, baby?" a feminine voice said from his rear. He looked over his shoulder and found the silhouette of his wife who happened to be holding their newborn child. The only thing that could be made out about the mother and her daughter were their silhouettes.

As soon as Calhoun's wife posed the question, Te'Qui and Kesha pulled up one after another. Te'Qui rolled down the passenger window and leaned over to holler out of the window.

"Yo', where you want me to park this mothafucka, Blood?" Te'Qui inquired.

"Pull into the back, at the garage door," Calhoun motioned with his hand. As Te'Qui followed his instructions, he turned around to his wife. "Close the door and go to bed, baby. I'll be back inside inna minute."

With that having been said, Calhoun's wife shut the door and went back inside. Once she was gone, Calhoun pulled his robe around his waist tighter and tied it around him. He then flicked his Black & Mild to the ground and mashed it out under his house slipper, leaving black ash and burning embers behind. Next, he jogged up the steps and grabbed what looked like a leather bowling bag stashed behind the balcony. He then headed to his backyard, hearing the slamming of car doors as he went along. By the time he rounded the corner of his house, he saw Te'Qui and Kesha looking in his direction, waiting for him.

"'Sup, man? I was beginnin' to worry," Calhoun said to Te'Qui, walking past him.

"Shiiiit, I'm pushin' a stolin' ride, I hadda take a couple of back streets to stay off the radar. You feel what I'm sayin'?" Te'Qui asked him.

"I feel you, big dawg," Calhoun switched hands with the bag he was toting and lifted the door of his garage. He then stepped aside and told Te'Qui to drive the Tahoe inside. Once he did, Calhoun and Kesha walked inside behind him. Calhoun closed the garage door behind them and sat the bag aside. He then grabbed a jack and pulled it over to the Tahoe, pumping the pole of the jack up and down. It took about fifteen pumps before the jack had the truck's back wheels off the ground. Once he'd done this, he popped open his tool box and removed a couple of tools, which he used to remove the muffler of the SUV.

Te'Qui and Kesha exchanged glances, wondering what the fuck Calhoun was doing. Te'Qui then turned to him and said, "What chu doin', my nigga?"

"You'll see, youngsta. Gimme a sec'," Calhoun walked the muffler over to the iron table at the corner of the garage. He put on a pair of workman gloves and protective eye wear. Next, he picked up the electric chainsaw and pulled its trigger, causing the jagged edged blade to spin around. The sound of the spinning blade filled the air. Sparks flew everywhere as he used the saw to cut open the muffler. He sat the saw aside, pulled his eye wear back at the top of his head and then pried the muffler open. A smile spread across his face as he feasted his eyes on six blocks of dope wrapped in aluminum foil.

Calhoun picked up one of the blocks and turned around to Te'Qui, smiling. "You see, the truck I couldn't give a rat's ass about. This is what I was really after."

"That's what's up. Now, where that paypa at?" Te'Qui asked, rubbing his hands together greedily. Calhoun pointed to the bowling ball styled bag on the ground and he picked it up. Holding it against his body, he unzipped it and marveled at the stacks of blue faces stuffed inside of it.

"You can count it up here, if you want," Calhoun told him.

"Nah, I trust you. We outta here, G," Te'Qui dapped up Calhoun and he and Kesha made their departure.

***

Te'Qui jumped out of his old school box Chevy and slammed the door shut behind him. He made his way around the grill of the vehicle and headed for the entrance doors of Rite Aid, hands stuffed into the pockets of his sagging jeans. He'd just crossed the threshold of the establishment when his shoulder was clipped by a man wearing a royal blue Nike sun visor cap and matching Nike basketball jersey. Instantly, a frown enveloped Te'Qui's face and he turned around scowling, pulling his jeans upon his ass. Right there on a spot, he got into a fighting stance. He planned to knock whoever had bumped his shoulder the fuck out if they bucked on him.

"Yo', my nigga, watch where the fuck you goin'!" Te'Qui mad dogged the man as he clenched his fists.

"Nah, nigga, you watch where…" The man's words died in his mouth once he saw who he'd bumped. The disdained expression dropped from his face and he took his hand from underneath his jersey. "Te'Qui? Is that chu?"

"Poochie?"Te'Qui took a closer look at the man and narrowed his eyelids.

Poochie adjusted the visor on his head and smiled, saying, "Yeah, it's me! I ain't seen yo' ass in a minute, fool! What that shit do, my boy?" he switched hands with the bag he was holding and slapped hands with Te'Qui.

"Ain't shit, dawg. How you been?" Te'Qui inquired as he took a step back and gave his old running buddy the once over. He could tell by his red nose and constant sniffling he was still snorting cocaine like a mothafucka. There weren't any doubts about it.

"Everythang is copacetic. You know a nigga workin' for Quervo now, so I stay witta grip. Know what I'm sayin'?" Poochie pulled on his nose and exposed the diamond and gold handcuff he was wearing and smiled. He then held up the gold necklace that was dangling down his chest.

The necklace held onto a gold dog milk bone which was flooded with diamonds and boasted his name, Poochie.

Te'Qui appeared to be astonished when he saw all the jewelry Poochie was stunting in. A year ago the nigga was posted up inside of a gas station asking people to pump their petro for spare change. Now here he was bragging, boasting and shining like new diamonds.

Te'Qui pulled into the Valero gas station off of Avalon with YG's - Why You Always Hatin? Rattling his trunk. Leaving his old school box Chevy running, he hopped out of it and walked around it pulling his sagging red Dickies upon his ass. He made it to the bulletproof partition which the clerk sat behind and paid for his gas as well as a pack of Newport shorts. After he pocketed his change, he walked back to his Chevy, seeing someone shuffling around it. He thought it was his homeboy Poochie who he hadn't seen in a while, but shook that thought from his head. You see, the dude he'd clocked was shabbily dressed and he could smell him from where he was. His homeboy Poochie was a clean cut, snazzy dressing nigga that was known to keepa pocket full of money and some fly-ass jewels around his neck. So he couldn't be him...or could he?

"Yo', my nigga, fuck you doin' around my car?" Te'Qui frowned up as he approached his hood classic car.

"Oh, I don't mean no disrespect, homie. I was just tryna see if I could pump yo' gas for whatever spare change you willin' to bless me with." the shabbily dressed dude cracked a dimpled smile. He smiled because he knew how important it was to be in high spirits when trying to earn a couple of dollars in the streets. He found out rather quickly that people were more likely to give their money to someone with an upbeat personality than someone who appeared to be sulking.

Te'Qui narrowed his eyelids into slits and leaned forward trying to get a good look at the nigga standing at the rear of his vehicle. "Yo', Poochie, is that chu, Blood?"

The man narrowed his eyelids and closer too. "Te'Qui?"

"Yeah, dawg, it's me." Te'Qui smiled broadly and approached Poochie. He slapped hands with his old road dawg and embraced him, patting him on his back. His face scrunched up as he got a whiff of him. Poochie noticed the look on Te'Qui's face and a look of embarrassment crossed his face.

"My bad, fam. I know a nigga fonky and shit. I look bad, too. You see my threads," Poochie looked over his tattered clothing. When he looked back up at Te'Qui, he could see the hurt and hopelessness bleeding from his eyes. He wasn't used to seeing his man like this. Poochie from off of 25th and Griffith was looking tore up from the floor up.

"It's alright, my nigga. I've been where you were. This is just a minor setback for a major come back." He told him as he watched him remove the nozzle to pump the gas into his car. While he was doing this, they chopped it up about the past and the present. Once the gas was done pumping, Poochie placed the nozzle back into its rightful place. When he turned back around, Te'Qui was holding out ten one-hundred dollar bills. Poochie

couldn't believe his eyes. He thought that he'd get a couple of bucks from his child hood friend, but not a g-stack.

"Thanks, dawg. I really appreciate this," Poochie said as he stuffed the money into his pocket.

"Don't wet it. You gotta pardon a nigga for being nosy, but I've gotta ask...what happened in yo' life that led you here?" he folded his arms across his chest.

"Well, you know I was already out here willin' and dealin', right? One night my curiosity got the best of me and I tried the shit. I wanted to see what it was about this shit that got niggaz hooked on it. Well, my ass found out. Now, I'm stuck on it. Doin' any and everything I have to to get high. A nigga like me that had the world at the palm of his hands fucked it off chasin' after some gotdamn coke. Who woulda thought?" His eyes grew watery and he shook his head, feeling ashamed that he allowed himself to go out over some drugs.

"Hold up." Te'Qui reached inside of his vehicle. He then looked around to make sure that there wasn't anyone watching him before he pulled out a small Ziploc of coke. He pulled Poochie closer to him and stuffed it in the pocket inside of his jacket. "That ain't much, but it should hold you until you get cho self anotha fix."

"Thanks, man." Poochie dapped him up.

"You ain't gotta thank me, Blood. I'm just lookin' out for a friend. I'm sho' you'd do the same for me, right?" Te'Qui asked as he jumped inside of his whip and pulled the driver's door shut.

"Most def'." he nodded as he stuffed the Ziploc further down inside of his jacket's pocket.

"That's what I know. Now, look, I want chu to do me a favor."

Poochie leaned down to the driver's window and rested his arms upon the windowsill. "Anything, my nigga."

"Don't spend alla that loot on yo' habit. I want chu to get cho self some clothes, somethin' hot to eat and a place to hole up for a while. Okay?"

"I got chu, dawg. I'ma do just that. I'ma pay you back to. I may be broke as a joke right now, but once I get right, I'ma repay you for lookin' out for a nigga. Mark my words."

"I believe you, homeboy. No doubt." He dapped him up and told him to stay up before pulling out of the gas station. Poochie stood where he was looking at Te'Qui as he drove off. Once he was out of sight, he pulled the small Ziploc from out of his jacket's pocket and looked at it in the palm of his hand. He then closed the bag inside of his hand and ran off into the night to get high.

***

Man, it's crazy how a nigga can be down one minute and then up the next. The drug game is bipolar as a mothafucka. That's why I stay on this ski-mask shit. A young nigga can't see his self shedding blood, sweat and tears while working a spot or corner for the next nigga. I ain't no hoe! Fuck I look like clockin' figures and then lettin' some other mothafucka check my dollas? Motha fuck that! Ain't nan nigga out here gon' pimp me!

"I see you, lil' daddy, doin' yo' thug thizzle out here in these streets. I ain't mad at chu, loved one." Te'Qui cracked a smirk which caused Poochie to smile broadly. He knew how niggaz like him loved to have their egos stroked and he didn't mind doing it. You see, to him, a real nigga should be able to salute another nigga'z accomplishments. He was proud to see any black man come up, whether it was on some street shit or some legal shit. "Get yours, and then some. You feel me? 'Cause ain't nobody out here gon' give you a damn thang."

"You ain't never lied, niggaz ain't gon' give you shit. Well, every nigga out here besides you. You always looked out when I ran into you. A nigga was fucked up out here in these streets, boy, so I 'fore sho' appreciate every goddamn dolla you blessed me with. You feelin' me, dawg?"

"Sho' you right." Te'Qui nodded.

"I don't know how I could ever repay you, G. For real, for real."

"I can think of a way you can pay yo' debt, if you know what I'm gettin' at." he smiled and rubbed his hands together greedily. He had a hunger in his eyes as he licked his lips. That nigga Poochie knew this look well. Te'Qui had came up with a scheme to get some money.

"You still on that kick doe shit, dawg?"

Te'Qui shrugged and said, "Aye, you know my M.O. You know any niggaz out here I can put that fiyah to and make 'em drop it like it's hot?"

There was a moment of silence as Poochie stared at Te'Qui, wondering what he should say to him. Once he came to his conclusion, he went on to speak. "Nah, I don't know anybody you could knock over, but I'll get at chu should I come across any. How's that?"

"Oh, fa sho."

Te'Qui watched as Poochie pulled his iPhone out of his pocket and went straight to his contacts.

"Shoot me yo' line," Poochie told him, eyes focused on the screen of his cell phone; its illumination shining in his face being that the foyer of CVS was dimly lit thanks to a couple of lights in the ceiling having blown out.

As Te'Qui gave Poochie his telephone number he studied his outfit as well as the jewelry he had on. In addition to the icy gold handcuff on his wrist and the iced out dog bone, he had huge square diamond earrings in his lobes and a gold, blue face Rolex watch, scarcely surrounded by diamonds. For the first time in his life, doing something scandalous to someone he had love for invaded his brain. He wanted to pull out and make Poochie's ass drop it like it's hot, and leave his ass right there in CVS's parking lot in his boxers. Now, as bad as he wanted to do something that foul, he wasn't going to execute those thoughts in his head. He had mad love for Poochie. They came up on free lunch together and ran the streets as adolescents. He, Baby Wicked and himself were like the Three Musketeers at one point. So, he couldn't bring himself to lay his 2-1-1 game down on him.

Nahhhh, Blood, how the fuck that look, me makin' this fool Poochie break himself? I'm fucked up, but I ain't that fucked up! You can't burn every bridge you cross. Besides, I'm sure he's gon' eventually bless me with a money move in the future.

"Alright. I locked you in," Poochie announced as he slipped his cellular back inside of his jeans. When he did this, Te'Qui took note of the Glock in his waistline. "I'll holla at chu once I get somethin', pimp. It's the least I can do for one of the realest niggaz in the streets, ya heard?"

"All day."

Poochie dapped up Te'Qui. In that moment, Te'Qui saw his nose dripping a mixture of snot and blood; a result of sniffing too much mothafucking coke. The nigga loved cocaine, and Te'Qui was sure he was going to die of an overdose one day if he didn't give his nose a break from it.

"Take it easy, my nigga." Poochie walked away sniffling and touching the moisture he felt below his nose. When he looked he saw traces of blood in his green snot which was on his fingertip and thumb.

"You do the same, homie." Te'Qui watched Poochie's back as he trekked through the parking lot, heading for a black on black BMW truck with all gold trimmings. That bitch had limousine tinted windows and gold rims. Te'Qui openly admired the SUV and saluted his nigga'z accomplishments.

Poochie fired up his truck and zoomed out of the parking lot banging RJ's *Get Rich*. Once he'd disappeared before Te'Qui's eyes, the young gangsta bopped off into CVS to get what he'd come there for in the first place. A home pregnancy test.

***

Te'Qui posted up outside the bathroom door waiting for Kesha to deliver the results from her pregnancy test. She'd been in the bathroom nearly twenty minutes so he couldn't help wondering what the hold up was. The suspense was killing him so he decided to see what was up with her. He was just about to knock on the door when he heard the lock coming undone. He stood in the doorway as the door was pulled open and he found himself standing face to face with Kesha. She looked up into his eyes and smiled hard as she held up the white stick. Te'Qui took the stick from her and looked at it. A smile spread across his face once he saw the blue plus sign on it.

"Oh, shit! I'm gonna be a father." Te'Qui said excitedly, like he couldn't believe it.

"That's right." Kesha nodded.

"And you gonna be a…"

"A mom." She nodded.

"I love you." He said as he looked into her eyes.

"I love you even more." She matched his gaze and threw her arms around his neck, kissing him.

Te'Qui was on his way home from a welcome home party for his homeboy Shottie when he first met Kesha. He'd pulled to a stop light when she'd crashed into the back of him. When he glanced up into the rearview mirror and saw an old school Buick Regal on them chrome thangz, he just knew it was a nigga as G as him behind those tinted windows and would more than likely want to show his ass. With that in mind, Te'Qui grabbed the paperwork to his vehicle out of the glove-box and snatched his Glizzy from underneath the driver's seat. After he tucked his shit on his waistline, he jumped out of his car mad dogging, hard as fuck. Approaching the rear of his vehicle, he glanced at the bumper and his shit was dented. His head snapped into the direction of the car of the mothafucka that hit him, wondering why the fuck he hadn't gotten out yet. Just as he was about to approach the car, the driver's door of the Regal swung open. The first thing that came out of the Buick was a pair of thick, shapely legs accompanied by short top burgundy Chuck Taylors. Right after came the head and body of a gorgeous woman. She wore her hair in dread locks and the 4Niners jersey she had on showed off her flat stomach and the diamond piercing in her navel. Te'Qui couldn't take his eyes off of her. Little momma was visually stunning.

Kesha approached Te'Qui rubbing the back of her aching neck and wincing. She looked at the damage to both cars before casting her apologetic eyes into Te'Qui's direction.

"I'm so sorry. This is my fault. This is what my ass gets for tryna text and drive," Kesha told him, feeling sorry for rear ending Te'Qui's car. She then looked him over to see if he had been injured. "Are you okay? Should I call an ambulance?"

"Nah, I'm, I'm…" Te'Qui stuttered having been struck stupid by Kesha's beauty. He then shook it off and continued with what he had to say. *"I'm good. Are you alright, though?"*

"My neck is killing me, but I'll be fine. I'ma head over to emergency once we get this taken care of. Limme grab my insurance papers out of the glove-box so we can exchange info. I'll be right back." Kesha walked off with Te'Qui eyes glued to her skin tight black jeans, watching her bodacious ass swing from left to right. He admired the sculp of her bottom as she reached inside of her vehicle through the front passenger window to grab her insurance papers out of the glove box. He observed her place some papers on the hood of her car and jot something down on it. Once she finished she advanced in his direction, looking over the papers. Kesha gave Te'Qui her insurance information and took down his for herself.

"Again, I'm sorry about all of this. I'ma call my insurance company as soon as I get home and let 'em know what happened."

"I appreciate that; good lookin' out."

Silence fell between Kesha and Te'Qui as they stood in the street staring into one another's eyes. Suddenly, Kesha decided to break the ice again.

"Listen, I feel awful about this. How about chu let me take you out to dinner to make up for it. What do ya say, huh?" she touched his hand affectionately, while holding his gaze and hoping he'd agree to go out with her.

"It's all good. You ain't gotta do that. I'm sure yo' insurance company will take care of me." He held up the paper containing her car insurance information.

"Please, I insist. Besides, it's the least I could do. I mean, look at cho shit. If I was you, I woulda jumped outta my car and beat my ass." She glanced at the dented bumper of Te'Qui's car and then focused her attention back on him. She looked at him with sad eyes and a pouty lip; fingers interlocked implying she was begging him. Te'Qui pretended to think it over a moment before answering. He was feeling Kesha but he didn't want to come off as thirsty. Once he figured he'd made her sweat long enough, he nodded his head and agreed to go out to dinner with

*her. As soon as he did a big ass smile spread across Kesha's
face and she jumped excitedly. She pulled her cellular from out
of the back pocket of her jeans and programmed Te'Qui's
telephone number into it. Once she'd locked his digits into her
cell phone, she gave him a friendly hug and promised she'd call
him soon to set up a date and time for them to go out for dinner.
This was one year ago.*

Te'Qui scooped Kesha up into his arms and carried her
down the hallway. He kicked open their bedroom door and
walked her over to the bed, where he laid her down. He slither
between her legs and cupped her face as he kissed her. Slowly,
they began peeling off one another's clothing until they were
nude. That night they made hot, sweaty, passionate love and fell
asleep, afterwards.

Later that night Te'Qui woke up to find Kesha asleep with
her arms around him. He smiled when he looked over his
shoulder and saw her beautiful face. He removed his arm from
around her and slid out of the bed, causing her to stir awake,
looking at him through narrowed eyelids.

"Where you going, bae?" Kesha asked him and yawned,
stretching her arms.

"I gotta piss, I'll be right back. Go back to sleep." Te'Qui
kissed her on the forehead.

"I love you."

"I love you more."

Kesha smirked and puckered her lips for a kiss. Te'Qui
chuckled and smiled before kissing her. Afterwards, she lay back
down in bed and fell right back to sleep. Te'Qui covered her
with the sheets and headed inside of the bathroom, flipping on
the light switch and shutting the door behind him.Once Te'Qui
relieved his bladder and washed his hands, he walked back
inside of his bedroom. He picked up the remote control and
turned on the flat screen which was mounted on the wall. As
soon as the television set came on it cast a light on Kesha and the
bed. Te'Qui looked to see if the illumination had disturbed her
but it hadn't.

Te'Qui walked back to the bed with the remote control. He
picked a club flyer up from off his dresser that someone had left

on the windshield of his car while he was in the super market with Kesha a few days ago.He sat the remote control down in place of the flyer and propped himself up in bed with his pillow. He used the light shining on him from the TV's screen to look at the flyer again.

On the front of it there was a big time drug dealer known around the city as Enzo. The nigga was holding a bottle of Ace of Spades in either hand and had four of the finest bitchez Te'Qui had ever seen in his life with their hands on him. The flyer was advertising the kingpin's birthday bash which was going down tomorrow night. As T.J. continued to study the flyer a jovial expression spread across his face. A plan had formed in his mind that would make his bank account even fatter.

Tranay Adams

CHAPTER THREE

T.J. stood inside of the tub with his head bowed and his hand pressed against the tiled wall. His eyelids were shut as the shower water beat down upon him, washing off the soap suds. He found his dick growing hard thinking about how he had Boo in the backseat of her car, beating her pussy up. He hadn't had any ass in a while and had forgotten what it was like to be with a woman, but damn did little momma give him a reminder. The only thing he hated was that he nutted so fast. He really didn't get a chance to enjoy the sex, and he was sure Boo didn't either. Right then he decided once he was done with his shower he was going to make up for his lackluster performance from earlier that day.

T.J. turned the dials and shut the shower water off. He slid open the glass sliding door and stepped his bare feet out onto the linoleum one at a time. He snatched his towel off the rack, drying his face and body. Next, he wrapped the towel around his waist and headed out of the bathroom. He'd just pulled opened the door and stepped out into the hallway when he clocked Boo hurrying past him with Cordary hanging over her shoulder asleep and toting a duffle bag. Instantly, his forehead creased with lines and he wondered what the fuck was going on. As he adjusted the towel on his waist, he sped walked down the hallway after her.

"Yo', Boo, where the fuck you going? It's one o'clock in the morning." A crinkled brow T.J. reminded her.

Boo suddenly stopped inside of the living room and turned around to him, holding her duffle bag at her side. T.J.'s brow crinkled further when he saw that the duffle bag she was toting was the same one he'd stashed his money inside of from the lick he'd hit.

"I'm sorry, T.J., but this isn't gonna work out. I'm leaving you." Boo looked at him like *It is what it is, nigga*.

"Bitch, you just had my dick in yo' mouth and in yo' pussy, now you 'bouta bounce onna nigga?" he raised an eyebrow in confusion. "Okay, cool. Fuck it! I can bust me another bitch, ain't no thang. You can get on, but what chu not gon' do is walk off with what I risked my ass for; leave my shit here!" he threw his finger at the bag. He'd be damned if he let her walk off with what he'd busted his ass for when she barely did shit to help him. If she thought that was going to happen then she had him fucked up.

"Nigga, I'm taking this shit! Me and yo' son gon' need it. Shit, you can kick some other dope boy's door down and get some mo'mothafuckin' money!" Boo spat with crazy attitude, moving her head like the true hood rat that she was.

"Hoe, you got me all the way fucked up! I tell you what though. I'ma give yo' ass 'til the count of three to step off! If you still here afterwards, I'ma go get my gun and I'ma shoot chu dead in that trifling-ass mouth of yours." his eyebrows slanted and he snarled, holding up three fingers. As he counted down, he dropped a finger with each number he called out. Boo didn't budge, she switched arms with her son and stood her ground. This caused an evil smirk to form at the corner of T.J.'s lips. "Youa brave bitch, you know that? Respect. But I'ma 'bouta show you I'ma nigga of my word," T.J. went to turn around to get his gun and the stock of a shotgun slammed into his face. The vicious blow spun him around, causing him to lose his towel, before crashing to the floor. He looked up at his attacker with blurred vision and blood creeping out of his nose. T.J. was in a daze as he touched below his nostrils and his fingertips came away bloody. When he looked back up at the nigga that had bust him in his face with the ass in of his shotgun, he saw two blurred images of him. Once the images combined and his vision cleared, he was able to see homie standing over him.

The mothafucka that had knocked T.J. on his ass was a tall, thuggish looking nigga. He looked to be in his mid to late sixties. He sported a black doo-rag with the flap on his head and his frame filled out a tan Dickie suit, which was opened to a black thermal. A platinum cable hung around his neck, holding onto his name, Drama. The D of the name was larger than the rest of the words and flooded with diamonds.

"Like she said, homeboy, we taking that shit." Drama looked down at T.J. mad dogging him as he twiddled the toothpick at the corner of his mouth. "Now, if you got anything else to say," he racked the chrome shotgun and pointed it in T.J.'s face. "You can say it to my friend here."

T.J. stared up at Drama with his face balled up, top lip twitching with hatred. His fists were at his sides and clenched so tight the veins in them bulged.

"I suggest you kill me, nigga. 'Cause I swear 'fore God, if you don't, I'ma find yo' ol' punk-ass and blow yo' fucking head off yo' shoulders! You hear me, nigga?" his eyes turned glassy and he clenched his jaws harder, causing the vein in his temple to twitch.

An evil smile spread across Drama's lips as he started laughing. His laughter was low at first, but then it grew loud and maniacal. The old thug looked back and forth between T.J. and Boo. His threatening eyes then settled on T.J.'s scowling face. "Loud and clear. Now, here's a lil' secret I'ma let chu in on, youngsta," Drama leaned down into T.J.'s ear and told him something that made his eyes bulge with surprise. He then stood upright smiling devilishly. Leveling his shotgun at T.J.'s chest, he went to pull the trigger but Boo called out to him.

"Baby, no! He ain't even worth it. We got the money and the bricks, let's just get outta here. Don't mind him. He's just talkin' shit, like he always do." Boo glanced in T.J.'s direction. The way she saw it, they were already breaking his ass for everything he had, it would be seriously fucked up if they were to kill him, too. Besides all of that, she still had a twinkle of love for the nigga. When he was out in the streets he was doing some of everything you could think of that was illegal to make sure they were well taken care of. She felt that by getting Drama to spare his life she'd be showing a little of her appreciation for his holding her down back in the day.

"You right, baby girl. This fat-fuck ain't worth the shell!" Drama spat the toothpick into T.J.'s face. T.J. shut his eyelids and slightly turned his head, as the toothpick deflected off his forehead. "Come on, momma, let's get up outta here."

Drama lowered his shotgun and took the duffle bag from Boo's hand. He then kissed her and headed out of the door. Boo looked at T.J. before following Drama out of the house, pulling the door halfway closed behind her.

T.J. scrambled to his feet as soon as Boo and Drama were out of his sight. He ran down the hallway and into the bedroom, flipping over the mattress. He grabbed both of his .9mm's and ran back up front. He kicked open the front door and ran out of the house. He came hurrying down the steps asshole naked with his dick swinging from left to right. By the time he reached the entrance of the yard, Drama was coming around in his Yukon Denali completing a U-turn. T.J.'s eyebrows slanted and wrinkles formed around his nose. He squared his jaws and came up with his 9 Double M's.

Blocka! Blocka! Blocka!
Blocka! Blocka! Blocka!

The shots shattered the black tinted windows at the back of the Yukon as it sped away. T.J. was so pissed off, that he hopped the short gated fence and ran out into the street. He chased after the SUV until he felt like he'd gotten far enough, then he stopped and pointed his guns at it.

Blocka! Blocka! Blocka! Blocka!

"Punk-ass nigga!" T.J. spat harshly, spit flying from his lips.

Blocka! Blocka! Blocka! Blocka!
Blocka! Blocka!

Drama's Yukon continued down the street until the brake lights disappeared into the night. T.J.'s eyes lingered in the direction that the SUV went in for a moment longer. He then turned around and marched toward his house, huffing and puffing out of breath. There was beads of sweat covering his face and body.

"Them bitchez are dead as soon as I find 'em. I swear 'fore God!" T.J. pointed one of his .9mm's into the air and busted it off, fire flickering from its barrel.

Blocka! Blocka! Blocka! Blocka!

T.J. skipped up the steps and went inside of the house, slamming the door behind him.

***

T.J. sat inside of Tam's Jr's on Hoover and Figueroa. He was hunched over a Styrofoam container of chili cheese pastrami French fries. His nose was twice its size thanks to Drama busting him in his face with the butt of his shotgun. He found it a little harder to breathe, but reasoned it wouldn't be a problem in time.

At the moment, he was thinking about his next move. He needed some money and he needed some money fast. He had about sixteen dollars in his pocket, and that wasn't shit. During his time out in the streets, he didn't have anything less than one-hundred thousand dollars stashed away. That wasn't counting the money he had on lock in case he got jammed up on a case.

You see, while T.J. was caged up, Boo ran through the money he'd put up to take care of her and his son. Now, she was only supposed to make sure she took care of the necessities, but her fake boujee-ass was breaking bread for designer labels and renting exotic cars. Needless to say, she blew through all of those bags.

T.J. was pissed off once Boo told him that she was broke. He'd told her to save him something to come home to, but obviously that shit went in one ear and out of the other. Basically, Boo wasn't trying to hear that shit he was talking. She still spent that nigga's shit up! This is why she made sure to set him up with a lick that would have him straight for a while. It was the profit from that same lick that Boo and that bitch-ass nigga Drama made off with earlier that night.

Scandalous-ass hooka! I shoulda knew better than to fuck around with her ass anyway! That's just what my fat-ass get! You can't make a hoodrat wifey material! It just ain't in the bitch! That's what my black-ass get tryna play Captain Save-A-Hoe. Ol' simp-ass nigga! It's okay, though. Soon as I catch up to ol' girl and her ol' wannabe young, fake thug-ass nigga, I'ma slump they asses. That's onna gang!

Hearing the bell over the door of the establishment ringing, T.J. looked up to see a quartet of people enter: two young men and two pretty young girls. The men had their arms hung around the girls' shoulders and their eyes were focused on the menu which sat high up behind the bulletproof glass. The bulletproof glass had niggaz' hoods scratched into it and drawn on it with permanent markers and/or white out pens. This didn't seem to matter to the youngstas though. They appeared to be ordering without any problems seeing the items they had in mind to purchase. Once they'd finished ordering, they kicked it around the tables shooting the shit. T.J. noticed that the young men were rocking heavy jewels and gold teeth. He reasoned they had to be into something illegal to afford such fly ass jewelry, and those bitchez they were with. Because the way he saw it, there wasn't any broads that fine looking to kick it with niggaz that weren't holding a little something, something.

T.J. ate his food and estimated the cost of the jewelry the young niggaz were sporting, as well as the bulges in their pockets which let him know that they were holding bankrolls. He knew that if he was to stick their asses up he'd come off with a nice chunk of change. As T.J. debated whether he was going to make those young balla niggaz break themselves or not, the cashier was calling them forward to get their orders. The quartet grabbed their respective grease stained bags and glanced inside of them to make sure their orders were right. One of the young niggaz popped a frie into his mouth and pushed open the glass door, making his way outside with the rest of the group on his heels. Seeing his meal ticket getting away, T.J. decided then that he had to bag them niggaz if he was going to eat. With that thought in mind, he closed his Styrofoam container, all the while keeping his eyes on the youngstas.

"Fuck this, them niggaz food," T.J. pulled out his gun and cocked it underneath the table. He then stuck it inside the pocket of his hoodie and pulled his hood over his head. Keeping his head bowed, he rose from the table and hastily approached the couples as they left out of the burger joint. From inside of the restaurant, the only patron left watched T.J. through the window as he ate his bacon cheese burger. He couldn't hear shit the fat nigga was saying, but whatever it was it must have been threatening, while he waved his gun around at the youngstas. All of their asses looked terrified, especially the women. T.J. had them mothafuckaz coming up off their money and jewelery. Afterwards, he made them lay on the ground, and bent down to one of them, taking what the patron believed were car keys. He then kicked whoever it was in the side and walked off. A second later, a pearly white Lincoln Navigator on some chrome "24 rims squealed out of the parking lot.

The youngstas that had just been robbed rose to their feet, looking disheveled and brushing the dirt from off their clothing.

The girls were crying and holding one another while the men swore to get revenge on the nigga that jacked them.

"As soon as I get a hold of my shit, I'm hittin' these streets and this nigga gone, just as soon as I find 'em. On my mothafuckin' grand momma, rest in peace." one of the young men swore as he dusted his Angels fitted cap off. While he was popping shit, his homeboy was holding his aching side and wincing, dialing somebody on his cellular.

The patron shook his head and picked up one of the fries from off the yellow wrapper that had once covered his burger. He dipped the fry into the slightly smeared pool of ketchup.

***

T.J. sped the big body Navigator into the automotive repair shop and pulled it up to a shutter, where he blew the horn twice. Shortly thereafter, the shutter rose up and a short fellow with big glasses and a nappy afro waved him in. He stepped aside to allow the Navigator to drive over the threshold before pressing the button that shut the shutter. As soon as he walked back inside, he circled the car taking a good look at it while gliding his fingertips over its sleek surface. He suddenly stopped and took a couple of steps back, massaging his chin as he thought of the bag he should drop into T.J.'s lap for the vehicle.

"I'll give you seven racks for it," the short fellow, whose name was Tiny, turned to T.J. and adjusted his glasses. Through his lenses T.J. could see the sparks flying from all over the shop as mechanics worked on several vehicles, removing their parts.

"Done deal," T.J. nodded in agreement of the payment he'd offered.

"Bet. I'll be right back." Tiny tapped him and headed off to retrieve the money. While he was gone, T.J. busied himself looking at car parts that had most likely been taken off stolen automobiles. He studied a shiny hub cap which was hanging from a wall at the furthest end of the garage. Seeing Tiny approaching him from behind, through the shiny hub cap, he turned around and the little fellow pushed a wrinkled brown paper bag into his hands. T.J. looked through the bag, pulling out one of the stacks that inhabited it and then dropping it back inside of it. "We good?" Tiny asked as he tilted his head to the side.

T.J. took the time to roll up the paper bag and tuck it inside the front of his Dickies before answering the question. "Yeah, we good." he dapped up Tiny and gave him a gangsta hug before he went on about his business. He disappeared into the night where he jacked himself another car so he could go see his man to fence the stolen goods.

***

T.J. entered his motel room and flipped on the light switch. He picked the remote control up from the nightstand and turned on the television set, flipping through the channels until he found something he was interested in watching. A moment later, The Jefferson's theme song erupted from the T.V.'s speakers and he sat the remote down on the small round table at the window. He then put his Popeye's chicken bag and his two liter bottle of Coca Cola down on the table. Still standing, he started pulling out the fat knots of money he'd made from that night's caper and the dough from fencing the jewelry. He dropped all of the money on the table top. When he went to sit down, he spotted something folded up and black at his feet. His brows wrinkled wondering what it was beside his sneaker. Right then he recalled it was a flyer for Club Vicious. He'd taken it out of the Navigator he'd stolen.

T.J. picked up the flyer and unfolded it, seeing a big time drug dealer known around the city as Enzo. The nigga was holding a bottle of Ace of Spades in either hand and had four of the finest bitchez he'd ever seen in his life with their hands on him. The flyer was advertising the kingpin's birthday bash which was going down tomorrow night. T.J. continued to study the flyer as he massaged his chin smiling, thinking of how he could make his next bag.

The next night

Te'Qui and Kesha bypassed the line that was wrapped around the corner for them to get inside of Club Vicious. Te'Qui hit the bouncer's hand with him and his lady's entree fee and a one-hundred dollar bill for himself. Having paid the tithe, the young couple was granted access to the establishment. As soon as they crossed the threshold, Te'Qui and Kesha were patted down and searched thoroughly by an individual of their respective sex, who was dressed in all black, like the gentleman working at the front door. Once this was done, Te'Qui and Kesha were free to walk into the club. Walking down the corridor, with their arms hooked with one another, they found Usher's *Yeah* growing closer and closer, until they were finally on the dance floor. There was a sea of people dancing and smiling; seemingly having a good old time. The colorful disco balls spinning from the ceiling flashed *on* and *off* the patrons.

Te'Qui spotted the bar and pointed it out to Kesha. He then walked over to it. The bartender, a tall, lanky white dude with bleached blond hair and a piercing that went through both nostrils, appeared to be hard at work preparing drinks and making mental notes of awaiting patrons' orders. There seemed to be one-thousand hands holding up $5, $10 and $20 dollar bills trying to get the bartender's attention. He looked like he was taking the orders of those that were offering to tip him big. With this in mind, Te'Qui whipped out a one-hundred dollar bill and called him over. The bartender looked down the bar at the young gangsta and took in his attire. Te'Qui was dressed in a red blazer, which he wore over a black turtle neck and red, suede Versace slip-ons. His accessories were gold designer frames, a gold crucifix, an A.P Rolex watch flooded with rubies and an icy gold pinky ring. To the bartender, Te'Qui looked like a quarter million dollars in drug money, so he couldn't pass him up. He approached him with a friendly smile while he shook up the metal canister containing the drink he was preparing.

"What's up, boss?" the smirking bartender asked.

"Gimme a Corona and a cranberry juice; the rest of this is yours, my man," Te'Qui held out the one-hundred dollar bill toward him and he took him. When the bartender went off to finish the drink he already was in the middle of making, Te'Qui and Kesha turned around to the dance floor. They leaned against the bar, holding hands and scoping the scenery. As soon as Te'Qui's eyes landed on the man he was looking for, he leaned close to the ear of his lady and whispered something to her. Kesha's eyes went right to where Enzo's ass was on the dance floor.

Enzo was in a crowd of dancing club goers. He was grinding against two exotic looking women and groping. One was at his back and the other was at his front. They were sharing a three way kiss with their eyes closed. From the looks of blissfulness written across their faces they appeared to be in their own world. Enzo stopped kissing the women and wiped his mouth with the sleeve of his shirt. He then grabbed the women by their hands and walked them towards the hallway. Te'Qui and Kesha kept their eyes on Enzo and the chicks until they disappeared through the men's room door.

"Cranberry juice and Corona, boss!" the bartender called out to Te'Qui. The young gangsta turned around and picked up the beverages, thanking homeboy. He passed the glass of cranberry juice to Kesha and kept the Corona. He interlocked his fingers with his lady's fingers and told her they were going to find a place to sit down. As they crossed the dance floor he kept his eyes on the men's room door.

"We can sit right here, babe." Kesha said to her man as she clocked a table in the shadiest part of the club. The table was hidden in the cut where not too many people could see it. There were half empty bottles of beer and a couple of glasses stained with alcohol occupying the table top because a waitress hadn't come by yet to clean it off.

"Limme get that for you," a white woman came out of nowhere, smiling. Her long brunette hair was pulled back into a ponytail and she was dressed in a black button-down, bowtie, slacks and matching apron. She went about the task of sitting the colorful beer bottles and glasses on her tray. She then sprayed the table with a cleanser and wiped it down. Afterwards, she hung the spray bottle on her belt, tucked the towel inside of her back pocket and picked up her tray. Te'Qui pulled out a wad of money and peeled off a bill, dropping it on the waitress's tray as she walked passed him, smiling. The woman thanked him and went on about her business.

Once the waitress was gone, Te'Qui and Kesha sat down at the table. They continued to watch the men's room door. A few minutes later, the door swung open and Enzo and those exotic looking bitchez came out. Enzo was zipping up his pants and buckling his belt while the women were fixing their hair and straightening out their dresses. Te'Qui and Kesha watched from the shadows as Enzo and the two women went into the V.I.P section. They lounged on a black leather sofa and smoked on hookahs, blowing smoke into the air.

At this time, D.J. Flip, the disc jockey for the night at the club was mixing Ron Browz' *Arab Money* and Jim Jones' *Ballin'*. He'd stop his mixing every now and again to shout out some shit to the mass of people on the floor dancing and grinding.

"Big shout out to Enzo, happy birthday, my nigga!" D.J. Flip called out from where he was posted, behind the turn tables, high up inside of the D.J. booth. He was a short, buff nigga that rocked his hair in short dread locks. A Gucci head band was around his forehead while his muscular form filled out a grey Gucci hoodie.

When Enzo heard the D.J. shout him out, he stood to his feet with four blocks of blue faces in each of his jeweled hands, looking around at everyone in the club, feeling like he was royalty and they were peasants or some shit.

"It's a real nigga birthday, bottles for everybody, on me!" Enzo announced and threw the money into the air, watching it rain down on everybody on the dance floor. The music came back on and he sat back down indulging in his hookah. He watched the scenary as the women he'd smashed inside of the men's room rubbed on him and shit.

Te'Qui and Kesha ventured onto the dance floor to get their groove on. They watched Enzo closely. It wasn't long before he was hitting the women he'd fucked earlier with a few dollars and sending them off. The remainder of his time in the V.I.P section he was guzzling expensive champagne and drunkenly dancing by himself. A big bald headed nigga that Te'Qui assumed was Enzo's chauffeur leaned over the velvet rope and said something to Enzo that he couldn't hear. Enzo glanced at his watch and sat the champagne bottle down on the table. He then pulled out a small wad of money that was held by a money-clip. He removed the clip and peeled off two one-hundred dollar bills, dropping it on the table top. Afterwards, he started for the velvet rope to get out of the V.I.P section. Seeing this, Te'Qui grabbed Kesha by her hand and led her towards the exit of the club. Te'Qui was going to get at that nigga as soon as he was out in the open.

***

Enzo made it to his Lexus truck and pulled out his keys. He pushed the button on the small remote and unlocked the driver's door. As soon as he pulled it open, he felt cold steel press against the back of his dome piece, and instantly the hair on the back of his neck stood upright and his body went rigid.

"Ah, ah, ah," Te'Qui began. "Now, I know you ain't cuttin' outta the party so soon without sayin' goodbye."

Enzo looked into the driver's window and saw a man wearing a red ski-mask. His eyes looked threatening, but a devilish smile was spread across his lips.

"Fuck! What the fuck you want, man?" Enzo slightly looked over his shoulder.

"What I want chu to do is to get into the driver's seat while I hop into the back. Yo' punk-ass gon' drive me to wherever the fuck you keep yo' money at. You try anything funny and I'ma turn the black tints in this fly ass whip red, you follow me?"

Enzo didn't say shit and that pissed Te'Qui off.

Te'Qui scowled and cracked him at the back of his head with the butt of his gun, causing him to bend forward, grabbing the back of his bleeding dome. He squeezed his eyelids and clenched his jaws, fighting back the throbbing pain he was feeling.

"Fuck you do that for, man?"

"Nigga, I ain't finna be sayin' what I gotta say two and three mothafuckin' times! I know you heard me! Now, get cho bitch-ass behind the wheel!" Te'Qui kept his banga on Enzo as he made to get into the backseat of the truck. As soon as he went to grab the door handle, he felt a gun press against the back of his neck. He stiffened up, and his eyes shot to their corners.

"Drop yo' gun, mothafucka, 'fore I splash you up against the side of this Lexus." A gravelly voice came from behind Te'Qui. It belonged to a big bald held nigga named Booney. He was Enzo's bodyguard. This was the same nigga that Te'Qui saw in the club talking to Enzo. He'd originally thought he was the kingpin's chauffeur. Booney was dressed in a navy blue turtle neck and a charcoal gray blazer. The mothafucka looked like Michael Clark Duncan. You know, John Coffee off The Green Mile movie?

Te'Qui dropped his gun like Booney's big ass had told him. The giant then patted him down. Once he didn't find any other weapons on him, he took his gun from the back of his head. Right after a wincing Enzo turned around rubbing the back of his head. He kicked Te'Qui between his legs which doubled him over. He followed up, grabbing him at the back of his neck and kneeing him in his face. Cocking his fist back, he punched him across the jaw and dropped him to the asphalt where he lay, bawling in pain.

"Damn, Booney, it took yo' ass long enough. This mothafucka coulda gotta 'way with my ass, man! Fuck was you doin'?" Enzo asked his bodyguard as he whipped out his handkerchief and used it to blotch the blood at the back of his head. Each time he touched the handkerchief to his dome, it came away bloodier and bloodier.

"My bad, boss, I lost you in the crowd. Luckily I got here when I did though." Booney pointed his gun down at Te'Qui, in case he tried some shit.

"It's alright, big man. All is forgiven." Enzo patted him on the arm. He then stuffed the stained handkerchief into his right back pocket. Afterwards, he turned his focus to a pained Te'Qui. "Ol' busta-ass nigga, gon' call yo' self tryna rob me," he pointed two fingers at his chest. "The mothafuckin' king of the streets. You gon' try to rob me? Oh, nigga, yo' momma musta drop yo' ass on yo' gotdamn head when you was born." he walked around him in a 360 degree turn, eyes looking down at him. He stopped once he reached his side and kicked him hard as shit in his stomach, lifting him off the ground. Te'Qui fell on his back wincing and holding his stomach.

Tranay Adams

"You chose the wrong one, homeboy," Booney stated, holding his gun on Te'Qui as his boss continued to stomp and kick him. "You see, the entire time you were playing the cut in the club watching my man, Enzo, I was watching yo' ass. I figured yo' ol' bitch-ass wassa jackboy which is why I pulled my man's coat tail to it. Now, here we are, in the parking lot, with you getting yo' monkey-ass handed to you. How 'bout that?" he cracked a one sided smile.

"He sho' in the fuck did!" Enzo gritted as he stomped Te'Qui in the stomach, causing his arms and legs to jump up from the ground.

"Uhhh!" Te'Qui made an ugly ass face as he felt Enzo's hard bottom dress shoe slam down against his torso.

"Get the fuck away from my, baby daddy!" A feminine voice rang out from behind Enzo and Booney. When they turned around, they found Kesha's crazy ass running at them with her gun up. She'd just pulled up and hopped out of her man's cherry red '64 Chevrolet Impala.

"Man, cap that crazy bitch, Booney!" Enzo pointed in Kesha's direction.

"Kesha, nooooooooo!" Te'Qui called out to his baby momma, outstretching his hand towards her, with a pained expression written across his face.

Blowl! Blowl!

Kesha let her gun talk to Booney and Enzo as she charged at them. Bullets whizzed by the men and over their heads.

"Keshaaaaaa!" Te'Qui called out to his unborn child's mother again.

Booney clutched his gun with both hands and angled his head. He shut one eyelid and took aim. He was about to end Kesha's life with one shot, that was until God intervened.

Blocka! Blocka! Blocka!

Three caps slammed into Booney and he grimaced, dropping his gun to the ground. Enzo looked to where the bullets had come from. At the end of his line of vision, he saw a fat nigga wearing a black bandana on his head and the lower half of his face. His eyes were covered by black sunglasses. He had two black .9mm handguns in his meaty hands, popping them both off.

As the bullets were flying around them, Enzo pulled Booney up by his arm and they took off running down the block. By this time, police car sirens filled the air; Twelve was heading to their location.

The fat nigga that was rocking the black bandanas ran over to Te'Qui. He leaned down and examined his body for wounds but he didn't find any. He asked him was he okay and he nodded yes. Next, the fat nigga stood up, holding one gun at his side and pointing the other at the fleeing suspects.

Blocka! Blocka! Blocka!

The fat nigga blasted his tool sideways at Booney and Enzo's fleeing backs, but they'd gotten too far for him to reach. Te'Qui's rescuer tucked his warm guns on his waistline and helped him upon his feet, throwing his arm over his shoulders. At this time Twelve's sirens were getting louder and louder as they closed in.

"Yo', follow me, lil' momma!" The fat nigga hollered out to Kesha. She was standing before him with her gun at her side, looking like she wasn't sure of what to do. She focused her attention on Te'Qui, who looked to be in pain, waiting for him to give her some instructions. Instead, he nodded, letting her know that it was okay for her to follow homeboy's order.

With the okay given, Kesha ran back to the Impala and jumped in behind the wheel. Once she'd gotten into the car, homeboy that had held Te'Qui down helped him over to the passenger side of his whip. He slammed the door shut and ran over to the driver side, jumping in behind the wheel. Shortly thereafter, he fired up his car and sped out of the parking lot, with Kesha following not too far behind.

The fat nigga took a few back streets and bent a few corners, with Kesha keeping up with him. He winded up in a dark ass alley where he murdered the headlights of his ride, and told Te'Qui to tell his baby momma to kill hers. Te'Qui didn't waste any time pulling out his cellular and texting Kesha the command he was given. Shortly, the lights of the Chevrolet were executed. By this time, Twelve's sirens were growing even louder, and the fat nigga was staring into the side view mirror. Through the reflection he clocked One Time whipping past him at his rear, red and blue lights flashing.

Once the sounds of the sirens disappeared down street, homeboy removed his sunglasses and his bandanas. He threw them out of the window and turned to Te'Qui.

"Ante up, my nigga," the fat nigga flexed his fingers, wanting Te'Qui's red ski-mask. Still holding his side, Te'Qui pulled it off, leaving his cornrows frizzy. "Yo' Glizzy too," he referred to his Glock as he held out his hand.

Te'Qui's face twisted and he looked homie up and down like, *Who the fuck are you?* "Blood, I gave you my mask, I'm ridin' in yo' whip hurt, and pretty much at yo' mercy. But it'll be a cold day in hell 'fore I give you my strap. Now, I appreciate you savin' my ass back there, don't get me wrong, but I don't know or trust yo' ass. You feel me?"

Old boy smirked and nodded his head, saying, "I feel you, Blood." he then went on to clean his guns off with the lower half of his shirt and tossed them out into the alley, along with the red ski-mask. Next, he fished a half smoked blunt from out of the ashtray and used a lighter to roast the tip of it, until it wafted smoke. When he sucked on the end of it, its tip glowed ember and he blew out a cloud of smoke. He turned on the lights of his vehicle. Switching hands with the bleezy, he swifted the gear into reverse and looked over his shoulder so he could back out of the alley.

"Hit cho girl up and tell her to follow me to the hospital." the fat nigga told Te'Qui as he backed out of the alley. Once T.J. was out in the street, he put his whip into drive and pulled off. Kesha was following right behind him.

***

Te'Qui was checked out at the emergency ward of the hospital. Besides his swollen and bruised face, he had fractured his ribs. The doctor wrapped his torso in bandages and gave him a prescription for some painkillers. With the examination having been done, Te'Qui was free to go home. When he emerged from the back he saw the fat nigga, who he later found out went by the name, T.J, sitting right beside Kesha. They looked to be conversing about something, but he didn't know exactly what. He found it suspicious that they suddenly stopped talking once they saw him walking up.

"Babyyyyyyy," Kesha sprung to her feet and ran over to Te'Qui wrapping her arms around him. She kissed on his lips and every exposed part of his face that she could. While she was busy smooching on him, he was looking over her shoulder at T.J. A crease fixed on his brows.

"Yo'," Te'Qui held Kesha back at arm's length, looking into her eyes. She frowned up, wondering what was up.

"What's up, bae? Something wrong?" she questioned with concern.

"Yeah, fuck was y'all choppin' it up about?"

"Who? Me and T.J?"

"Yeah, you and T.J." his eyebrows slanted, as he looked back and forth between her and T.J.

"Oh, look at my booski, getting all jelly and shit. That's so cute," she smiled, grabbing him by his bottom jaw and puckering his lips up. She gave him a quick peck on them. "We just talking about you and the baby, silly. Ain't nothing to be worried about. You know who all of this," she placed his hands on her breasts and then her bodacious ass. "This, and this," she placed his hands on her heart. "Belongs to."

"Who?" he angled his head, looking at her side ways like she wasn't about to say his name.

"You. My king. Who else?" she smirked and threw her arms around his neck.

Te'Qui placed his hands on her waist, staring her in the face. The animosity vanished from his face and he finally cracked a smile. "It better be me. Had you said any other nigga'z name, I woulda stanked yo' ass."

"Oh, really?" she smirked harder, coming closer to him. Their noses were nearly touching. "So, you gone kill me while I'm carrying yo' baby, nigga?"

"Nope. I'ma wait 'til you have 'em, then I'm nod yo' ass." he smiled harder, looking into her eyes lovingly.

Kesha smacked him in the back of his head playfully and said, "Stop playing, boy, and gimme a kiss."

Te'Qui and Kesha turned their heads counterclockwise as they kissed deep and passionately.

"You know I love you, right?" he stared deep into her eyes, meaning every word he'd just spoken to her. He'd never loved any woman in the world more than he loved her. He'd smashed mad bitchez and didn't any of them mean shit to him but pussy. Kesha had his heart and his undying loyalty. There wasn't anything in the world that he wouldn't do for her. Little momma was his ride or die, for sure.

"You better 'cause if you don't, after I have this baby, I'ma kick yo' ass." Kesha swore, holding him by the collar of his hoodie as she brushed her nose up against his, affectionately. She then kissed him three times, mashing her lips against his the third time. "I love you too, baby."

Te'Qui threw his around Kesha's shoulder, wincing when he did so. Her face frowned up as she looked to him wondering what was wrong. "You okay?"

"Yeah, it's just my ribs, I'm be good though. Come on." he ushered her towards the emergency room exit. Coming across T.J., he motioned for him to follow them outside. Once they were outside, he turned to Kesha. "Baby, go get the car, I'ma holla at T.J. for a minute."

"Okay." Kesha smiled and kissed him. As she turned to walk away, Te'Qui smacked her on her ample bottom. She stopped mid-walk, looked over her shoulder grinning, and twerked for him a little.

"Alright, now, don't get the shit fucked up out cha when we get home." Te'Qui cracked a one sided grin.

"Nigga, please, you ain't scaring nobody." she walked on.

"Alright, bet." he watched his woman as she continued to stroll towards the parking lot, observing her big old booty rocking back and forth.

Right then, T.J. stepped beside him. Instantly, Te'Qui's demeanor changed. His face took on a more serious expression and he looked to homeboy.

"First off, homie," Te'Qui began. "I wanna thank you for savin' my ass. If it wasn't for you, them fools woulda laid down me, my lady and our unborn child."

T.J. nodded his head and said, "Don't mention it. It's all love."

"Nah, you don't know me, homie. You didn't have to stick yo' neck out there for me like that. You don't owe me jack shit. You feel me?"

"I feel you."

"Which brings me to my other question, what were you doin' out there any way?" he looked him square in his eyes, trying to read what kind of nigga he was. That nigga T.J. didn't even flinch. There wasn't any hoe in his DNA. That's for damn sure.

"Look, I'ma keep it a g-stack witchu, Blood," T.J. started off. "A nigga 'bout the ski-mask business, I stay hitting licks and shit. When I saw that nigga Enzo, knowing that he basically a mothafucking crack king, I saw a pay day. I was gon' snatch that ass up and have 'em take me to where he holding all his money and dope at. Right when I was finna bust my move, I saw you making yours. I saw you in trouble, and decided to step in, you feel what I'm saying?"

"Like I said earlier, dawg, I appreciate chu lookin' out for a nigga." he dapped him up. "Listen, limme bless you with a lil' somethin', somethin' for yo' trouble."

"Nah," homie put his hands up, letting him know he didn't want anything from him. "I can't take that from you. What I did was just good lookin' out."

"You sho'? 'Cause I could lay somethin' on you tonight."

"As fucked up as I am out here, I don't know how the hell I'm fixing my mouth to tell you no." he shook his head and ran his hands down his face. He couldn't help thinking about how close to broke he was. The lick he'd hit the night prier netted him a little change but it would only last for so long. He was counting on the loot he'd make snatching up Enzo keeping his pockets straight for a minute, but that hit was botched on the account of Te'Qui getting to his victim before he did.

Te'Qui's forehead creased with a line as he stood upright and folded his arms across his chest. He looked at T.J like he was generally concerned about his problems. "Look, homie, I'm not tryna get all up in yo' B.I., but what's up witchu?"

T.J took a deep breath before beginning. "Blood, to make a long story short, my baby momma and some old nigga hit me for six birds and sixty bands, stuck me for all my shit." he shook his head thinking about the haul he'd come up on, only to have some low life hoodrat rape him for it. From the look in his eyes, Te'Qui thought the nigga wanted to cry. If he would have, he wouldn't have blamed him. The way he was talking, homegirl must have hit him for something real nice. "Bitch fucked me with no vaseline, dawg."

"I'm sorry to hear that. I know how it is to lose it all, then have to figure out how to get it all back again." Te'Qui assured him. "Limme hit cho pocket with a lil' somethin' tomorrow though. You know, a lil' somethin' to hold you over 'til you get back on you feet."

"I can't let chu do that. I'ma man. I can't be out here taking no hands out." He told him. "Check this out though. You know what chu can do for me?"

"All you gotta do is name it, homie."

"If you really wanna help a nigga out, look out fa me the next time another lick falls into yo' lap. I'd greatly appreciate it." T.J. looked at him with sincere eyes.

Te'Qui stared at him for a moment, weighing his options as he thought things over, massaging his chin. Making up his mind, he pulled his cellular from out of his pocket and outstretched it towards T.J. "I got chu, my nig. Just program yo' math into my cell, and I'ma holla at chu once I come up on something."

"Fa sho," T.J. programmed his telephone number into the cell phone and handed it back to Te'Qui, who stashed the cellular inside of his pocket. "Good looking out, my nigga." he dapped him up and moved to head towards his ride. He stopped and turned around once Te'Qui called out to him. "'Sup with it?"

"Where you from, Blood?"

T.J. told him the blood gang that he was from.

"I'm from Eastside 20s Bloods." Te'Qui replied.

"Blood Love," T.J threw up the Bloody B. Te'Qui returned the gesture.

Right then, Kesha pulled up in front of Te'Qui and unlocked the passenger door. He snatched the door open and jumped into the front passenger seat. He gave his baby momma another kiss and she drover off, passing T.J as he trekked towards his whip. She honked the horn and they waved at him. He waved back and continued towards his ride, fishing his keys out of his pocket.

"Looks like somebody made them a new friend." Kesha glanced at Te'Qui and smiled.

"Ain't no new friends, baby. That nigga back there saved my life, so I owe him one. I'ma pay that debt, after that we square."

"Aww, come on. You could always use some new friends."

"Baby, I don't even have any old friends." Te'Qui told her. "The only friend I have ever had in life besides Poochie was my nigga, Baby Wicked; one of the downest, truest, realest young niggaz to have ever walked the earth. I don't trust nan' other nigga outside of 'em."

"I guess it's just you and me against the world, huh?"

"Me, you and that bun you got bakin' in that oven." he glanced at her slightly protruding belly, rubbing on it gently. He then interlocked his fingers with hers, lifted her hand and kissed it. Next, he kissed her hand and laid his head back against the headrest, staring out of the window.

Tranay Adams

CHAPTER FOUR

Te'Qui was stirred awake by the ringing and vibration of his cellular. He turned on the lamp light as he twisted his knuckle at the corner of his eye. He picked up his cell phone and looked at the display. Recognizing the number, he frowned up wondered why homie was banging his jack at that time a night.

"What's brackin', Big?" Te'Qui spoke groggily into his cell phone.

"Man, my bad fa wakin' you up at this hour, but I needa holla at chu, ASAP." Big Will said into the cellular.

Te'Qui glanced at the digital clock on the nightstand. It was two o'clock in the morning.

"It's all good, Big, speak onnit." he told him as he lay back in bed. Kesha laid her head against him and rubbed on his chest.

"It's best that I holla at chu in person. A nigga ain't really tryna blast his bitness over the phone. You think we can meet up?"

"When?" Te'Qui asked, looking down at his lady and rubbing his hand up and down her arm. He then kissed her on the top of her head.

"Shit, right now if you can."

There was silence and Big Will knew that Te'Qui was thinking about it, so he decided to sweeten the pot for him.

"Look, here, I know you gotta lil' one onna way. If you can holla at me right now, I'll drop a lil' somethin', somethin' on you. How 'bout that?"

"Alright, bet. Where you wanna link up at?"

Big Will ran him the address where he wanted to meet him at. It was the Denny's parking lot at Universal Village by USC College.

"You got it, dawg?"

"Yeah, I got chu. I'll see you at, like, 2:30."

"Alright. No doubt."

Te'Qui disconnected the call and slipped out of bed. His moving caused Kesha to stir awake. She lay on the space he once was fluttering her eyelids and watching her man get dressed. Te'Qui slipped on his red Dickie shirt and matching pants.

Afterwards, he took his Glizzy from underneath his pillow and tucked it on his waistline.

"Where you going, baby?" Kesha inquired. She then yawned and stretched his arms, hearing her bones crack.

"I gotta make a run." Te'Qui said as he stood before the nightstand mirror, buttoning up his Dickie shirt.

"A run where, nigga?" She twisted her face up and angled her head.

"I gotta go see this dude; a Money Man. You know don't shit get me outta bed butta dolla or conflict."

"Unh huh, limme find out." she gave him a side eye as she folded her arms across her bosoms.

"Let chu find out what?" he turned around from the nightstand to her, having just picked up his red *T* fitted cap.

"That chu finna go lay up with the next bitch."

"Hahahahahahaha!" he laughed his ass off. "Yo', on Bloods, yo' ass really be trippin'. I ain't finna go see no bitch, right now. And if I was, best believe that hoe 'bouta come offa check. Shiiit, I gotta mothafuckin' baby onna 'way. Like them pimp niggaz say, 'bitch better break bread or play dead.'"

"Mmmmhmmm," she gave him a look like she knew he was trying to run game her. "Anyway, I'm finna grab my strap 'cause I'm rolling witcho ass." she threw the sheet from off her and jumped out of bed.

"Are you serious, man?" he asked her as she walked past him, headed towards the closet.

"Yep. 'Cause I don't trust a damn thang." she said, looking through the clothing hanging on the rack inside of the closet.

"Alright," he plopped down on the bed. "But cho black ass is drivin'." he pointed his finger at her.

"Whatever, nigga, don't try to deter me from coming." she said, slipping on her clothes.

Te'Qui chuckled as he watched her get dressed.

2:27 P.M.

Kesha pulled up inside of the parking lot and looked out of the front passenger window, just as Te'Qui was. At the end of their line of vision was a big bald headed ass nigga in an all red suit that looked something like the one Neo wore in The Matrix Reloaded movie. He was posted up beside a black on black Cadillac Escalade truck on some big ass chrome rims. Posted at the grill of the SUV was a tall cat, dressed in all black. He wore his hair in short twisties and had a goatee that outlined his mouth perfectly. He wore a serious face, and appeared to be keeping an eye on everything surrounding him. Homie was wearing a black bandana tied around his head, Tupac style, and black shades. His slightly muscular frame filled out a black wife beater, which he wore under a black jean jacket. Although Te'Qui couldn't see the burna for himself, he knew he was packing heat because he was Big Will's bodyguard, Drama.

"That big Suge Knight looking nigga is who you 'pose to be meeting with up here?" Kesha looked to her man.

"Yeah, that's Big Will, pull up over there by 'em." Te'Qui told her, eyes still on Big Will.

"Alright." she said, turning around inside of the parking lot and pulling up two parking spots down from Big Will's truck.

"Bae, you good?" Kesha asked Te'Qui just as he was about to jump out of the car.

"'Sup?" he looked over his shoulder at her.

"You want me and my friend to roll witchu?" she tapped her purse, referring to her gun she'd brought along just in case some shit cracked off at this little meeting of his.

Te'Qui chuckled and said, "Nah, baby. It's all good." he kissed her on the lips and then hopped out. Unbeknownst to him, Kesha was still eyeballing him and holding onto her purse. If drama arose, she was putting some holes in Will's big ass.

"Big mothafuckin' Will, what's brackin' witchu, Blood?" Te'Qui slapped hands with the big man and patted him on the back.

"Ain't shit. Maintainin'. You know how I do."

"Right, right, right." he nodded.

"You remember Drama, right?" Big Will nodded to his bodyguard.

"Yeah, I remember, Blood." Te'Qui turned to him. Throwing his head back, he said, "'Sup with it, homie?"

Drama looked Te'Qui up and down, then turned back to his scanning of the parking lot.

"Don't mind 'em. He's the strong silent type."

"Sho' you right." Te'Qui said, still staring at the side of Drama's face. He did his homework on the OG killa. He was a sixty-five-year-old cat, and was in excellent shape, for a man his age. Let the streets tell it, and Drama made his bones knocking off niggaz for mafia big wigs back in the day. There wasn't a dome he wouldn't split for the right change. The only reason he slowed down on the murder shit was because his nephew, Big Will, pulled him in off the streets to become his bodyguard and chauffeur. Still, every now and then the CEO of Hood Rich Records would let him bust his gun whenever there was some mothafucka that just couldn't seem to get right.

Big Will took a breath before going on to say what was on his mind. "I gotta situation that requires yo' level of expertise." he told him straight like that.

"Oh, yeah, what's that?" Te'Qui asked as he made a serious expression and rubbed hands together in anticipation of what he had to say.

"First off, I told you I was gon' hit chu off with a somethin' 'fore meetin' up with me, so limme gon' and get that out the way." Big Will took a brief look around the parking lot and pulled out a folded manilla envelope that had a thick stack of money impression on it. He then passed it to Te'Qui on the sneak.

Te'Qui stuck the manilla envelope into the small of his back, looking around to make sure there wasn't anybody watching him.

"Good lookin' out." Te'Qui dapped up the giant.

"Don't mention it." Big Will told him. "But, look, you know I got my own indie label, Hood Rich Records."

"Yeah, man, y'all doin' y'all thang out here, for real, for real." he folded his arms across his chest, nodding his head. "Salute to yo' team and y'all success." he saluted him.

"That's love; appreciate that shit, especially with all of these hating ass niggaz out here."

"Oh, most def'."

"Anyway, man, my artist, the biggest artist on my label, Killa Tay. Well, Blood, got jumped and robbed of his shines."

"Onna real?" Te'Qui frowned up and angled his head. He couldn't believe someone had the audacity to put hands on dude. He knew that whoever brought harm to him was going to pay their weight in flesh and blood, because what he gathered from his music and his persona, homie was one of the coldest gangstaz to have ever touched a microphone.

"Yeah, family, they done a real number on my nigga, too. Come here fa a second," Big Will motioned for Te'Qui to follow him with his meaty hand. They made their way around the Escalade truck and stopped at the front passenger door. He knocked on the black tinted window. A moment later, the window descended, to display a light-skinned nigga that had been riding shotgun. The side of his face was swollen, his left eyelid was swollen shut, his lips were busted and he had black and blue bruising below both of his eyes. On top of that, his arm was in a sling. This was the multi-platinum recording artist, Killa Tay. And somebody had beaten the dog shit out of homie. He was so ashamed of his appearance that he couldn't even look Te'Qui in the face.

"Damn, my nigga, who the fuck caught you down bad?" Te'Qui asked curiously, looking homeboy over. Seeing how fucked up he was made him mad for him. He just knew he was ready to soak the shirts of the bitch-made-ass niggaz that had pounded him out.

"I don't know exactly, but them niggaz gotta pay. Mothafuckaz thinking it's a joke wit' me, homie. I want some get-back, and the big homie says you the one to get me just that." Killa Tay looked to Big Will.

"Limme show you the footage these clown-ass niggaz posted up all over social media, dawg." Big Will pulled out his cellular and pulled up footage on VladTv of Killa Tay getting stomped out and robbed for all of his jewelry.

Te'Qui watched as Killa Tay walked out of the Galleria Mall with shopping bags, heading towards his vehicle. Just as he reached his car, out of nowhere two dudes came out of nowhere. The larger of the two fired on Killa Tay. The swift blow sent the gangsta rapper spilling to the ground, spilling some of the contents out of his shopping bags. The nigga filming the whole shit hollered out 'WorldStar' as soon as the gangsta rapper was dropped. From there, the other masked fool joined the fray. Together, they stomped, kicked and punched the multi-platinum rhyme spitter. They snatched off all of his icy gold jewelry and his presidential Rolex watch. They then, grabbed his shopping bags and kicked him in his side as he struggled to get to his feet. The impact from the kick dropped him on his back, where he lay bloody and bruised. The nigga'z face looked like bloody hamburger meat and shit.

The nigga filming it all ran over to him and got a good close up of his face, telling anyone that would eventually view the footage what rapper it was that had just caught the L. Right after Killa Tay was stomped in the stomach, and the screen went black.

"You see that shit there, Blood? Mothafuckaz done my nigga dirty. This whole shit, makes my company look bad," he put his cell phone back inside of his suit's jacket. "So, I need for you, for a nice price of course, to make my company look good. You feel me?"

"Niggaz caught me lacking, but that shit won't ever happen again though. That's on mommas." Killa Tay spoke up once again, holding up his Glock and wagging it. He then glanced in the sun-visor mirror to check out his wounds.

"Niggaz wouldn't have caught chu lackin' if you woulda took unc witchu, like I told you to. Instead of tryna play supa gangsta and shit." Big Will frowned up at him. "I told you once you signed on that dotted line that cho life was finna change forever. You can't be out in the streets, kickin' it in the hood and in hole-in-the-wall fuckin' clubs, when you done sold twenty million records and shit, dawg. Youa mothafuckin' celebrity now, so these clout chasers, overzealous fans and goon-ass niggaz are gon' be lookin' to make yo' ass go viral. But, nahhhh, yo' hardheaded ass don't wanna listen to me. You know every-fuckin'-thing, but I bet that ass listen now, though."

"Whatever, Big Will, I'm not tryna hear that shit!" Killa Tay made a nonchalant face as he waved the boss of his record company off.

"Whatever, Big Will, my ass! I'll tell you what, you gon' and get cho ass smoked out here. Everybody knows a dead rapper makes mo' money than an alive one anyway," Big Will mad dogged Killa Tay as he slipped on a pair of shades, covering up his blackened eyes. Soon after, the gangsta rapper held down the button that made his window go back up. Once he'd done this, Big Will focused his attention back on Te'Qui. "Anyway, Blood, I need you to check these mothafuckaz for me, and get it all on video so we can upload the shit. I gotta show the world what happens when you put hands on one of mine, you feel me? I put my gangsta on the shelf once I started this label, but niggaz and bitchez gotta know I can pick it back up whenever need be."

"You know where these niggaz hang at, Big?" Te'Qui posed the question as he folded his arms across his chest again.

"Yeah, I know where they at. Mothafuckaz onna Gram been hittin' up Tay with some of everywhere these niggaz be at since the video went viral. I can give you this dumbass nigga'z password and shit," the giant looked at the passenger side window that Killa Tay was behind, heatedly. He wanted to open the door and smack fire out of his smart mouth ass, but truth be told, he loved the young nigga. He wasn't just his artist; he loved him like a brother. It hurt his heart having seen what those fool-ass niggaz had done to him at that parking lot at the mall. "So, you can hit the field with 'em."

"Alright, I can fuck with that." he rubbed his hands together in anticipation.

"Cool. How much you tryna get for this work?" Big Will inquired as he took the time to pull out a big ass Cuban cigar and light it. He took a pull from the end of it, causing its tip to turn ember before blowing out a cloud of smoke. He then watched as Te'Qui massaged his chin, thinking of how much he should hit him over the head with for the job he was asking him to do.

"Hmmmm," Te'Qui continued to massage his chin, as he stared out of the corner of his eyes, deep in thought. His mind was on what kind of time he'd be faced with if these fools he was going to holler at on the behave of Big Will decided to snitch on him, or if he got bagged by The Boys. Having finally coming up with a fitting price for the assignment, he dropped his hand at his side and addressed the giant. "Slide me a hunnit kay, big dawg."

"Okay. You got that." Big Will nodded. He didn't even bat an eyelash as he agreed to Te'Qui's payment. The young nigga gathered it was because he was a multi-millionaire, and one-hundred grand was a drop in the bucket to him. "I'll hit chu with half of that tomorrow mornin' and the other half once the job is done."

"My nigga." Te'Qui said in the same vain as Denzel Washington as he dapped up Big Will. "I'll hit chu up with the address to the meet spot once I get back to the crib."

"Fa sho'." Big Will took another pull from his Cuban, causing smoke to waft around him. He then looked beside Te'Qui and waved at someone, smiling. When Te'Qui looked to see who he was waving at, he found Kesha. She had her eyes on him and her hand inside of her purse. "That's yo' queen, homie?" he asked Te'Qui about Kesha, pointing with the hand that held his cigar.

Te'Qui turned back around to Big Will and said, "Yeah, that's my queen."

"You keep that one, dawg; lil' momma a rider, fa sho'." Big Will said. He'd noticed Kesha clocking him since she and Te'Qui had pulled up. This let him know that she was looking out for her man, and if some shit jumped off, she'd lay down that hold parking lot just to protect him. He had a wife that was ride or die just like that. He loved that gangsta love. To him, there wasn't anything like it. Fuck what you heard!

"I already know. I'ma gon' and get outta here, man. Shoot me ya man's password and shit so I can get at these fool's for y'all." he slapped hands with Big Will and patted him on his back.

"I got chu." Big Will watched as Te'Qui jumped into the front passenger seat and slammed the door shut. Right after, Kesha was driving off with him.

Big Will took another pull from his cigar and blew out a cloud of smoke. He then climbed inside of the Escalade truck. Drama slid in behind the wheel, cranked that big mothafucka up and drove out of Denny's parking lot.

The next night

Kesha lay in bed counting up the bag that Te'Qui had gotten, which was his first half of the payment for the job Big Will had hired him for. While she was busy doing all of this, Te'Qui was standing before the nightstand mirror strapping on his Kevlar bulletproof vest. He looked to each side that he strapped down, with red webbed, weed slanted eyes. Once he finished putting on the body armor, he adjusted it so it would fit him comfortably. Next, he slipped a black sweatshirt over his head and tucked his red ski-mask into his right back pocket. He grabbed his Glizzy and slid it inside of his deep pocket. Then, he picked up two extra magazines and slid them into his other pocket. Right after, he picked up the throwaway cellular that Big Will's people had dropped off along with the money. He was to use the cell phone to record the shit he was going to do to them old buster-ass niggaz that had ambushed Killa Tay. He had already gotten the username and password to Killa Tay's Instagram, so he was ready for the night's mission at hand.

Te'Qui sat down on the bed and looked at Kesha count up the last of the money. Once she was finished, she wrote the amount down on the small notepad lying beside her leg. Once she finished, she scooted over to Te'Qui and showed him the total amount he'd saved. Smiles spread across the couples' lips staring at nearly one million dollars.

"You see that, babe? We're $350,000 away from your goal." Kesha put her arm around Te'Qui's shoulders as she held the notepad before his eyes. He took the notepad from her hand and took a good look at it.

"That's hard work right there, baby, hard-mothafuckin'-work." Te'Qui declared, still looking over the numbers before him in black and white.

"Yep. My baby don't play when he sets his mind to something. I got myself a hard working, strong, handsome black man," she stared at him admiringly. She genuinely loved any and everything about him, even his flaws. Little momma couldn't see herself being with anyone else besides him. As far as she was concerned, he was going to be the man that she spent the rest of her life with.

"Once I get that million, I'm done. We gettin' the fuck outta the hood. We gon' raise our lil' family in the A." he switched hands with the notepad and rubbed on her stomach. Kesha chuckled and rubbed the opposite side of her stomach, looking down at it smiling.

Te'Qui had been knee deep in the streets snatching up every dollar that he could to obtain that million dollar goal. The plan was for him and Kesha to move down to Atlanta, buy a nice affordable six bedroom house and a Benz station wagon for their family. They had it in mind to open up their own soul food restaurant. It all had been Kesha's idea. She had wanted to be a chef and run her own spot ever since she was twelve-years-old. Now, here Te'Qui was, trying to make it all come true for her. There wasn't any wonder why she loved the young nigga as much as she did.

Kesha put the rubber bands back around the money she'd counted up and shoved it inside of the Gucci knapsack that Big Will's carrier had brought it in. She then passed it to Te'Qui who carried it over to the closet, opening it. Once he pulled the drawstring that turned on the light bulb hanging from the ceiling, he moved the clothes back that were hanging on the rack. He then kneeled down to a digital safe, glancing over his shoulder to make sure Kesha wasn't there trying to get a peek at the pass code he was about to enter. Although little momma was his heart, he wasn't anybody's fool. He knew a mothafucka, no matter how much they claim to love you, would body your ass for enough money.

Once he didn't see Kesha peering over his shoulder, Te'Qui went back to the key-pad before him. After he cleared his throat, he punched in the code to access the digital safe. The door popped open, and he started placing the g-stacks inside of the safe, alongside the other stacks of money already there. Once he was done unloading the knapsack, he sat it inside of the closet and shut the door of the safe. He put the clothes on the rack back in their rightful place and shut the closet door behind him.

"Baby." Kesha called out to the father of her unborn child.

"'Sup, momma?" Te'Qui asked.

"Well, you said there gonna be like three niggaz you gotta G-check, right? Well, I was thinking that maybe you should holla at T.J. You know, to have someone there to watch cho' back? You know he ain't no punk about his shit, and he won't hesitate to bust them thangz if he gots to."

"Hold up. You holdin' this nigga'z dick or somethin'?" Te'Qui gave her the side eye. He wasn't feeling her complimenting another nigga'z gangsta.

Kesha's brows furrowed and she waved him off like he was talking non-sense, saying, "Boy, please. Only nigga dick I'm holding is yours. All I'm tryna do is look out for you. I don't want nothing to happen to yo' black ass 'cause I know I'd be sick."

"Ain't nothin' 'bouta happen to me. I'm straight. You just worry too much."

"With the life you caught up in, can you blame a bitch for worrying about chu. The last thing I want is for something to happen to you and our child grows up without a father, like I did. When I think about him or her growing up without a father, it breaks my heart all over again and I get sad, babe. Real sad." Her vision obscured as her eyes pooled with tears and her bottom lip trembled. "Why you think I'm always tryna roll with you to have yo' back? At least I know if something happens to you, then I'll be there. That way, if niggaz take you out, then they gon' have to see me to. 'Cause I'd rather be dead than live in this world without chu." She became teary eyed.

"Lil' momma," Te'Qui stared into her eyes as he caressed the side of her face. He watched as she blinked back tears. "You ain't ever gotta worry about livin' in this world without me. 'Cause I ain't goin' nowhere without you and that lil' one of ours. That's on my momma and daddy's grave."

"Promise me, then." she said. Her eyes were focused on the collar of his sweatshirt as she fondled with it.

"Promise you what, beautiful?"

"That chu never gonna die, and leave me and our baby alone."

"Look at me," Te'Qui told her. She looked right up at him. "I promise I'm not gonna die and leave you and our baby. I'ma real-ass nigga, and I'm too hard to kill. These busta-ass niggaz I'm goin' to holla at can't fade me."

After telling her that, Te'Qui cupped her face and kissed her on both cheeks and then her forehead. Afterwards, he threw his hood on his head and grabbed his trench coat from off the bed. After he slipped the trench coat on, he lifted up his mattress and removed the long, black shotgun with the strap. *Chick-Chick!* He cocked that fat mothafucka and gave his lady a kiss goodbye. Heading towards the door, he hid the shotgun inside of his trench coat and kept on strolling. He'd almost disappeared through the doorway when Kesha called him back, stopping him in his tracks. He looked over his shoulder at her.

"What's up?" Te'Qui asked as he threw his head back.

"I love you." she told him as tears rolled down her cheeks.

He grinned at her and said, "I love you, too. I'll be back soon. Okay?"

"Okay."

Te'Qui flashed her a smile and she flashed him a weak one back. He then continued out of the door to carry out his mission.

***

Te'Qui hit up all of the locations that Killa Tay's fans had DM'd him through his Instagram. The last one he went to was a house below the poverty line. The house looked like it was in terrible need of a paint job. Its fence was rusting and it had a dirt patch lawn. A '76 navy blue Buick Regal on "24 chrome rims was parked inside of the driveway. The lights were on inside of the house and Te'Qui saw someone walk past one of the windows. Seeing this, he knew that there was a good chance that the fools he was looking for were inside. So he parked two houses down from the house he was scoping out and murdered the engine.

Te'Qui popped open his glove-box and removed his red ski-mask. He then hopped out of the car and slammed the door shut.

He walked around to the rear of the vehicle, opened the trunk and pulled out the shotgun. Once he held the shotgun down low, he looked around to make sure that no one had seen him remove it from his trunk. Having seen the streets was clear of lurking eyes, Te'Qui moved up the sidewalk cautiously, keeping a close eye on his surroundings. He snuck inside of the yard of the house that the fools were at that robbed Killa Tay. Hunched over, he hurried over to the side of the house and pulled his ski-mask down over his face. Using one hand, he adjusted the mask so that he could see out of the eye holes. Once he'd done this, he turned around and slowly peered over into the window. Through it, he saw a nigga playing X-Box while another one was cooking something on the stove. Exactly what he was cooking? He didn't know, nor did he give a fuck. He was there to make an example out of niggaz.

Te'Qui took his head from out of the window and crept to the front of the house. He placed his ear to the door and listened in for a minute. He could hear Future's *Fuck up some commas*, as well as Madden which homeboy was playing from the couch. Te'Qui cradled his shotgun and took a step back from the front door. He lifted his leg and bent it back, aiming to kick the door in at its lock.

Boom!

Te'Qui kicked the front door in and nearly knocked it off its hinges. His forceful entree caused Mann to drop his controller and say 'Oh shit'. When the nigga went for his gun, which was lying on coffee table, Te'Qui blasted the table top. The pint of Hennessy it held exploded and the shreds of a magazine went up into the air. Seeing Skinny, the nigga who was standing over the stove cooking something, move out of the corner of his eye, Te'Qui whipped his shotgun around. As soon as he did, Skinny threw a coffee pot of murky water and crack at him. The coffee pot connected with his head and he let off a frivolous round at the carpeted floor. Te'Qui staggered back, wincing. By the time he regained his equilibrium and turned around, he discovered the nigga that was playing Madden charging at him.

Before Te'Qui could blast on his monkey-ass, Mann was grabbing hold of his shotgun. The men gritted and frowned at one another as they tussled over the weapon. While they were in their power struggle, Te'Qui saw Skinny pull his gun from the small of his back. He observed him cock it and point it. A danger alarm rang loud and angrily inside of Te'Qui's head. He saw Skinny with his gun trying to draw a bead on him. Acknowledging this, Te'Qui tried his best to keep Mann within firing range of his homeboy's gun. That way, he wouldn't wind up getting shot himself.

"You fucked up and broke into the wrong house, cuz! Now, that's yo' ass!" Mann told Te'Qui as they wrestled for control over the shotgun. "Skinny, shoot 'em! Shoot this mothafucka!"

"I can't draw a bead on 'em! You in the way!" Skinny said, trying his best to get a shot at Te'Qui. "Fuck it." he lowered his gun at his side and sped walked towards them so he could shoot Te'Qui in the head at point blank range.

"Awww, hurry up, this mothafucka strong!" Mann called out to his homeboy.

Seeing that Skinny was getting dangerously close to them, Te'Qui knew he had to do something fast or that was his black ass. He kneed Mann in his balls which doubled him over, making him grab a handful of himself. Right after, he blasted Skinny in his leg. The nigga threw his head back wailing at the top of his lungs, displaying all of the teeth inside of his mouth. He then fell to the floor, dropping his gun and bawling in pain.

When Mann looked back and saw his homeboy was at the nigga in the ski-mask mercy, he knew he had to act fast or they both were going to be dead. He hollered out a battle cry and tackled Te'Qui up against the same door he'd kicked open, slamming it shut. Te'Qui, then, slammed the stock of his shotgun into his back, causing him to holler out in pain. He then kneed him in the stomach and struck him across the jaw with the stock. As soon as he fell to the carpeted floor, Te'Qui took the liberty to stomp his fucking head.

"Bitch-ass mothafucka!"

Blam! Blam! Blam!

Te'Qui's head was thrown back from the impact of bullets crashing into his chest. He staggered backwards, dropping the shotgun and falling slumped against the wall. His head was bowed and his right hand was lying on his lap. His movements had ceased and he was silent.

The only sounds inside of the living room were the Madden video game and Mann and Skinny's groans of agony. Half Dead, the nigga that had just opened fire on Te'Qui, lowered his long nose nickel plated revolver, as its barrel wafted with smoke. He was in the bathroom taking a shit when everything popped off inside of the living room. He sat his pistol down on top of a tall speaker and went about the task of zipping up his jeans and buckling his belt.

Half Dead looked around at his homeboys as he slipped his leather belt into its metal buckle. From the expressions on his homeboys' faces he could tell that they were in a great deal of pain. "Y'all niggaz all right, man?" he asked of their current conditions.

"Fuck no; I ain't all right, fool!" Skinny winced as he held his busted, bleeding leg. "That cocksucka shot me in my fucking leg! Aaaahhh!"

"Shiiiit, nigga, you leaking something awful, I'ma call 9-1-1." Half Dead went to grab the telephone, but Skinny calling him back stopped him.

"Don't call 'em yet! We gotta get this dead mothafucka outta here, and stash that dope somewhere." Mann said as he scrambled to his feet slowly, holding the side of his head. He was a little dizzy from Te'Qui whipping his ass.

He's right, Half Dead, get that shit from off the kitchen table." Skinny, who was still holding his busted leg, wincing, threw his head towards the kitchen. "Once you hide that shit, help Mann dump this nigga somewhere." he spoke of Te'Qui, who was still sitting slumped against the wall.

Half Dead grabbed his revolver and tucked it at the small of his back. He then ran inside of the kitchen where he saw a box of bacon soda, razors, sandwich baggies and a digital scale. Skinny was in the middle of cooking up coke to serve to the crack fiends around the way, when Te'Qui kicked down the door.

Half Dead put away the items on the kitchen table that was going to be used to prepare the crack. He then snatched the package of coke, which was wrapped up in duct tape, from off the table and ran back inside of the living room. He kneeled down to the speaker box he'd sat his revolver on top of earlier, and removed the bottom speaker from out of it. Next, he stuffed the kilo inside of the hollow space and replaced it with the speaker. Once he was done, he turned around to help Mann move the dead body.

Half Dead's eyes doubled in size and his mouth dropped open. He saw Te'Qui kick Mann across the chin which knocked blood out of his mouth and dropped him to the carpeted floor. Seeing this, Half Dead reached around his back to grab his .44, but Te'Qui had already came from off his waistline with his Glizzy, spitting fire at him. The first shot ripped through Half Dead's kneecap, while the second shot ripped through his left bicep. Te'Qui picked up his shotgun and hoisted its strap over his shoulder. Still pointing his gun at Half Dead, he sped walked over to him and took his revolver. Afterwards, motioning with his gun, Te'Qui commanded Mann to help Half Dead over to Skinny and lie on his back beside him. Once homeboy had done what he was told, Te'Qui pulled out the throwaway cell phone that Big Will's carrier had given him.

"Alright, you ol' busta-ass niggaz, I'ma 'bouta tell you how this shit gon' go," Te'Qui began, holding his gun at his side. "I'ma record y'all apologizin' to Hood Rich Records and Killa Tay."

"Now, why in the fuck would we apologize to them fools foe?" Skinny asked as he lay on his stomach, still wincing from his busted leg.

"'Cause if you don't I'ma empty this Glock out on you and yo' busta-ass homies." Te'Qui kicked Mann in his side hard as shit, causing him to howl in pain. He squeezed his eyelids shut and gritted his teeth to combat the aching in his ribs. "Now, do you have any more questions?"

"Y-yeah, are you gon' kill us?" Half Dead asked with a pain streaked face, bleeding all over the goddamn carpet.

"Nah, I ain't gon' crush y'all fools. Big Will just wanted me to spank y'all and record the apology."

"Man, how we know you not lying? Put that on God!" Mann looked up at him from where he was lying on the floor.

Te'Qui tucked his gun on his waistline and swung his shotgun around, locking one into its chamber. He tapped Mann at the top of his head with its barrel and told him to open his mouth. Once he obliged him, Te'Qui stuck his shotgun in that nigga'z grill, looking down at him with animosity in his eyes.

Cool and calmly, Te'Qui addressed Mann, "My nigga, the next time you open them fat ass lips, I'ma blow yo' entire fuckin' head off yo' shoulders. Do we have an understandin'?"

"Uhn huh," Mann said with a mouthful of shotgun.

"Good." Te'Qui took the shotgun from out of his mouth and whipped out his Glock again. "Alright, fuck-niggaz, this is exactly what I want y'all to say…"

Te'Qui recorded the fools lying on their stomachs apologizing to Hood Rich Records and Killa Tay. He then recovered all of the jewelry and money they'd stolen from off of Killa Tay. Next, he took the dead faces they had on them and all of the drugs they had in the house, including the kilo Half Dead had stashed inside of the speaker box.

He was going to call an ambulance for them niggaz, but once he heard Twelve's sirens heading to the location; he got the fuck out of dodge.

***

Kesha was lying in bed watching television when she heard the front door open. She hopped out of her bed and ran towards the door to meet Te'Qui. As soon as he crossed the threshold, she threw her arms around his neck and kissed him all over his face. Te'Qui winced against her embrace and pushed her back gently. She frowned up at him, wondering what she'd done to hurt him.

"What's the matter, baby?" Kesha questioned with concern, looking him up and down.

Te'Qui didn't bother answering her. He walked over to the nightstand with the mirror attachment and sat his shotgun down on it, along with the package of coke he had on him. Next, he pulled out the throwaway cell phone and Killa Tay's jewelry, both of which he sat down on the nightstand beside the other shit he'd put there.

Te'Qui, what's the matter?" she placed her hand on his shoulder.

"Gimme a sec', babe," Te'Qui squeezed his eyelids shut and clenched his jaws, fighting back the pain he was feeling. He peeled off his trench coat and then his sweatshirt, handing it to her. Looking back up, he saw the bullets mashed up against his bulletproof vest. He started unstrapping the Kevlar armor.

"Oh, my God, bae, you were shot?" Kesha's eyes grew big. She knew that Te'Qui could have been killed that night if he'd been shot, and that scared her. In fact, it scared the living shit out of her. Her eyes got moist but she didn't cry.

"Yeah, nigga came outta nowhere and threw three at cha boy. Luckily I was strapped up," Te'Qui took the bulletproof vest off and sat it up against the nightstand's mirror. Looking at his reflection, he saw the reddish purple bruising from where he'd been popped in his vest.

"That looks bad. Do you want me to put some ointment on it?" she asked as she examined the bruises on his chest.

"Yeah. And fix me a drink, will ya?" he asked her.

"Sure, bae, what would you like?" she asked over her shoulder as she slipped his trench coat on a hanger to hang it on the rack inside of the closet. She had his holy sweatshirt over her shoulder and was going to dispose of it shortly.

"The usual, momma." he responded as he picked up his cellular and lay back in bed.

"Okay." Kesha walked past him to go make the drink he'd requested.

As soon as Kesha had left the bedroom Te'Qui got on the jack with Big Will. He told him he'd handled the job and asked him where he wanted to meet, so he could collect his other half of the money.

"Alright, you wanna meet up there at what time?" Te'Qui asked Big Will as he took the glass of alcohol from Kesha who'd just sat down beside him in bed. She was beginning to twist the top off a small jar of ointment. "Cool. I'll holla at chu, then. Peace." he disconnected the call and sat the cell phone down beside him in bed. He then took a sip of his drink and licked his lips. "Aahh!"

Te'Qui winced in pain feeling Kesha's fingers rub the ointment on his bruises. He looked at her like she was the devil.

"I'm sorry, boo, I wasn't tryna hurt chu. Here, limme kiss it and make it better." She leaned down and kissed his injuries, then went back to rubbing the ointment onto his chest, gently this time. "How's that?"

"I got somethin' you can kiss and make feel better," he looked at her with a smile and freaky thoughts on his brain.

"I bet chu do." she smiled and playfully slapped him on the shoulder, before going back to applying the ointment onto his bruises. He continued to sip from his glass as she performed her duty.

"You know, bae, you were right. I shoulda hit that nigga T.J. up so he coulda rolled out with me, to have my back." he took the time to scratch his nose with his thumb before continuing, "Shit got realll thick up in there. I thought them fools had me back there. I came close to checkin' out, especially when that fool threw them three at me. Through the grace of God, a nigga still here, but I coulda been gone."

"See," she began, blinking back the tears that had formed in her eyes. "I told you, but you weren't tryna listen to me. Maybe you'll listen to me now, and take 'em along the next time you gotta go up against more than one head."

"I am. As a matter of fact, the next lick I get I'm bringin' homie with me."

"Good." she replied, twisting the lid back onto the ointment. "There. All done."

"Gimme a kiss." he placed his hand behind her head and pulled her closer. He kissed her long, deep and passionately.

The next night

Te'Qui was five minutes away from the meeting spot that he and Big Will had agreed upon, when he'd gotten another call from him changing the location. He gave him the address to some house out in Compton. Te'Qui didn't ask why he'd changed his mind about meeting at the other location. He just figured he had his reasons. Besides, it wasn't like it was a big deal to him. The only thing that bothered him was the way the nigga sounded on the jack. Big Will sounded as if he was frustrated and angry about something. What it was, he did not know, nor did he give a shit, just as long as that nigga had his paper.

Te'Qui parked four houses down and across the street from the house Big Will told him to meet him at. Reaching underneath his seat, he grabbed his gun and cocked a hollow tip into its brain. He then hopped out of the car and shut the door behind him. He gave his surrounding a quick scan before tucking his banga on his waistline. Te'Qui jogged across the street looking up and down the block for any oncoming vehicles, which he didn't see. He entered the yard of a tan house with a brown rooftop. Its greenish brown grass was unkempt and dying.

Te'Qui was about to make his way up the steps to ring the doorbell when he heard a menacing voice above his head.

"Who are you, Blood?" The voice rang aloud.

Te'Qui looked up to find two gunmen on the rooftop, one sitting and another standing. The one that was speaking to him was wearing a red bandana laid over his head, with a fitted cap on to of it. Another red bandana was over the lower half of his face. He sported a bulletproof vest underneath a windbreaker. Homie was pointing something long, black and dangerous at Te'Qui, with a banana clip in it. The murder in his eyes led Te'Qui to believe that if he said the wrong thing he'd lay him down where he was standing.

"I'm Q-Ball, homie." Te'Qui answered with his hands up in the air.

"Who you here to see, nigga?" The nigga sitting down on the rooftop asked. He had the exact same weapon that his homeboy standing beside him had, and he was pointing that big mothafucka down at Te'Qui just like he was.

The other nigga on the rooftop was rocking a red beanie with Compton emblazoned on it. A red bandana was around his neck and he had one hanging from the end of his assault rifle's barrel. He was wearing a bulletproof vest on top of his long sleeve T-shirt. His eyes were also filled with murder, begging for Te'Qui to flex so he could add another body under his belt.

"Big Will."

"Blood, know you was comin' through?" he asked. When Te'Qui nodded, he pulled out his cellular and hit up Big Will. They had a quick conversation before he lowered his weapon and turned his eyes back to Te'Qui. "You good, my nigga, gon' to the back and knock on the door."

When the blood sitting down on the rooftop lowered his weapon, his comrade did too.

With the go ahead having been given, Te'Qui made his way to the back of the house. Pushing open the double black iron gates, Te'Qui entered the backyard to be greeted by two hulking pit bulls. One of them was white with a pink nose while the other was brown and striped. The beasts went crazy on their chains when they spotted Te'Qui's ass, growling and barking madly. The very moment the hounds went off, the light bulb above the back porch came on. As soon as it did, Te'Qui looked up at it. Right after, he heard the doors of the black iron door coming undone. Once the door finally opened, he came face to face with Big Will. He was wearing a wife beater and slacks. He was shiny from perspiration. He was clutching a fist full of money in one hand and a small brown leather bag in the other. The very familiar smell of marijuana filled the air and taintilized Te'Qui's nasal senses.

"'Sup, homie?" Big Will dapped up Te'Qui with the fist he clutched the money in.

"Ain't shit. What chu got goin' in there?" Te'Qui nosily peeked over his shoulder to see niggaz shooting craps at the kitchen table. There was niggaz smoking fat ass blunts and drinking dark liquor from out of plastic cups too. In fact, one of them was Drama; he was holding a cup of alcohol and shooting dice with the other, oblivious to the presence of Te'Qui.

"Gambling. Here. This you." He passed him the brown leather bag.

"So, that's why you were tight when I holla'd at chu earlier tonight." Te'Qui said, having put two and two together.

"Hell yeah, man, niggaz been tearing my big black ass up in there. It's okay though 'cause I gotta 'nough paypa to shooting 'til these niggaz' arms fall off." He reached into his back pocket and pulled out a red bandana, wiping the sweat from off his face and neck. Afterwards, he tucked the bandana back inside of his pocket. "You tryna get in on this crap game?"

Before Te'Qui answered, he peeked over Big Will's shoulder again. This time he found Drama wincing and shaking his head having just crapped out. He threw down his money for his fade and looked back up. His eyes were focused on the new shooter on the dice, and he was about to take a sip of the alcohol in his cup, when he looked at Te'Qui. Drama's face balled up with anger and he looked at him like *What the fuck are you looking at?*

"Why don't chu take a picture? It'll last longer, mothafucka!" Drama spat at him heatedly. Te'Qui switched hands with the brown leather bag and pulled out his gun. He went to enter the house, but Big Will moved into his path and pulled the door shut behind him.

"Whoa now, cowboy, don't pay unc no mind. He's just in his feelings 'cause them niggaz in there tapping them pockets. You know how it is when you losing money on them tables; niggaz be mad at the world."

Te'Qui nodded his understanding and tucked his Glizzy back up. "I hear you. But cho people and their attitude, man. You and me are good money, Big, but I ain't gon' keep lettin' shit with that nigga fly. For real, for real, old head better start respectin' mine, 'fore he find himself wearing one of them tags on his toes."

Big Will tilted his head to the side as he scowled at Te'Qui. He didn't like that the young nigga had threatened to body his uncle, but then again, he understood where he was coming from. They were all gangstaz and demanded respect. Every last one of them was willing to kill and die behind their reputations.

"I feel you. I'ma holla at my peoples and get his mind right."

"Good."

"You got that footage for me?"

"Oh yeah, I almost forgot." Te'Qui reached into his back pocket and pulled out the throwaway cellular he'd used to film the fools that had beat down Killa Tay apologizing. He pulled up the footage on the device and passed it to Big Will. Big Will pressed play on the cell phone and watched the footage, a smile forming across his lips. He patted Te'Qui on his shoulder and gave him his props for handling his business. Afterwards, he slipped the cellular into his pocket and dapped him up.

"Good shit. I'ma have my people load up the footage with the quickness. I bet this shit go viral and getta million hits. Mothafuckaz will know notta fuck with Hood Rich records and their affiliates." Big Will said with confidence.

"Sho' you right. Limme gon' and get up outta here though. I'll get up witchu later." Te'Qui told him.

The gangstaz dapped up and parted ways.

Tranay Adams

CHAPTER FIVE
Two weeks later

Te'Qui sat up in a tub of murky, hot, sudsy water taking the occasional pull of a bleezy. While he indulged in the gas, Kesha went about the task of washing him up. Once she was finished, she'd go on to dry him off, dress him and feed him. Kesha treated her man like a fucking king, and he in turn treated her like a queen.

"I can tell you thinking about something. What's on yo' mind, baby?" Kesha inquired.

"About this next money move I'ma make." Te'Qui answered.

"Oh, yeah? What's next up for us?"

"Us?" he looked to her with one eyebrow rose.

"Yeah. Us. As in you and me." she cracked a slight grin.

"Nah, whatever I do from here on out, I'll be doin'it solo. I'm not bringin' you along for the ride again, puttin' you and my seed at risk." he rubbed on her stomach again. "Hell, I was a fool for lettin' yo' lil' ass talk me into lettin' you come along on this last lick. I coulda lost you that night if it wasn't for that nigga T.J." he kissed her on her stomach.

"Yeah, I guess you right. I was kinda of scared for you. I thought I wasn't gonna make it in time to bust blood melon, but luckily T.J. showed up." she said, looking down at him, rubbing her stomach. "He came outta nowhere like The Angel of Death, flying from out of the shadows with two guns up," she made her hands into the shape of guns and pretended to shoot them. "He really saved the day, 'cause that coulda been both, well, all three of our asses."

"I know. That's why I'm thinkin' about bringin' 'em in on the next lick I get to pay 'em back."

"Bae, for real?" she asked, stroking the side of his face.

He nodded and said, "Yeah. Homie said his pockets hurtin' and he needa get back on his feet, so I told 'em I'd put 'em down If I caught wind of somethin'. What chu think, momma?" he looked into her eyes as he continued to rub her stomach.

"I think it's a good idea. You need someone out there watching yo' back. I know you not tryna have me out there witchu, so why not T.J.? He seems like he's an okay dude."

"Yeah, you do gotta point." Te'Qui kissed her lips and then her forehead. He then killed the lamp light and lay back in bed, shutting his eyelids. Kesha laid her head against his chest and her arm over his torso. She shut her eyelids and they both drifted off to sleep.

The sounds of gunfire awoke Te'Qui from his sleep. He threw the covers from off him and tip tied to his bedroom door. Gently, he twisted the doorknob and pulled open the door. He stuck his eye in the opening he'd provided and watched as his father, Faison, was blown off his feet by a woman in disguise. Seeing his old man slumped and bleeding, brought tears to his eyes and his bottom limp quivered. He could feel his heart breaking into one million pieces. Te'Qui observed the woman that had chopped his old man down, check the pulse in his neck as he stared off at nothing with the dead face. Afterwards, she swung around and pointed her shotgun at him, finger settled on the trigger. Te'Qui was fully prepared for her to blow him away, but she suddenly lowered her shotgun and fled the hallway.

Once she was gone, Te'Qui crept out of his bedroom into the hallway. He snuck over to his dead father, coming across the opened bathroom door. When he looked inside, he discovered his mother, Chevy, lying slumped dead inside of the tub with the shower water still pelting against her. Her eyes were wide and vacant, while her mouth hung open. There were two big ass holes in her body and they were pouring blood that mixed with the hot shower water, swirling down the drain.

"Momma, oh momma," Te'Qui cried out to his mother, tears streaming down his cheeks. He rushed inside of the bathroom and twisted the dials, shutting off the water. He then snatched a towel off the rack and draped it over her, kissing her on the forehead. Next, he stood upright and crossed himself in the sign of the Holy crucifix, running back out into the hallway. He didn't waste any time grabbing the revolver from Faison's chubby dead hand and checking its chamber. Seeing that he had enough bullets to avenge his parents, he shut the chamber and ran out of

the hallway. He made his way inside of the kitchen and peered out through the window over the kitchen sink, seeing the woman that had popped his parents running along the side of the house. Quickly, he snatched his face from out of the window and ran out of the back door.

He made his way on the side of the house just in time to see the woman crossing the front lawn. Right then, he ran as fast as he ever had after her. Once he'd gotten so close, he snuck toward her, holding his .357 Magnum revolver at his side with both hands. He watched her make her way across the street toward what he assumed was her vehicle. Te'Qui looked up and down the street for any oncoming cars, before hurrying across it himself, bare feet smacking down against the cold asphalt.

Te'Qui saw the woman at the driver's door of her car trying to open it. Seeing his chance to exact revenge, he snuck up behind her and pointed his gun at her back with both hands. His eyebrows arched and his nose scrunched up. He licked his lips and bit down on his bottom one. Then, he pulled the trigger of his weapon, chamber twisting as it unleashed fire.

Blam!

"Aahhhhh!" Te'Qui rose up in bed hollering aloud, eyes wide, mouth open, face and upper body covered in beads of sweat. He looked to Kesha and she was still asleep. He threw the sheets from off him and got out of bed, walking into the bathroom. He turned on the dials of the faucet and water poured out. He cupped his hands below the flowing liquid until his palms filled and splashed it upon his face, twice. Afterwards, he took a good look at himself in the medicine cabinet's mirror. He then dabbed his face dry with a towel hanging on the rack. Just then, he heard his cellular vibrating on the dresser. When he glanced into his bedroom he could see its screen lighting up. His brows furrowed wondering who it could be hitting him up at that hour.

Te'Qui flipped off the bathroom light as he crossed the threshold into his bedroom. He picked his cell phone up from the dresser and looked at the display. It read, Poochie. It answered it.

"What's brackin'?" Te'Qui asked.

"You ready to eat, my nigga?" Poochie said.

"Shiiiiid, I'm always ready to eat. What's up with it?"

"Quervo. I'm not finna say to much on this jack. We can link up somewhere and chop it up."

"Alright. Cool. Where at though?"

"That Valero gas station on the corner of El Segundo and Crenshaw."

"What time?"

"How does ten o'clock in the morning sound?"

"I can fade that. I'll holla at chu then."

"Fa sho'."

Te'Qui disconnected the call and sat his cellular back on the dresser. He then lay back in bed, put his arm around Kesha and kissed the back of her head before shutting his eyelids. He took a breath and before he knew it he had fallen back to sleep.

10:00 A.M

As soon as Te'Qui pulled into the AM/PM gas station, he noticed Poochie posted up. He was standing beside a purple '95 Honda Civic smoking a withering Newport. The nigga looked fucked up. He had a big ass knot on his forehead, bluish black rings on his eyes, a swollen nose and busted lips. There was also a cast on his right arm. The nigga was dressed down too. He didn't look nearly as fly as he did that night he ran into him at CVS. That day he was wearing a dingy black tanktop with the Toxic Crusader on it, light blue jeans with tears in their knees and some mothafucking sandals. It was from his appearance that Te'Qui knew that the nigga was broke than a mothafucka, because any time he had money, he made it his business to broadcast it through his jewelery, clothing and cars.

Poochie's habit had gotten the best of him. He'd lost all of his money and assets thanks to his addiction to coke. When he found himself struggling to support his habit, he started stealing product from Quervo's spots. Once he was caught, Quervo and his goons' pistol whipped him and stomped him out. The only reason why the niggaz didn't kill him was because he begged and pleaded with Quervo to spare his life. Feeling sorry for his ass, Quervo granted him clemency, provided he left the city and never returned. Poochie agreed. He then packed his belongings into his car and drove away. As soon as he left the house,

Poochie pulled out his cell phone and hit Te'Qui up with a plan to rob Quervo.

This wasn't the story he'd told Te'Qui though. Nah, he told him that someone had lied and told Quervo that he was stealing and that's why he'd gotten his ass beat. You see, he led the young gangsta to believe that his wrongfully getting punished was his reasoning behind wanting to set his ass up.

Poochie dropped the Newport at his feet and mashed it out underneath his sandal. He then snatched open the back door and sat down, pulling the door shut behind him. His forehead creased when he noticed T.J. sitting in the front passenger seat. He didn't have any idea that Te'Qui was bringing someone along with him. As far as he knew, it was only him and Te'Qui that were going to be in on the lick. Having someone else there in on the caper meant that his slice of the pie was going to get considerable smaller. He wasn't tripping off of it though. The dough they were going to get for the hit would still be more than enough to keep him happy.

"Who's this?" Poochie inquired.

"Oh, pardon my mannas. Poochie, this my man T.J. T.J. this my homeboy Poochie."

"'Sup witchu, Blood?" T.J. asked as he sucked on a cherry Tootsie Roll pop, looking over his shoulder at him and holding out his fist.

Poochie touched fists with T.J. and said, "Ain't shit, tryna see about securin' this bag."

"I can feel that. I'm all about my money."

"Sho' you right." Poochie nodded.

"Gimme the skinny on this fool Quervo. Where this nigga stash at?"

"Well, my girl says he keeps his shit inside the wall in his crib. What wall? That I don't fuckin' know, but that's where y'all come in. When y'all run up in his shit y'all gon' have whip off in his ass to get 'em to come off the location of where them bands at. Now, if you know Quervo like I know Quervo, he's a stubborn, prideful bastard, so that's gonna prove to be tough."

"Oh, he'll talk, best believe that. I done went at some of the hardest mothafuckaz in these streets and they all buckled under my gun. Once I lay my G down on his ol' wannabe gangsta-ass, he'll tell me exactly where that paypa is." Te'Qui assured him.

"Now, when y'all go in there, he gon' try to throw y'all off with that safe inside of his closet. It has money in it, but all that shit is fake. That's a dummy grab. He got that shit there in case mothafuckaz are lookin' to get at 'em. That way they think they leavin' with somethin', but they really got some ol' bullshit."

"I'll give it to homeboy, he is a clever mothafucka," T.J. said as he massaged his chin and surveyed his surroundings.

"That he is." Te'Qui nodded and continued to indulge in his Tootsie Roll sucker.

"Here, limme give you this nigga info," Poochie fished a piece of paper out of his pocket and handed it to Te'Qui. He continued to talk to him as he looked over the piece of paper. "Homeboy's birthday is tomorrow night. They goin' out to celebrate. My lil' white bitch said she gon' make sure they're home and in bed 'round eleven o'clock. She gon' leave the back door open for y'all niggaz to creep in. Now, I don't give a fuck what y'all do to Quervo, fuck him! Just don't kill my bitch. Rough her up if you have to, but don't kill her ass. I love that bitch! I ain't goin' to be able to hack it out here if somethin' happens to her."

"Alright. We ain't gon' splash her, but we gon' have to rough her up to make it look good though. I'm sho' you don't want this nigga on yo' ass if he gets the feelin' she was in on the shit, right?"

"Yeah. Like I said 'if you gotta rough her up then handle yo' business'. Just don't kill her, that's all I'm sayin'."

"Don't worry about nothin', bro, I got chu faded." Te'Qui assured him.

"Cool." Poochie responded. "Yo', Qui, you think you can bless me with a lil' somethin' 'til we secure this bag, man?"

Te'Qui was silent for a minute as he thought about what Poochie had just asked him. He knew that if he gave him some money that he was going to snort it right up his fucking nose. He didn't like the idea of giving a nigga some money to support his habit, but then again, homie was a grown-ass man. If the nigga wanted to play with his nose then let him play with his nose.

Tomorrow night

A masked up Te'Qui and T.J. hopped out of their car and tossed their pickaxes over the fence. They then scaled over the fence and jumped down into the backyard of their intended victim. They looked around to make sure there weren't any dogs around, although they'd been told that there wouldn't be any hounds on the premises. Seeing that the coast was clear, they grabbed the tools they'd tossed over the fence and jogged across the lawn to the backdoor. Te'Qui was the first nigga at the back door; he placed his ear against it and listened closely. He didn't hear anything so he opened the door and crept inside over the threshold. He didn't have any trouble getting the door open because Poochie's inside woman had left it unlocked for them.

The only light on inside of the house was the one inside of the kitchen. No one was down stairs but Te'Qui and T.J. could hear R. Kelly's *Sex me* playing upstairs loudly. They propped their pickaxes up against the refrigerator and exchanged glances. Te'Qui gave T.J. the signal to follow him up the staircase and he nodded his understanding. They snuck through the dark living room and crept up the steps as quietly as they could. Once they reached the landing, the music seemed even louder. With knowledge of which bedroom R. Kelly was crooning from, Te'Qui and T.J. made their way down the hallway, with their guns held up at their shoulders. Reaching the master bedroom, they took their places on either side of the door. Te'Qui gave T.J. another signal that let him know exactly what he had in mind. Again, he nodded his understanding.

Te'Qui counted down to three inside of his head. He then swung out before the door and kicked that mothafucka wide open. He flipped the light switch *on* and he and T.J. rushed into the master bedroom. They found a nigga with what looked like an S-curl fucking the white bitch that was in on the lick, doggy style. Her name was Jane, and as soon as she saw them masked up niggaz, she started screaming hysterically.

"Ahhh! Ahhh! Ahhhh!" Jane screamed over and over again as she cowered against the headboard, pulling the covers over her bosom.

"Bitch, shut the fuck up 'fore I shoot chu in yo' trick ass mouth!" T.J. commanded as he and Te'Qui pointed their bangaz at Jane's hollering ass.

Seeing movement at the corner of his eye, Te'Qui's head snapped in the direction of the dude with the curly hair. He clocked him reaching for the chrome .45 handgun with the pearl handle on the dresser. Swiftly, Te'Qui pointed his gun and shot the lamp which was beside the gun, shattering it into pieces. The shock of almost being shot caused homie with the curl to snatch his hand away from the dresser. He quickly threw his hands up in surrender and looked Te'Qui in his eyes, defiantly.

"Fuck!" He cursed under his breath wishing he'd gotten to his gun before the masked up nigga had noticed him. He knew that if he was lucky he'd walk away from the home invasion alive, but if he wasn't, his black ass would be getting fit for a suit and casket by next week.

"You must be Quervo," Te'Qui walked in his direction with his gun pointed at him. "The half black, half Puerto Rican bitch we gon' squeeze for everything he's got. Where the money at, nigga?"

"I ain't giving you shit, puto! As a matter of fact, nigga, suck my dick!" Quervo snarled and spat at his feet. The nasty yellowish glob that flew from his mouth splattered against Te'Qui's sneaker. Angry, Te'Qui exchanged glances with T.J.; neither of them could believe the size of Quervo's balls.

Te'Qui flipped his gun over in his hand and whacked Quervo upside the head with it. The vicious blow knocked Quervo off the bed and he landed on his side hard as shit. Lying on his side, he winced and held the side of his bleeding head. Te'Qui straddled him and continued to pistol whip him until he gave up the whereabouts of the money he had stashed. Right after, Te'Qui grabbed Quervo by his ankle and dragged him towards the bedroom door.

"Grab that bitch and bring her ass down stairs, too!" Te'Qui ordered T.J. He then glanced over his shoulder to make sure he wouldn't bump into the wall as he dragged Quervo down the hallway, kicking and screaming. T.J. was right behind them, pulling Jane along by her long stringy hair. Her face was red and she was holding on to his wrist. His grip was so tight that it felt like he was going to rip her hair from out of her scalp. She winced and whimpered, but she never complained about what was happening to her for fear she'd get her face blown off.

Bunk! Bunk! Bunk! Bunk!

Quervo's head banged off each step as Te'Qui drug him down the staircase by his ankle, not giving a mad ass fuck about the injuries he'd sustain. Once they reached the landing, he continued dragging his ass inside of the living room, where he eventually released him at the center of the floor. Afterwards, he tucked his gun on his waistline and went inside of the kitchen to get the pickaxes. T.J. entered the living room behind him, throwing Jane to the floor, roughly. He then walked over to the light switch and flipped it *on*, restoring light to the living room.

While this was going on, Jane was looking around the living room, terrified. Teardrops fell from her eyes and her bottom lip quivered. As she begged and pleaded for her and her man's lives, Te'Qui returned to the living room with two pickaxes whistling Dixie. He sat the pickaxes on the couch. Next, he pushed the couch and the love seat out of the way, leaving a clear path to the portrait of Malcolm X hanging on the wall.

Once he was finish doing this, he picked up one of the pickaxes and spared a glance over his shoulder. He found T.J. holding Jane and Quervo at gunpoint. Turning back around, Te'Qui knocked the Malcolm X portrait off the wall with the pickaxe. He gripped the pickaxe with both hands and slammed it into the wall, yanking out plaster and shit. Chunks of the wall and residue spilled down onto the floor at his sneakers. But he didn't waste any time as he continued to attack the wall, pulling out chunks of it along with plaster. As he continued to hack away at the wall, bricks of money wrapped in plastic began to appear. Having grown exhausted, he turned around to T.J. breathing heavily, chest expanding and then compressing.

Bloody faced and bruised, Quervo stood upon his knees beside Jane holding his aching head. His shit was throbbing from being bumped against the steps when Te'Qui dragged him down the staircase. Seeing Te'Qui tear his stash of money from out of the wall enraged him. His face twisted into a mask of hatred. He couldn't believe Te'Qui and his punk-ass homeboy was in his house jacking him. The entire situation made him feel like a straight up bitch! And he didn't like that shit one bit.

"You niggaz is dead, you hear me? Both you bitchez!" Quervo pointed a bloody finger at T.J. and then Te'Qui. "I'm puttin' stacks on you bitchez heads; fiddy grand each! You fucked with the right one this time! The right goddamn one!" he smacked his hand up against his chest as he emphasized, leaving a bloody hand impression on his bare chest.

"Yo', big mouth," T.J. called for Quervo's attention and his head snapped in his direction. His eyes bled his mortal hatred for the masked man standing over him. "You forgetting something."

"Fuck is you talm 'bout, fat boy?" he frowned curiously.

"You gotta be alive to put that change onna nigga'z brain."

Quervo's eyes bulged and his mouth dropped open, displaying his teeth. Right then, he realized that T.J. planned on bodying him on the spot.

"Wait..." Quervo lifted his hand to shield his face as T.J. pointed his gun at him. Before he could finish what he had to say, T.J. was pulling the trigger of his banga. His gun bucked and a slug ripped through the bones and ligaments of Quervo's palm, splitting his wig and splattering his brain fragments on the kitchen floor. The dope man's body collapsed to the linoleum and Jane screamed in horror over and over again, with her trembling hands pressed to her face.

"Poochie said-Poochie said you weren't going to kill anybody!" Jane said as she looked up into the menacing eyes staring out of the holes in T.J.'s ski-mask. Tear spilled down her cheeks and threatened to drip off her chin. She felt like she was going to piss on herself right then, feeling her bladder growing hot.

"I don't give a fuck what that nigga told you, bitch! Don't nobody run this nigga here!" T.J. tapped the barrel of his gun against his chest. "Now, you gon' shut cho up with all of that gotdamn screaming, or I'ma leave yo' skinny white-ass lying right beside this nigga!" he pointed his gun at Quervo's dead ass. "Is that understood?"

Jane nodded as she sniffed back snot and wiped her dripping eyes with her fingers. Her body quivered as she tried to pull herself together. She was falling apart before her eyes. She was an emotional wreck. All she wanted to do was get payback and a little bit of money for Quervo always fucking around with other women behind her back. She thought Poochie's niggaz were just going to scare Quervo. At least that's what he'd told her. So, imagine her surprise when the heftiest of the masked men blew his brains out on the kitchen's floor.

Oh, my God, oh my God, what the fuck have I gotten myself into?

Jane thought as she stared at her shaky hands once again. She balled them into fists and they continued to shake uncontrollably. It was as if they had a mind of their own.

"Good. Now, take the pick from my homeboy and finish knocking down that wall so we can get them coins up outta there!" T.J. pointed to Te'Qui with his gun. He then watched Jane take the pickaxe from Te'Qui and start hacking at the wall. Once she had finished, her face was shiny from perspiration and she was breathing huskily. She wiped her moist face with the lower half of her shirt.

"Now, that's what I'm talkin' 'bout, baby. Show me the money." Te'Qui grabbed two duffle bags. He tossed one over to Jane and ordered her to help him fill the bags with the stash they'd uncovered inside of the wall. They got right down to business filling the duffle bags and zipping them up.

"Alright now, let's get outta here." Te'Qui said as he hoisted the strap of the duffle bag on his shoulder and headed for the door. Jane was right behind him with the other duffle bag, and T.J. was on her heels.

"You try to run and I'm smash yo' ass. You got that?" T.J. whispered into her ear as he followed closely behind her, banga pressed into her back. She nodded rapidly when he asked the question, fearing for her life.

Te'Qui jetted over to that nigga Poochie's spot. He pulled in through the alley and Poochie unlocked the gates to let him inside of the backyard. He closed and locked the gates once Te'Qui had pulled inside on the dirt patched lawn. He then motioned for everyone to follow him as he headed back inside of the house and led them down inside of the basement. They pulled up chairs to a round table. Te'Qui stood upright dumping the blue faces from out of the duffle bags onto the table top. With the help of Poochie, he tore the plastic from off the money and removed the rubber bands from off them. They were about to start counting up the money by hand until Poochie remembered that he had a money counter upstairs inside of his bedroom closet.

"Hold up, fam. We're liable to be down here all fuckin' night countin' up this bread." Poochie told Te'Qui. He then turned to Jane. "Baby, run upstairs and get me that money counter off the top shelf inside of my bedroom closet. It's behind that old Nike sneaker box. You can't miss it."

"Okay." Jane replied. She looked like she was trying her best to keep calm having witnessed Quervo getting his head blown off. Seeing someone she'd known murdered had really shaken her up and she was trying desperately to appear normal.

Jane pushed herself away from the table and rose from her chair. She then hurried up the staircase to do like Poochie's bidding.

Poochie watched Jane climb the staircase until she'd gone out of his sight. He then leaned back in his chair and pulled out a syringe which he bit down on. Next, he took out a small bottle of something that looked like its contents were insulin. Te'Qui and T.J. exchanged frowns and looked back to Poochie.

They watched as he stabbed the needle of the syringe into the small bottle and withdrew some of its contents. Once he was done, he stuck the bottle back inside of his pocket and held the syringe before his eyes. He pushed on the plunger and squirted some of the contents out of the syringe. Hearing Jane coming back down the steps, he looked to Te'Qui and T.J. and placed his finger to his lips, signaling to them to be quiet about what they'd seen him do. Te'Qui and T.J. went back to counting up the money, pretending like they didn't just see some suspect shit a few seconds ago.

"You got it, boo?" Poochie asked Jane as she reached the landing with the money counter.

"Yeah. It was exactly where you said it would be." Jane handed him the counter.

"Thank you, baby," He puckered up his lips.

"You're welcome, honey." She kissed his lips and sat down at the table. With slightly trembling hands, she went on about her business, turning on the counter and dropping stacks of money inside of it. While the task at hand consumed all of her attention, Poochie gave Te'Qui and T.J. a knowing look and pulled the syringe from where he was hiding it underneath the table.

"I gotta take a piss, y'all, I'll be right back." Poochie pushed his chair back from the table and stepped behind Jane as she was running dead presidents through the money counter. As she watched the machine flicker the cash rapidly before her eyes, Poochie smacked his hand over her mouth and yanked her head aside. Her eyes bulged and she tried to gouge out his eyes but he turned his face, frowning and gritting. Out of the corner of his eye, Poochie spotted the pronounced vein in her neck and brought the syringe into play. The pointed needle tip of the medical instrument twinkled before it pierced Jane's vein, causing a burgundy cloud to taint the contents of the syringe.

"Mmmmmhmmmm!" Jane struggled against Poochie's powerful grip. She thrashed her arms around and kicked her legs, causing herself to fall out of her chair. Poochie held fast to her though, and pushed the poison into her system. Jane's eyes rolled to their whites. All that could be seen were the red webs set against her moist eye balls. Once Poochie had pushed all of that shit into her bloodstream, he let her drop to the floor. Te'Qui and T.J. who were holding stacks of money that they were pretending to be counting, stepped back from the table and looked at Jane's body.

Jane's dying body danced on the floor wildly. Blood ran from out of her eyes and ears and red foam formed inside out of her mouth. The foam slid out either side of her mouth and dripped to the floor. She continued to dance on the floor until she eventually went still. Her head fell to the side and she took her final breath. Her eyes were as big as baseballs and foam was still running from out of her mouth.

Poochie stared down at Jane remorsefully as he held the empty syringe. His chest rose up and down as he breathed. He sat the syringe down on the table top and leaned down, touching the pulse in her neck. He then looked to Te'Qui and T.J. confirming her death. Next, he brushed Jane's eyelids shut and stood upright, capping the syringe. As he continued to stare down at her lifeless body, he took a deep breath like he'd done the hardest thing in his life. He then crossed himself in the sign of the holy crucifix and turned to Te'Qui and T.J. The young gangstaz were surprised to see that he had tears in his eyes.

"That was my lil' suburban white bitch, man, I loved her to death. I didn't wanna do what I did, but it was a necessary evil." Poochie explained to them. "I know if The Boys ever came around questioning her, she'd eventually breakdown crying and tell. She's always meant well, but she was soft. She don't know nothing 'bout this street shit. I shoulda never gotten her involved in it. She wasn't cut out for this shit. You feel me?" he snorted back snot that oozed out of his left nostril and then wiped his dripping eyes with the lower half of his Clippers jersey. "Alright, man, y'all come on so we can finish countin' this paypa up."

Poochie sat back down at the table and placed the syringe down upon it. He picked up where Jane left off, feeding the money counting machine cash. As soon as a stack would finish, he'd remove the money out of the counter and tangle a rubber band around it. Afterwards, he sat the stack on top of other stacks of money. Every now and then, he'd stopped running money through the machine and used one of the stacks to fan his face. He would then take a breath. It was hot as a mothafucka down in the basement.

Before Poochie knew it, he was finishing counting up the blue faces. Once he laid down the last g-stack, he'd lean back in his chair and look over the stacks of dough lined up before his eyes.

"Alright, my niggaz," Te'Qui began rubbing his gloved hands together. "What we have here is three-hundred and fifty thousand dollas in blood money. Now, T.J. and I will split a buck seventy-five each and you'll hold the change." He looked at Poochie to see if he'd buck, but he didn't. The way Te'Qui saw it. Although Poochie put them down on the lick, he and T.J. had done all of the work so they deserved the biggest slices of the pies. "Okay then. I'ma divide the spoils." Te'Qui bagged up he and T.J.'s cuts of the blood money and left Poochie's share out on the table. "You okay, my nigga?" Te'Qui asked as he hoisted the strap of the duffle bag over his shoulder. He couldn't help seeing the hurt in Poochie' eyes.

"I'll be straight, my nigga. Y'all gon' and get up outta here." Poochie told them as he mashed out the cigarette he'd lit up while they were counting up the mula. His eyes were red webbed and moist. You could tell that he was suffering from a broken heart.

"You don't want us to help you dispose of lil' momma's body?" Te'Qui asked.

"Nah, I got it. Don't even wet it."

"Alright, dawg, we outta here," Te'Qui dapped up Poochie and so did T.J. With the exchange having been made, the gangstaz made their departure.

***

"Yo', I think yo' man is gon' snap." T.J. said to Te'Qui in a hushed tone as they came out of the house through the backdoor.

"For real?" Te'Qui's forehead wrinkled. "How you figure that?"

"Yeah, him killing that white broad really fucked up his head."

"I guess so. The way I see it, I didn't twist his arm for 'em to go ahead with this lick. He brought it to me and included his bitch."

T.J. nodded his understanding as he massaged his chin, looking to be thinking about something. He then looked to Te'Qui and said, "You think he might rat us out over a guilty conscience?"

"Nahhhh." He frowned up and shook his head.

T.J. looked him dead in his eyes and said, "You willing to bet cho freedom on that?"

Te'Qui looked at him and then focused his attention back on the road. He didn't say another word, which let T.J. know the answer to his question.

"I thought so." T.J. looked out of the passenger window, with the scenery of the streets reflecting on its glass.

CHAPTER SIX

When Te'Qui pulled up in front of T.J.'s house they dapped one another up and pledged to link up again for another lick. T.J. hopped out of the car and slung the strap of the duffle bag over his shoulder. He looked around at his surroundings as he made his way inside of his yard. As he fished around in his pocket for his keys, he could still feel Te'Qui's presence. Seeing that he was still idling at the curb, he figured he was making sure he was getting in the house safely before he pulled off.

Once T.J. made his way inside of the house, he poked his head outside of the door and waved goodbye to Te'Qui. Te'Qui honked the horn and drove off. As soon as his ass was gone, T.J. retrieved his .357 Magnum revolver with the tape around its handle from underneath his mattress and threw on another hoodie. He then went inside of his kitchen where he fixed the barrel of his gun with an Idaho potato. Afterwards, he crept out of his house and hopped inside of his car, pulling out of the driveway. Once he reached his destination, he hopped out of his whip and made his way inside of the yard. He rung the doorbell and looked over his shoulder to see if there were any eyes on him, but as far as he could see there wasn't. Just then, he heard a voice from the other side of the door.

"Who is it?" the masculine voice sounded muffle from the other side of the door.

"It's me. T.J." he told him. "Man, niggaz caughta flat and ain't no donut in the trunk. I'm tryna see if you'll let us hold your donut 'til tomorrow, since we pushing the same model."

"Hold up."

T.J. listened as Poochie left the door. A couple of minutes later he returned to the door and opened it, slipping his arm into the last sleeve of the shirt he was putting on. At this time, T.J. could only make out his silhouette but he knew without a shadow of a doubt it was him. Homie opened the black iron door and stepped out onto the porch, looking up and down the street for the car T.J. and Te'Qui drove over there in. His forehead creased when he didn't see the vehicle and he looked at T.J.

"Where the car break down at?" Poochie inquired curiously.

T.J. mad dogged him and pointed the .357 Magnum with the potato on its barrel at his face. Poochie's eyelids stretched wide open and he gasped. Before he could say a mothafucking word, his brain fragments flew from the back of his skull and he fell awkwardly inside of the house. The nickel size black hole in his forehead wafted with smoke as a slither of blood ran from out of it. T.J. scanned his surroundings again to make sure there wasn't anyone watching him. Confirming that he wasn't being watched, T.J. lowered his smoking gun at his side and stepped over Poochie inside of the house. Tucking his revolver in his belt, he grabbed Poochie's lifeless limbs and pulled him completely inside of the house. He shut and locked the door. Next, he raided his bedroom where he found a black garbage bag stashed underneath the bed. When he opened it he found Poochie's cut of the money inside from the lick him and Te'Qui hit earlier that night.

"That's what I'm talking about, baby." T.J. smiled happily and tied the black garbage bag up. He then made his way out of the bedroom. As soon as he crossed the threshold out in the hallway, a light at the corner of his eye caught his attention. When he looked he saw that the light was shining out from the bathroom. Pulling out his revolver again, he crept his way down the corridor. Once he reached the bathroom's doorway, he poked his head inside, and what he saw in inside of the tub would be etched in his mind forever. Jane's limbless body was sitting up inside of the tub, bloody. Her severed head sat on the ledge of the tub next to a stained meat cleaver and one of her legs.

On the floor, by the tub, on top of a blood stained carpet were a few things wrapped in black garbage bags, which T.J. assumed was the other parts of her body. Sitting on the porcelain bathroom sink were two long spray cans: one white and the other aluminum. T.J. came to the conclusion that Poochie was draining the blood from Jane's cadaver and hacking her up to bury her. Afterwards, he was going to use whatever chemicals in the spray cans to get rid of the DNA inside of the bathroom.

T.J. pulled his head out of the bathroom and strolled down the hallway, tossing his revolver inside of his garbage bag. He opened the front door and fled out into the night, disappearing from the grotesque scene he'd created.

***

Te'Qui pulled into the grounds of an apartment complex that was still under construction. He took a glance out of the driver's window and headlights flashed twice. When this signal was given, he knew that it was his ride waiting on him. Quickly, he got undressed and sat his pile of clothes on the front passenger seat. He grabbed his extra pair of clothes from out of the backpack he'd brought along and slipped them on. Next, he snatched his duffle bag from off the backseat and hopped out of the car. After sitting the duffle bag at his feet, he pulled out some lighter fluid and a match book. Once he soaked the interior of the car with the flammable liquid, he struck a match and tossed that shit in through the driver's window. Frooosh! The golden orange flames ignited inside of the vehicle and spread throughout it.

Te'Qui observed the fire for a second before picking up his duffle bag and making his way towards the car that was waiting for him. He casually strolled towards the vehicle like he didn't have a care in the world. Just then, the car he'd set on fire exploded in the background and he didn't even flinch. He snatched open the passenger door of the car waiting for him and jumped into the front seat, slamming the door shut behind him.

"Everything went okay, bae?" Kesha asked as she glanced back and forth between Te'Qui and the windshield.

"Yeah. We made off good, too." Te'Qui reported.

"That's what's up. What about cha boy, T.J.?"

"Oh, he did his thang. He set the tone as soon as we went up in that mothafucka. I can most definitely see myself gettin' down with 'em again on some shit."

Kesha nodded and kissed Te'Qui. Afterwards, he sat his duffle bag down between his legs on the floor and let his seat back. He laid back and shut his eyelids, folding his arms across his chest. He drifted off to sleep. Kesha looked at him grinning, enjoying the peaceful look on his face as he slumbered. She reached over and played with the cornrows dangling down his neck. When she pulled to a stop light, she leaned over again and kissed him on the temple.

"I love you." She said with a grin.

"I love you, too." He replied in his sleep and smacked his lips. He then adjusted himself in the seat and drifted back to sleep.

***

The day was warm and beautiful so Te'Qui had decided to take Kesha shopping for a few things for the baby. They hit every store in the mall, buying everything you could dream of that a baby would need. Te'Qui found himself ten stacks down, but that wasn't shit. He could still afford to spend more on his unborn seed, and Kesha had every intention on making him do it. If it was one thing the girl loved, probably as much as her nigga, it was shopping. The girl could spend hours in the store, which made Te'Qui hesitant to hit a couple of stores with her. But when he thought about it, it had been all work and no play since he'd been on his grind, jacking niggaz for everything they had. It was about time he got out with his lady and enjoyed the fruits of his labor.

After tearing up the mall, Kesha decided she wanted to get the baby some undergarments and grab a few things for their house from Walmart. So that's where they found themselves, piling shit up inside of the shopping cart.

"Babe, you got like half the fuckin' baby section in this basket," Te'Qui said as he picked up a baby bottle, examined it and drop it down inside of the shopping cart along with the other stuff that was piled up in there.

"Aye, you never know what our lil' one gon' need," Kesha said as she held up two baby outfits which were on a hangers, looking at them carefully. She then placed it to her torso and turned around to Te'Qui, showing him the outfit. One of the outfits was blue and the other was pink. Since they didn't know what the sex of their child was they decided to purchase clothing for both sexes. "What chu think, bae?"

Te'Qui looked the outfits over and said, "They cool."

"Cool?" her forehead wrinkled. "Nigga, please, either of these lil' fit will look cute as fuck on our baby. I'm getting them both." she sat the outfits down inside of the shopping cart and continued to look at the baby clothes on the rack.

"I'm finna getta strawberry milk shake from that Mickey D's in here. You want somethin'?"

"Yeah, get me a McChicken sandwich; no lettuce."

"Alright," Te'Qui moved to walk away but what she said next halted him.

"Now, I know yo' ol' trifling-ass ain't walking away without giving me a kiss. I just know you not, you must won't cho mothafucking wig split up in here, fool." she turned around to him with her hand on her hip and her lips twisted, looking appalled by his actions. "Bring your black ass here." she called him over to her, curling and uncurling her finger.

Te'Qui chuckled and smiled before walking his way over to his boo. She grabbed him by the front of his shirt and pulled him down towards her, kissing him. She kissed him on the lips once more before releasing him. As he turned to walk away, she smacked him on his ass causing him to stop and turn around to her. A slight frown was on his face.

"Aye, you better gon' somewhere with that gay shit." he spat with annoyance in his tone.

"Hey, when you see a fat ass, you gotta smack it." she smiled and openly admired her man's butt.

"Alright now, gon' fuck around and make me clap that ass in here," he playfully threatened her as he patted the impression of the gun on his hip.

Kesha laughed and said, "Whatever, boy! You ain't gon' do nothing. You love me and this baby way too much." she held her stomach as she referred to the life growing inside of her.

"Is that what chu think?" Te'Qui questioned as he walked away.

"That's what I know," she called out to him as he widened the distance between them. She then turned back around to the clothes on the rack smiling as she went through them.

Te'Qui walked across the floor, leaving the baby section and coming across racks and racks of clothing in the boy's section.

Seeing someone at the corner of his eye, he turned around to see a stunning vision. Te'Qui clocked a sexy-ass chick ten feet away from him. She looked hood as fuck, but she was very enticing to the eye. She was a dark caramel complexioned honey that was thick in all of the right places, with a big old ass. She was wearing a royal blue halter top and jeans so tight they looked like they were painted on her. The jeans had tears going down the legs of them, giving anyone that looked at her a peek at her succulent thighs.

The woman was focused on a little boy who was standing in front of her, holding up different shirts to him trying to see which one looked the best on him.

"How you like this one, Cordary?" the woman asked the little boy who Te'Qui assumed was her son. This was because she had the same name she'd called him inked on her right breast.

"I want the Spider Man one, mommy." the boy anxiously pointed at the shirt with the Spider Man character on it.

"You sho'?" she lifted an eyebrow, trying to be sure of her son's choice. He had a habit of saying he wanted something and then he'd change his mind once they got home.

"Yes, I'm sure." he said excitedly as he took the shirt by the hanger as she gave it to him. "Can I get the sneakers that go with it,too?"

"Yep." the woman responded, and continued to look at the other shirts hanging on the rack.

Te'Qui's forehead furrowed when he saw an older man, who had his back to the woman while on his cellular, turn around to her. He disconnected the call he was on and stuck the cell phone in his jacket pocket as he wrapped his arms around the woman's shoulders, kissing her on the neck. The man had a bandana wrapped around his wrist and around his neck. This was Drama, Big Will's uncle's style when it came to fashion. As a matter of fact, when Te'Qui took a closer look, he realized that it was that old ass gangsta nigga.

Small world! Very, very small world, Te'Qui thought to himself as he kept on about his business. On his way back to Kesha, he clocked Drama, the woman and her son with their backs to him as they walked down the main aisle. Approaching Kesha, Te'Qui passed her the McDonald's bag and sipped his shake, keeping his eyes on Drama and them.

"What chu looking at, babe?" Kesha asked as she unwrapped her McChicken sandwich and took a bite.

"Nothin'. Nothin' at all," Te'Qui replied, keeping his eyes on Drama and them. The gangsta, his bitch and his kid looked like one big happy family to him.

***

After Te'Qui had come back from shopping with Kesha that day, he dipped over to T.J.'s crib and honked the horn for him to come outside. As he waited for him to come out, he busied himself with the task of rolling up a fat ass blunt. By the time T.J. was pulling the passenger door closed, Te'Qui was blazing up the bleezy and blowing out a cloud of smoke. Once T.J. had gotten into the car he dapped up Te'Qui and they shared the gas he had on deck.

"Yo'," Te'Qui started off. "You ain't gon' believe this shit."

T.J.'s brows dipped with wonder. "What's up?"

"Blood, I think I ran into yo' B.M and that nigga you told me about that ran off witcho shit."

He sat up as if he was interested in what he had to say. "Dawg, you fucking with me?"

"Look, I'm pretty sho', I ran into the bitch while I was out clothes shoppin' with my girl for the baby."

"How she look though?" T.J. sat up in his seat.

"The broad I saw was crazy thick. I'm talkin' 'bout big ass titties, great big ol' ass," Te'Qui described with his hands. "She hadda mole above her upper lip and she rocked cornrows down her back. She also hadda tattoo on her right tittie. It read somethin' like," his brows furrowed and he snapped his fingers trying to recall the ink on the woman's breast. He started throwing out names in hopes that one of them may get him to remember. "Codoroy or some shit."

"Cordary?" T.J. looked him in the eye hoping he'd say that was the name on the broad's breast he'd seen. The description he'd given him of the woman was definitely one that fit his baby momma, but he had to be sure.

Te'Qui snapped his fingers and pointed to him, excitedly. "Yeah, that's it. Cordary. That's the name that was on her breast."

"That's my son's name, Blood. Fonky-ass bitch!" T.J. slammed his fist down on the dashboard and threw his back against the passenger seat. He ran his hand down his face and expelled his hot breath. He then looked at Te'Qui and said, "Bro, finish telling me the story."

Te'Qui ran down everything that had happened back at the mall between T.J.'s baby momma, Boo, and Drama. The more of the story that Te'Qui told him, the more pissed off T.J. appeared to get. The nigga had bit down on his bottom lip so hard that blood trickled down at the corner of his mouth. When Te'Qui mentioned the blood to him, he licked it away and continued to listen to him.

"Scandalous ass, trifling ass, no good, hoodrat, gold digging bitch!" T.J. slammed his fist into his palm, angrily. His eyebrows were arched and he was clenching his jaws. "I'm smashing that bitch and that bitch-ass nigga you said you seen her with. On Bloods!"

"I know you are and I'ma help yo' mothafuckin' ass, too."

"For real?" he looked to him like *Are you serious?*

"Hell yeah," Te'Qui replied, as he passed the blunt back to him.

"'Preciate it, homie, but chu ain't gotta do that."

Te'Qui took a few more puffs of the bleezy and polluted the vehicle's interior with smoke. With his lungs holding the smoke hostage, he said, "I know. But I fucks witchu, hardbody." He tapped his fist against his chest. He then blew out smoke making the interior of the car look like someone had been pimp smacked with a handful of powder. "Now, hit this bleezy a couple of mo' times, you needa calm yo' ass down. You too fired up." he passed the blunt to T.J. and he took it without complaint, indulging in it.

"This shit pretty good."

"I only smoke the finest, bro. That gas."

T.J. passed the bleezy back to Te'Qui and he took a few more puffs of it before he started chopping it up with him again. "Right now, we gon' focus on getting this money. But afterwards we getting at Boo and that faggot-ass nigga that snatched my shit."

"Fa sho'." Te'Qui nodded and dapped him up.

Two weeks later

Te'Qui lay in bed asleep with Kesha lying on his chest. He was snoring aloud and drool had run from the corner of his mouth, soiling his pillow. He was tired than a mothafucka. He and T.J. had been jacking and extorting niggaz all over the city. Them niggaz was hitting back to back licks. They were on a paper chase, and didn't show any signs of slowing down. But the minute they decided to fall back and let the streets cool off, Te'Qui's sleepless nights caught up to him.

Homie had lie across the bed to talk to Kesha about their plans, when he fucked around and fell asleep. It tripped Kesha out how he drifted off so fast. He appeared to be wide awake when he was talking to her, but deep down he must have been exhausted. She wasn't surprised that he had crashed though. He had barely been home since he'd been on the grind trying to make sure their family had enough dough when the baby arrived.

Kesha's eyelids twitched hearing the vibration of a cellular nearby. Once she peeled her eyelids open, she looked to the nightstand beside Te'Qui and found his cell phone. Leaning over him, she picked up the cell phone to see who was on the display. It was T.J. Seeing his name she knew what he was calling about and she wasn't ready to let her boo go just yet. She wanted to be under him just a little while longer before she gave him up. With that in mind, she went to press the decline button, and that's when Te'Qui woke up.

"Babe, who is that?" Te'Qui asked groggily, face fixed with a frown having stirred awake.

"Nobody, baby, go back to sleep." she told him.

At that moment, Te'Qui took the cell phone away from her and checked the display. When he saw that it was T.J., he disconnected the call. He was as tired as a runaway slave and didn't exactly feel like running the streets with him again.

"Man, I'll get at that nigga later. I'm tired as a bitch right now." Te'Qui confessed, sitting the cellular back upon the nightstand. He then lay back in bed and shut his eyelids. When Kesha lay her smiling face against his chest and shut her eyelids he wrapped his arm around her. The couple was drifting off to sleep when they heard someone beeping their car's horn like they'd gone mad.

Beep! Beep! Beeep! Beeeep! Beeeeeeeeeep!

"Yo', Te'Qui, it's time to roll, dawg! Brang yo' ass outside! Come on!" T.J. called out. He was so loud that his voice carried from the streets, to inside of Te'Qui and Kesha's house.

Beep! Beep! Beeep! Beeeeeeeeeep!

"Come on now, Blood, it's time for us to shake and move! We got bitness to handle!" T.J. called out again.

Kesha shot up in bed, face frowned, lips twisted, as her individual braids hung over her face, little momma was hot than a mothafucka. "What the fuck, Te'Qui? Is yo' fucking friend crazy?"

Te'Qui sat up in bed and looked to the digital clock on the nightstand. It was 2:30 A.M. "I don't know, but homie better have a damn good excuse 'fore showin' up atta nigga crib at this hour for real, for real." he blew hard and ran his hands down his face.

Beeep! Beeeep! Beeeeeeeep!

"Yeah, this negro done definitely lost his gotdamn mind!" Kesha hopped out of bed, slipping on her house slippers and grabbing her housecoat. The entire time she was putting her shit on she looked pissed off.

"Where you goin'?" Te'Qui looked over his shoulder at her with a crinkled brow.

"To check this disrespectful ass nigga!" she told him, pulling her dreads from out of the collar of her housecoat and letting them fall down against her back. She started her march towards the door, but stopped once he called her back.

"Hold up, Keesh. Limme go see what this nigga want. It could be about some serious shit." Te'Qui said as he hopped out of bed and grabbed his Glock underneath his pillow. He tucked that bitch on his waistline and grabbed his hoodie from off the back of their bedroom door.

"If it ain't life or death, get in that ass, bae." Kesha told him as she stood by the door. Her brows were lowered and her lips were twisted, with her arms folded across her bosom. She was displaying mad attitude, like hood chicks do when they feel a nigga disrespected them.

"Fa sho'." He kissed her on the forehead. As soon as he graced her forehead with his lips, there was pounding at the front door.

"Bae, you hear this shit? This nigga knocking at the doe like he goddamn police." she looked back and forth between her man and the front door.

"Open up, nigga! I know you up in there 'cause yo' shit parked outside! Don't make me kick this bitch down, Blood! You know I'll do it!" They heard T.J. at the door. After he made his announcement, he continued to pound on the door.

Bang, bang, bang, bang!

"Unh unh, my nigga doing too much, gimme yo' strap, Te'Qui. I'm fitsna shoot this mothafucka!" Kesha tried to grab Te'Qui's gun from off his waistline, but he grabbed her wrists and pinned them to her sides.

"Relax, bae. I got this, okay?" he looked in her eyes and waited for her response. From the expression on her face he could tell that she was on ten, so he wasn't about to let her go until she told him that she was straight. Her eyes were focused on the front door and she was seething. Seeing this, he turned her chin towards him so that they'd have each other's gaze. "Okay?"

Finally, Kesha took a deep breath and shut her eyelids briefly, calming herself down. She looked to the carpeted floor and then back up at her man, saying, "Okay. Go handle your boy."

"Thanks, babe." he gave her a quick peck on the lips and headed for the front door.

Bang, bang, bang, bang! The front door rattled from the pounding of T.J.'s fist.

"Come on, dawg, we gots shit to do! Crack this bitch open!"

Bang, bang, bang, bang!
Again, the front door rattled from the pounding.
"Alright, nigga, I'm comin'. Hold the fuck on!" Te'Qui called out. All that mothafucking noise had gotten to him. Te'Qui unchained and unlocked the door, pulling that bitch open. As soon as he did, T.J. started in over the threshold. When he looked up and saw Kesha's scowling face, he greeted her. "'Sup, Keesh?" T.J. threw his head back like *What's up?* She responded by rolling her eyes and slamming the bedroom door on him. T.J. raised an eyebrow and looked to Te'Qui, pointing at the bedroom door. "Fucks wrong witcho bitch?"

Te'Qui's brows slanted and his nostrils flared. He stepped to T.J. with hostility. He didn't play that shit about Kesha. He'd blow a nigga'z brains out over her. "My nigga, my queen not gon' be too many mo' bitchez, ya hear? Watch cho mothafuckin' mouth."

T.J.'s face balled up and his lips slanted. He looked Te'Qui up and down like *This is not what you want.* He then waved him off, like he wasn't tripping off of him. "Whatever, nigga, I ain't even finna go there witchu. You know how I get down. I need you to bust this move with me. I know somebody that can tell me where that hoe-ass bitch Boo at. So, grab yo' shit and let's roll."

"Nah," Te'Qui shook his head. "I ain't goin' any where 'til you apologize to my queen for disrespectin' our home."

"Blood, you serious?" T.J. narrowed his eyelids and angled his head. He looked him square in his eyes trying to figure out if he was playing with him. From the expression on his homeboy's face he looked like he was dead ass serious about what he'd said.

"You mothafuckin' right, I ain't budgin' 'til you handle that." he held his gaze. He had a straight face and he wasn't bullshitting either.

T.J. stared at him for a minute. He nodded his head and licked his lips. He knew he was doing too much with that shit he pulled earlier, and if all it took for Te'Qui to roll out with him was an apology, then he'd give him that.

"Alright, fuck it. A nigga violated, I'll give you that. Tell wifey to come up in here." he motioned for the bedroom door.

"Bet."

Te'Qui walked inside of his bedroom and told Kesha something that T.J. couldn't quite make out. T.J. watched as Te'Qui searched his closet for something while Kesha got out of bed and came out into the living room. She stopped just outside of the doorway and folded her arms across her breasts, leaning the weight of her body on one leg. By the look on her face T.J. could tell that she wasn't interested in anything that he had to say, but if he had to smooth things over with her so his homeboy would ride out with him, then fuck it.

"Yo'," T.J. began as he placed his hand against his chest, "a mothafucking nigga apologize for blowing up y'all spot like I did earlier. That shit was mad disrespectful and it won't happen again. On God." he kissed his fingers and crossed himself in the sign of the holy crucifix.

"Hmmph," Kesha looked him up and down like he wasn't shit. She then headed back inside of the bedroom.

T.J. waved her off and sat down on the arm of the living room couch, folding his arms across his chest. He watched Te'Qui from where he sat. The nigga had just emerged from out of the closet, slipping on a bulletproof vest. Kesha helped him strapped it down to his body and slip his sweatshirt over his head. Afterwards, she gave him a hug and a kiss. With that out of the way, Te'Qui came out of the bedroom, pulling the door shut behind him.

"You ready to roll, bro?" Te'Qui asked him.

"Yeah, let's go." T.J. rose from off the arm of the couch and followed his right-hand man out of the house.

***

Boom!

Te'Qui kicked open the door and rushed in, with T.J. bringing up the rear. As soon as Broadway saw them, he went to grab the banga lying on the table beside the money he was counting up. Before his hand could grasp the handle of his weapon, Te'Qui was putting some hot shit through him. *Bloom!* The blast from the shotgun knocked Broadway's chair over and made made his ass wince. His blood dotted up the wrinkle bills he was counting, and he made a loud thud when he hit the carpeted floor.

As soon as the front door had flown open, Tangela took off running towards the kitchen to get out through the backdoor. She'd almost cleared the kitchen doorway, when T.J. grabbed the floor runner rug she was making hurried footsteps on and gave it a strong tug. Tangela did a flip in the air and landed hard on her back, wincing.

"Fuck you think you going, bitch?" T.J. asked with a scowl as he approached her, tucking his banga into his waistline. He grabbed a handful of Tangela's dookie braids and dragged her ass back into the living room, kicking and screaming. A pained expression was written across her face as she held tight to T.J.'s wrist and thrashed her legs. Her thrashing kicked off one of her high heel pumps in the process.

"Aaaaaaah!" She belted out with tears in her eyes, which spilled down her cheeks.

"Bitch, shut the fuck up!" T.J. pulled Tangela around and punched her in her mouth hard as fuck, bloodying her grill. He then grabbed a chair and smacked it down on the living room floor, planting Tangela's ass in it, roughly. "Yo', check the upstairs, it could be some mo' bitchez up in here." He called out to Te'Qui as he duct taped Tangela's torso and ankles to the chair.

"Alright," Te'Qui nodded and ran up the staircase. He kicked open the first bedroom door, but there wasn't anyone inside. He then made his way down the hallway towards the only bedroom left. He placed his ear to the door and listened closely for any movement. Afterwards, he took a step back and kicked that bitch open with so much force that he nearly tore it off its hinges.

"Aah! Aaah! Aaaah!" One of the girls screamed.

"Please, don't kill us!" a second girl cried.

"Y'all bitchez shut the fuck up, and bring y'all asses downstairs 'fore I make shit bloody in here!" Te'Qui threatened. Having heard his homeboy barking orders, T.J. looked to the staircase. He found Te'Qui marching four half naked women down the steps at gunpoint. All of their faces were wet with tears and they appeared to be quivering.

"Make they asses get on their knees, right there!" T.J. pointed at the center of the living room floor, as he pulled a jar of liquid substance from out of the back pocket of his jeans.

"Y'all heard the man, get on yo' mothafuckin' knees, right there!" Te'Qui commanded the bitchez, pointing his shotgun at the exact spot T.J. wanted them to kneel. Once they'd done like they were told, Te'Qui went down the line of them looking at their faces. They were all fairly attractive, but he could tell that the street life was catching up to most of them. They looked disheveled and aged in the face. In fact, some of them even had track marks on their arms. Hell, one in particular wore denchers, but they weren't in her mouth because Te'Qui hadn't given her time to put them in. This was three of the women; the fourth and final girl didn't look a day over sixteen. Although her body was developed like a grown-ass woman, anyone could clearly see she was a minor.

Te'Qui stopped at the young girl and looked down into her face. She was sniffling and crying like all the other girls. She quickly looked away from Te'Qui, not wanting to look him in the eyes for fear she'd give him the incentive to kill her.

"What's yo' name, lil' momma?" Te'Qui asked.

"A-Asia." she stuttered, making sure to keep her head bowed.

"How old are you?"

"Fourteen." she whimpered.

Te'Qui shook his head like it was a goddamn shame, having heard Asia's age. He then looked back at Broadway's dead body. His eyes were wide and his mouth was stretched open. "That nigga'z a real piece of shit, Blood, pimpin' this young-ass girl." he then turned to T.J. and said, "Yo', you know lil' momma is only fourteen-years-old?"

"Oh, yeah? Well, I didn't know, and now that I do, I can't say that I give a shit." T.J. whipped out his gun again. "My only concern is finding out where that bitch Boo is, and this skank scaliwag-ass bitch is gon' tell me." he yanked Tangela into him by her hair and drew a shriek from her. He gave her the evil eye and clenched his jaws, looking her in the face. "Ain't that right, hoe?"

"Fuck you, nigga! I ain't tellin' you jack shit!" Tangela scowled and spit at him. A nasty gooey glob of saliva hit his ski-mask and dripped off the brow of it.

T.J. wiped the dripping goo off of his ski-mask with the back of his gloved hand. He then looked down at Tangela, smiling devilishly. "Oh, youa gangsta bitch, huh? Youa gangsta?"

"Yeah, nigga, I'm the most gangsta bitch up in here!" She mad dogged him, as he held a fistful of her braids.

"Hoe, the only G's in here is me and my mothafucking homeboy! Bow down to something greater than yo' self, trick!" T.J., still holding Tangela by her braids, took his gun by its barrel and beat her in the face with it. He grunted each time he crashed the hard metal into her face, dotting his clothing with her blood. T.J. was beating her so viciously, that the other hoes turned their heads, cringing. Once he finished whipping her ass, he took a step back and looked at her closely. Tangela's face was bloody and dripping on her lap. One of her eyes was swollen shut and her nose was twice its size. Her good eye looked around aimlessly. She moaned in pain and spat out a bloody, broken tooth. "Now, who's the gangsta, bitch?"

"I-I-I am." Tangela managed to say with a smart-ass smirk.

T.J. looked back at Te'Qui and said, "I must admit, I respect this bitch's G." he then looked back to Tangela and shot her in the kneecap.

"Aaaaaah! Aaaaaah!" Tangela whipped her head back, screaming bloody murder. Tears welled up in her eyes and spilled down her cheeks. She brought her head back down and looked T.J. in his eyes, still talking that big, bad gangsta shit. "Fuck you, fuck you! Fuck you, you fucking bitch made-ass nigga!"

At this time, Asia was looking back and forth between T.J. and Tangela, wondering what he was going to do to her next. Tears were in her eyes and her heart was thudding. She was scared for the older whore.

"I salute cho' gangsta," T.J. saluted Tangela and pointed the gun at her forehead.

"No, don't kill my sister!" Asian called out.

T.J. and Te'Qui frowned up and looked at Asia. They were shocked at the revelation that she'd made.

"Bitch, you were letting this nigga pimp out cho lil' sister? Awww, man, neither one of y'all ain't shit. But neither am I 'cause I'ma 'bouta do something that may guarantee that I won't go to heaven." T.J. wiped his blood stained gun off on Tangela's clothing and walked over to her younger sister and the whores. Without warning, T.J. shot all three of the women that were on their knees in their foreheads at point blank range.

They fell flat on their face and their blood poured out of their heads. His action caused Asia to tremble harder than she did before. She squeezed her eyelids shut and tears jetted down her cheeks. Using the sleeve of his thermal, T.J. wiped the blood from the whores that had splattered against the side of her face. He then turned back around to Tangela who had a shocked expression on her face.

"What the fuck is the matter with chu, you fuckin' monster?" Tangela hollered out as tears slid down her cheeks.

Te'Qui looked down at the dead bodies of the whores and then back up at T.J. He was as ruthless as they came, and he hoped that one day he didn't have to turn his gun against him. But should that day come, he wouldn't hesitate to take his head off his shoulders.

"That was just to let chu know that I'm not playing witcho ass. I mean bitness out this bitch!" T.J. said as he placed his hand on Asia's trembling shoulder, walking around her until he was at her back. The young girl's heart was thudding crazily and she found her palms growing moist. With her head bowed and her eyelids shut, she silently prayed to God to spare her life.

Wait a minute, I know this nigga ain't 'bouta do what I think he's about to do, Te'Qui's brows creased as he thought to himself. He had the feeling that T.J. was about to bust a cap in Asia's head, and that wasn't something he was down with. Bodying grown mothafuckaz was one thing, but killing little girls was another.

"Now, let's try this again," T.J. started over, placing his gun to the back of Asia's skull. "Where the fuck is Boo? I'm not gon' ask yo' ass again." He looked up at Tangela as he held his banga to the back of her younger sibling's dome piece.

Tangela was silent. She didn't say anything. She appeared to be mulling things over. It was hard for her to give up Boo because the two of them were as good as blood sisters. They'd been tight since the second grade. They'd never even had so much as an argument so it was hard for her to come up with a reason to sell her out.

"Times up," T.J. went to put a bullet in the back of Asia's head, but Tangela called out to him.

"Waiiiiit!" Tangela shouted. "I'll tell you-I'll tell you where she's at, just don't kill my sister, okay?"

Te'Qui sighed with relief. He didn't want young Asia to get popped. She hadn't lived her life yet.

T.J. took his gun from the back of Asia's head and walked over to Tangela. Stopping before her, he said, "Talk."

Tangela told T.J. the address where Boo was holed up at. As soon as she finished spilling her guts, he put a hot one in her brain.

Blocka!

Tangela's head flew backwards and her braids went up into the air, blood spraying out of the back of her dome. Blood and brain fragments dripped out of the back of her skull, as she stared up at the ceiling, wide eyed, mouth open.

"Noooooooo!" Asia jumped to her feet and shoved T.J. aside, running up the staircase. Before T.J. could fall, he righted himself. He then aimed his gun up at Asia as she fled for her life up the staircase. He tried to draw a bead on Asia, but he couldn't get her in his sights. Realizing this, he lowered his gun and charged up the staircase after her. Te'Qui chased after him, lugging his shotgun along the way.

Asia ran into the bedroom and tried to get push the window open. She winced as she struggled to push the window open, occasionally glancing over her shoulder to see how far behind the masked men were. They were right on her ass so she started screaming for help, hoping that someone would hear her and call the police.

Asia managed to push the window open. She was about to climb out of the window until she heard T.J.'s threatening voice behind him.

"Ah, ah, ah, lil' bitch!" T.J. taunted her, pointing his gun at her back.

Asia knew that he had the drop on her. Therefore, she was at his mercy. Acknowledging this, she whimpered and put her hands up in the air, slowly turning around to face him. She was so afraid that she'd wet her panties.

"Please, don't kill me. There's no reason to, I haven't seen your face! I haven't seen your face!" Asia broke down sobbing, shoulders rocking back and forth.

T.J. pulled off his ski-mask and held it down at his side, revealing what he looked like beneath it, and saying, "Now, you have." he told Asia and pointed his gun at her chest.

Blocka! Blocka! Blocka! Blocka!

"Nooooooo!" Te'Qui called out as he reached out to stop T.J. from shooting the young girl but it was already too late.

Asia's blood splashed against the windowpane and she fell back on the carpeted floor. She lay there lifeless, staring out of the side of her eyes vacantly.

"What the fuck is yo' problem, man!" Te'Qui shoved T.J. hard as fuck, causing him to stumble backwards.

"Yo,' watch who you put cho fucking hands on!" T.J. shoved him back more aggressively, causing him to stumble backwards as he did. Both of the gangstaz had mad dog stares plastered across their faces, looking like they were ready to pop off at any moment then. "I don't give a fuck about none of these bitchez up in here! That bitch, Boo, ran off with my money and my dope, now a nigga on one. The way I'm feeling, anybody can get it behind mine! You feel me?"

"Lil' momma wasn't nothin' but fourteen, man, she was a lil' fuckin' kid." Te'Qui reasoned as he walked over to Asia's corpse, looking down at her. He crossed himself in the sign of the holy crucifix. Afterwards, he sat his shotgun down on the nightstand and snatched the white sheet from off the bed, draping it over Asia's body. As soon as the sheet covered her body, her blood started seeping through it, leaving crimson stains behind.

"Come on, Blood. Let's grab that money down stairs on the table and get the fuck from outta here." T.J. told Te'Qui. He then pulled his ski-mask over his head and adjusted it so that he could see out of the eye holes of it. Without waiting for Te'Qui to follow him, he headed out of the bedroom and headed down the staircase.

CHAPTER SEVEN

After Te'Qui and T.J. disposed of the car they'd driven over to Tangela's house in, they hopped into a rental and headed out to Te'Qui's crib. T.J. drove and smoked on a fat ass blunt, stinking up the interior of his ride. He found himself glancing over at Te'Qui whose attention was focused out of the passenger window. There was a frown fixed on his face and he looked hostile.

"'Sup, Blood? You tripping off that lil' bitch back there that I offed?" T.J. asked him.

"That girl was only fourteen, my nigga, fourteen-mothafuckin'-years-old." Te'Qui told him.

"Limme ask you something, homie," T.J. said as he made a right turn at the light. "How old were you when you put ten toes down in these streets? How old were you when you lost yo' homeboy, Baby Wicked? How old were you when you caught yo' first body?"

"I was ten-years-old, but what the fuck does that have to do with anything?"

"You was ten before you got knee deep in these streets, and that lil' hoe back there was fourteen. Shiiiiit, she was probably far mo' seasoned than you. You know bitchez mature faster than niggaz, right?"

"What's yo' point?" his brows wrinkled.

"My point is this, these streets don't love nobody. They don't give a fuck how old you are or who you kin to." T.J. told him, straight up. "As far as these streets are concerned, if you got sense enough to play in 'em, then you fair game. It's fucked up, but that's just how it is, you feel me?" he tried to pass Te'Qui the bleezy, but he didn't want to hit that shit. He waved that nigga off.

"Youz a coldhearted ass nigga, man. Straight up. You don't give a mad-ass fuck!" Te'Qui told him how he felt. "You know who you remind me off, Blood? You remind me of my mom's ex-boyfriend, Tiaz. He was a ruthless, cold blooded mothafucka just like you."

"Oh, yeah?"

"Yep."

"Well, I'd like to meet, Blood."

"You can't. He's dead. My uncle peeled his ass in jail."

"For what?" T.J.'s forehead wrinkled with curiosity.

Te'Qui went on to give T.J. the rundown on Tiaz and his mother's relationship, as well as how everything went down. The fat nigga listened closely to everything he was being told, and appeared to be intrigued by it all.

"Damn, Tiaz didn't play. Y'all better be happy yo' unc got 'em up outta here, or else that woulda been y'all ass."

"Man, fuck that nigga! I ain't no lil' ass boy no mo', if he was alive I'd have somethin' for that ass."

"My nigga, spoken like a true gangsta," T.J. smiled and tried to dap him up, but he left him hanging. Instead, he focused his attention back out of the passenger window.

T.J. shrugged and kept on driving, puffing on his fat ass blunt. About thirty minutes later he was pulling up at Te'Qui's house and he was jumping out. Te'Qui slammed the door behind him and leaned down into the passenger window, making eye contact with T.J.

"Check this out, dawg. You my man and all and I fucks witchu hardbody, but after we get cho trap back, I can't fuck witchu no mo'." he told him seriously.

"What chu mean?" T.J.'s forehead creased.

"What I mean is, once we get cho shit back, you and me are through. I see the future right now, and fuckin' with a nigga like you, I'ma either wind up dead or fightin' a life sentence, and I can't fade either one of 'em."

With that having been said, T.J. mad dogged Te'Qui, looking like he was ready to bite his fucking face off. He didn't say shit back though. He pressed the button on the door panel and rolled the passenger window up, causing Te'Qui to pull his head back. When T.J. took off, Te'Qui stood there in the street watching the back brake lights of his car. Once the red lights disappeared, he headed towards his house.

***

Te'Qui closed and locked the door behind him once he entered his house. He pulled off his shirt as he headed to his bedroom door, hearing the television as an infomercial playing. He opened the bedroom door and found Kesha lying underneath the covers on her side asleep. Te'Qui sat on his side of the bed and unlaced his sneakers, sitting them aside on the floor. Afterwards, he rose from the bed, pulling thick wads of blue faces from out of his deep pockets and dumping it on the bed. As he was doing this, Kesha stirred awake and looked at him through sleepy, narrowed eyes.

"Hey, baby, when did you come in?" Kesha asked groggily.

"Just now," Te'Qui replied. From the sound of his voice Kesha could tell something was up with him. So she turned around to him in bed to see what was up.

"What's the matter? What happened out there?" she asked with concern.

Once Te'Qui finished emptying his pockets out on the bed, he turned on the lamp on his nightstand. He then sat up on the bed and grabbed a handful of the money that had Broadway's blood splattered on it. He and T.J. had busted it down the middle, so he went home with quite a few thousand dollars.

"I can't tell you exactly what happened, you know that, Keesh. In my business, it's always best that you don't know too much of shit. That way if The Boys snatch you up, you ain't got shit to tell 'em 'cause you don't know shit. You feel what I'm sayin'?"

"Yeah, I feel you. You keeping certain things a secret is for both of our protection."

"That's right." he started counting up the money.

"It's 'cause of something that nigga, T.J. did, huh?" she inquired as she joined him in counting the money up.

"Yeah." he admitted, shaking his head as he thought about the fourteen-year-old Asia that T.J. clapped. He then said under his breath, "That stupid fat mothafucka."

"Okay. I know you can't tell me shit, but I can at least guess, right?"

"If you want too." he replied with a tone higher than a whisper, as he counted up the blue faces.

"Well, being that it's T.J., I know he's a ruthless ass nigga. So, I'ma say he capped somebody that you feel that he shouldn't have. Also, the person was young and most likely female. A young girl, probably barely old enough to date?" she looked up at him.

Te'Qui stopped counting and took a deep breath. Staring ahead, he tried to decide whether he should tell Kesha what was up or not. Coming to a conclusion, he looked her right in her eyes and said, "Yeah. That's exactly what it is."

"I'm sorry, baby." she sat the stack of money down on the bed and caressed the side of his face.

"Me too. 'Cause although I didn't pull the trigga I was there. So, my hands are just as much stained with baby girl's blood as his are."

Kesha nodded her understanding, but she didn't agree with the girl's blood being on Te'Qui's hands. See, she knew her man was a cold blooded wig splitta in the streets, but she also knew that he had a heart. A big heart.

Maybe you should fall back from dealing with dude. I mean, it seems like y'all don't live by the same moral code, so y'all gon' end up bumping heads. And if he's the G that he seems to be, they y'all gon' wind up killing each other."

"Shit, I thought that was gon' go down tonight, after that girl lost her life."

"For real, bae?"

He looked at her and nodded. "Yep."

"If that nigga would have done anything to you, I woulda took that choppa out that closet and went looking for that ass."

Te'Qui looked at Kesha and smiled. He the caressed her cheek and kissed her on her forehead. He loved the fact that she'd ride out for him. "That's my baby."

"You goddamn right, don't nobody fuck with my man or my baby." she looked down and rubbed her stomach.

Te'Qui and Kesha finished counting up the blue faces. They then rolled them up and put rubber bands around them. Afterwards, he got up from the bed and opened the closet. He opened the digital safe and placed the money inside. He picked up the small notepad and ink pen, writing down the amount he'd just put inside of the safe. Once he sat the ink pen and notepad back inside of the safe, he shut it.

"I tell you one thing I'ma do though, babe," Te'Qui started up again, closing the closet door behind him.

"What's that?" Kesha asked curiously.

"Like I told homie once he'd dropped me off, after we get his money and shit back from this broad, I'm severing ties with 'em. I can't afford to play for the stakes he's playin' for in this game. You feel me?"

"Sho' you right, baby."

"I'm finna go take a shower." Te'Qui disrobed and kissed Kesha.

"Alright, I love you." she watched his back as he headed for the bathroom door.

"I love you too, momma." he replied, shutting the bathroom door behind him.

Once Te'Qui was out of sight, Kesha got down on her knees on the side of the bed. She shut her eyelids and put her hands together, praying that her fiance made it out of the streets before he met his death in them.

One night later

Boo was inside of the kitchen sweeping the floor and singing Boo'd up, when she looked up and seen her four-year-old son, Cordary, peering out of the curtains. Just a second ago he was sitting on the floor playing with his toys and watching television, so she wondered what had stole his interest. Her brows deepened with grooves as she propped the broom up against the wall and walked inside of the living room.

"Cordary, what are you looking at out there?" Boo inquired as she took her nickel plated .22 from underneath the middle cushion of the couch. A strange feeling had come over her so she decided to grab her gun.

Cordary was startled by his mother calling his name. He turned around to her with a puzzled look on his face holding one of his toys. His innocent eyes darted to the gun in his mother's hand and his brows scrunched up, wondering what she was doing with it. He'd saw guns before on television and he knew exactly what they did. So it worried him that his mother was packing one. The first thing that came to his young mind was that they were in danger.

"What's the matter, momma? What's going on?" the little dude asked with genuine concern.

"Did you see someone out there, baby?" Boo asked, ignoring the boy's question. The first thing she thought was T.J. had found out where she was staying and had come to murder her scandalous ass. She looked out through the curtains and scanned the outside, but she didn't see anyone in sight. "Cordary, who did you see outside?"

"I saw a man in all-black; he was creepin' around the side of the house." Cordary reported.

Boo took her face from out of the window and turned around to her son, kneeling down to him so they'd be at eye level. "You said he was creeping where?"

"Around the side of the house, bitch!" A strong masculine voice came from the back of Boo and her son.

Boo's heart dropped and she whipped around to where she'd heard the voice come from. She spotted a masked up nigga, who was pointing a gun at her. She went to point her gun at him, and he shot her in the thigh. She hollered out in pain and fell on the floor, grimacing.

"Mommy!" Cordary called out to her, running to her aid. "Are you okay?"

Right then, the masked up nigga, T.J., yanked Cordary aside and pointed his gun at Boo's face. "Drop that burna, bitch, you already know what time it is!"

Boo obliged T.J. and he kicked the .22 aside. The small gun spun around in circles as it slid across the floor.

"Uhhhh!" T.J.'s eyes bulged and he grabbed his aching balls with one hand. He doubled over in pain, having been kicked in his crotch by Boo.

"Run, baby, run!" Boo called out to her son. The boy took off running. He'd cleared the kitchen threshold, when a masked up Te'Qui snatched his little ass up. The boy kicked and screamed as Te'Qui carried him back inside of the living room.

"Aaaaah, sssss, you fucking bitch! You gon' pay-oh, yeah, you gon' pay for that one." T.J. swore as he winced in excruciation, holding himself. He stood upright, and pointing his gun at Boo's kneecap.

"Nooooo, don't hurt my mommy!" Cordary hollered out, and that's when it happened.

Blowl!

Boo's kneecap exploded upon impact of the hollow tip slug. She grabbed it with both hands and threw her head back, screaming in agony. Tears rolled out of her eyes and blood seeped between her fingers. Lying where she was on the shiny waxed floor, she bawled and whined like a toddler.

Seeing that she was already in great pain, T.J. took the liberty to stomp on her thigh, adding to her suffering.

"Fonky-ass hoe! That shit, hurt don't it?"

"Please, T.J., stop! No more!" Boo begged him.

"Daddy, why are you doin' this? Stop, you're hurting mommy!" Cordary called out, with tears spilling down his cheeks. He was afraid for his mother.

"Welp, since he knows who I am anyway," T.J. pulled off his ski-mask and stuffed it into his right back pocket, letting it hang like a gangbanger would his bandana. He then turned around to his son, saying, "I know I'm hurting mommy, she's been bad. This is her punishment for being bad. You know, like how you getta spanking for acting up?" Cordary nodded and wiped the tears from his dripping eyes. "Don't worry, this'll all be over in a bit, lil' man. Just have a seat at that table over there. Then, I want chu to shut your eyes and cover your ears for me."

Te'Qui released Cordary and he pulled out a chair at the dining room table, sitting down in it. He then did exactly like his father had told him, shutting his eyelids and covering his ears.

"Back to this hoe," T.J. turned around to Boo and kicked her in the stomach.

"Uhhhhh!" Boo's body jerked from the kick. Her eyes widened and watered. She held her stomach, having gotten the wind knocked out of her.

"Now, where my money and dope at?"

"If-if I tell you-you gon' kill me anyway. So, fuck you, gon' head and do it!" Boo told him, as she continued to bawl on the floor, dripping blood.

"Boy, I tell you, you and yo' homegirl Tangela. I see where we at with it. I guess I gotta go there," T.J. tucked his banga at the front of his Dickies and made his way inside of the kitchen. Te'Qui kept a watchful eye on Boo and Cordary while listening to his homeboy rifle through the kitchen drawer. He heard the sound of silverware clinking together, and then a moment later, T.J. came marching out of the kitchen, meat cleaver in his gloved hand.

"Yo', go over there and watch that bitch. I got lil' man from here," T.J. told Te'Qui.

"What chu 'bouta do, dawg?" Te'Qui looked back and forth between the meat cleaver in T.J.'s hand and the sinister look in his eyes.

T.J. looked at Te'Qui in annoyance, saying, "My nigga, what's up with the questions? Just hold me down."

Te'Qui went to do what he was told. He stood over Boo with his Glizzy at his side. If his homie told him to nod her ass, then that's exactly what the fuck he was going to do. What was making him uneasy now was T.J. having that meat cleaver out around Cordary. The only reason why he was going to let the scenario play out was because the boy was of T.J.'s blood, and he didn't think he'd harm him. Te'Qui had it in his mind that homeboy was just going to use the meat cleaver as a scare tatic.

"Limme see yo' hand, lil' man," Te'Qui sat the meat cleaver down on the dining room table and rolled up Cordary's sleeve. He then placed his hand flat down on the table top and picked up the meat cleaver.

"What-what're you doing to him?" Boo whined.

A scared Cordary looked back and forth between the meat cleaver and his outstretched hand. He trembled and tears ran down his face.

"Daddy, no, no! Please!" Cordary pleaded, green snot bubbling out of his nose. His head snapped over to his mother. "Mommy, stop 'em, stop dad! He's goin' to hurt me!" He hollered hysterically, trying to yank his small arm from his father's grasp. T.J., being the adult, was much stronger than him though, so he couldn't pull himself free from his grip.

"T.J., stop! Don't hurt 'em, he's your son! He's your son for Christ sake!" Boo screamed and yelled from the floor. The tears seemed to be cascading down her cheeks and snot was threatening to drip from her right nostril.

"He's my son? My son, huh?" T.J. looked at her and laughed maniacally.

"Yes, yes, he's your son! He's your blood!" Boo hollered out to him.

"Hahahahahahaha!" T.J. laughed even harder this time. This caused Te'Qui to look back and forth between Boo and T.J. He didn't know why the fuck that nigga was laughing like that. "Bitch, this lil' big eared mothafucka ain't come from out my dick! He that Compton nigga son you was fucking...Drama!" When he said this, recognition flashed in Boo's eyes. It was from this that he knew that it was undoubtedly true. Drama had told him that Cordary was actually his 'son' before he attempted to blow a hole in him. "You didn't think a nigga knew that, huh? Well, I do! The streets talk, baby girl, and I just so happen to be listening." he lifted his meat cleaver above his head in a striking motion.

"Noooo, noooooo, nooooooo!" Boo screamed and screamed, outstretching her bloody hand towards her son. Little Cordary was looking at her pleadingly, slimy snot sliding over his lips. His face was shiny from crying.

"Mommy, pleeeease, please, stop 'em! Stop 'em!" Cordary screamed and cried. He was screaming so loudly that he was starting to grow hoarse.

"Yo', stop, man, stop!" Te'Qui told T.J. as he advanced towards him. Things had gone too far and he couldn't allow him to chop off little Cordary's hand.

"I'll tell you, I'll tell you!" Boo told him over and over again, afraid for her son.

"Where the fuck is my shit?" T.J. slammed the meat cleaver down and the entire living room fell silent. Still lying on the floor, Boo stared at T.J. and her son, breathing heavily. Her heart was thudding madly. Cordary was staring at the meat cleaver, which was lodged into the wooden table. His chest jumped up and down, as he breathed huskily.

"Where's my shit, Boo? I'm not gon' ask you not one mo' mothafucking time!" T.J. spoke sternly as he held his finger up.

Boo shut her eyelids briefly and took a deep breath. She silently thanked God for stopping T.J. from chopping her son's arm off. Once she peeled her eyelids back open, she looked up at T.J. "Okay. Look, that nigga, Drama, sold all the dope to some niggaz in Compton. We spent some of the money, but we got some left."

T.J. pulled the meat cleaver out of the table top with two tugs. He then said, "Where that shit at?"

"It's inside of the deep freezer, inside of the kitchen." she pointed to the kitchen with a bloody finger.

"How much is left?" T.J. inquired.

"About forty gees." she admitted.

T.J. looked back and forth between Boo and the kitchen. He wagged his meat cleaver at her as he talked to her, saying, "If I open up that freezer and find anything less than forty bands, I'ma waltz back in her and chop yo' mothafucking head off."

T.J. sat the meat cleaver down on the dining room table and walked into the kitchen, stopping at the deep freezer. He opened the deep freezer and peered inside, rifling through the frozen packages of meats. A smile spread across his lips when he uncovered a block of money sealed tight in plastic. He then removed the block of money and shut the freezer. Afterwards, he walked back inside of the dining room with the block tucked under his arm, like a baseball. Looking at Boo, he said, "I'm not even gon' bother to count this shit up. Although you a trifling, no good, rotten skeeza, I'ma take yo' word for it."

"Bag that shit so we can go, my nigga," Te'Qui told T.J.

"I am ol' impatient-ass nigga. First, I wanna raid this bitch's bedroom. She was laid up with a street nigga, so I know he's gotta stash somewhere in this bitch." T.J. responded. "Hold this shit down 'til I get back."

T.J. disappeared inside of the bedroom, turning over all of the furniture and flipping the mattress. He came up on twenty g-stacks, a couple of Rolex watches and some other jewelry. He stashed the goods and the money inside of a Nike duffle bag which he found at the back of the closet.

"Awww, fuck!" T.J. heard Te'Qui holler out in pain from the living room. He hoisted the strap of the Nike duffle bag over his shoulder and ran back inside of the living room. His eyes widened with surprise when he saw Te'Qui kneeled on the floor. He was wincing and holding his bleeding arm, with the meat cleaver beside it. T.J. looked to the dining room table and Cordary was long gone.

"My nigga, what the fuck happened?" T.J. asked concerned, forehead creased with worry.

Lil' mothafucka chopped me in my arm with that cleaver and ran out of the backdoor." Te'Qui was gritting as he nodded to the blood stained meat cleaver and then towards the kitchen, where the backdoor was located.

"How the fuck you let that lil' nigga do that? He was way over there?" T.J. said. He didn't wait for Te'Qui response. He snatched his ski-mask from out of his back pocket and pulled it down over his face. "Come on so we can catch this mothafucka, man." he pulled Te'Qui back upon his feet and then picked up the meat cleaver. He wiped the blood stained cleaver off on his pants leg and tucked it in his belt. See, forensics was a mothafucka and he wasn't trying to get caught up on the account of DNA being left behind.

"Please, don't kill 'em, T.J. Don't kill my son, he doesn't have anything to do with this!" Boo begged for T.J.'s mercy. By this time she was sweating and pale from having been shot. Her face was shiny from crying and the slimy green snot from her nose had dried.

"You don't want me to slump that lil' nigga, then tell me where homeboy at that helped you rob my ass." T.J. told her.

Boo gave T.J. the address to where Drama was at.

"Good looking out." T.J. pulled out his banga and blew her brains out. He then tucked his gun and nudged Te'Qui to follow him out of the backdoor. At this time, police car sirens wailed loudly, heading to their location.

T.J. and Te'Qui made hurried footsteps across the lawn of the backyard. Looking ahead, T.J. saw Cordary drop down from the gate, having just climbed over it. He watched as the little dude hauled ass down the alley.

"There that lil' mothafucka is!" T.J. pointed out to Te'Qui, who was running beside him holding his wounded arm. T.J. tossed his duffle bag over the gate. He then scaled it alongside Te'Qui. Once they were halfway down on the opposite side of the gate, they jumped down to the graveled ground. T.J. picked up the duffle bag and tossed it into the backseat of the getaway car. He and Te'Qui then jumped into the vehicle, and he sped off after Cordary. While speeding after Cordary, who was running as fast as he could down the alley, they glanced to their right. In between the houses, they saw several police cars with their flashing lights racing to the house that they'd just left.

"Lil' fucka!" T.J. said, staring ahead at Cordary as he fled. He smiled devilishly and gripped the steering wheel, mashing the gas pedal down to the floor. The engine of the getaway car revved up and ripped down the alley, leaving debris and loose trash in its wake.

Te'Qui's head whipped back and forth between the windshield and T.J., fearful of what he was about to do to young Cordary.

"Fuck is you doin', bro?" Te'Qui asked.

"Fuck you think? I'm finna mow his lil' ass down." his eyebrows arched and he bit down hard on his bottom lip.

Right then, Te'Qui grabbed hold of the steering wheel. He and T.J. tugged back and forth for control of it. Realizing that his efforts were useless, T.J. tried a different approach. He elbowed Te'Qui in his stomach which doubled him over. Following up, he chopped him in the throat, which caused him to gag. Te'Qui's eyes bugged and watered, as he grabbed his neck with both hands. He slid over to the passenger side window struggling to breathe.

With Te'Qui out of the fight, T.J. floored the gas pedal again, ripping down the alley. The bright headlights of his getaway car shined on Cordary, putting him in the spotlight. The sweaty boy looked back and forth over his shoulder at the car at his rear. His eyes were wide with terror and his heart was beating insanely. His tiny chest jumped up and down with every terrified breath he took.

Ba-dunk! Bunk!

The getaway car rocked from left to right as he ran over Cordary's body. T.J. could hear the boy's bones snapping and popping as it was crushed by the four ton vehicle. Having mowed down the small child, T.J. adjusted his rearview mirror and looked at what was left of Cordary. He saw the boy's brains mashed against the asphalt and his severed leg lying not too far from it.

Still breathing funny, Te'Qui pulled himself from the passenger window and looked out of the back window. Sadness poisoned his eyes and anger swelled his heart, seeing Cordary splattered on the ground behind them.

"What the fuck you do that for, man? He was just a kid!" Te' Qui screamed at him, spit leaping off his lips.

T.J. scowled hard and slammed on the brakes, causing the car to jerk. At the exact same time, he and Te'Qui snatched the ski-mask from off their faces and drew their bangaz. They pointed their guns in one another's faces. They stared one another down, nostrils flaring and jaws clenched.

"You helped that lil' nigga escape the house, didn't chu?" T.J. questioned him, but he didn't answer. "Didn't chu, you soft-ass nigga?"

"I told you, I ain't down for splashin' no kids!"

"That lil'nigga saw my face!"

"Ain't nobody tell yo' dumbass to take off yo' mask!"

"Nigga, his momma said who I was before I took my shit off!"

"I don't give a fuck, Blood! I ain't down with killin' no babies!"

"Fuck all this talking! Are we dying tonight or what's up?" T.J. asked. He didn't give a mad ass fuck if he lived or died as long as he was buried a mothafucking G.

Slowly, Te'Qui took his gun from out of T.J.'s face and T.J. did the same.

"After we dump this G-ride, slide me to the house, Blood, I'm cool on you." Te'Qui turned around in his seat. He pulled up the sleeve of his sweatshirt and checked his wound. Seeing how deep it was, he was definitely going to need stitches.

T.J. put the car in drive and peeled off.

After discarding the guns used in the home invasion, T.J. and Te'Qui dumped the getaway car and set that bitch ablaze. They then hopped into another whip and drove to Te'Qui's crib. As soon as they pulled up in the front of the young nigga'z house, Te'Qui jumped out of the car and leaned down inside of the passenger window.

"Yo', limme park so I can come in and we can bust that money down the middle." T.J. told him. He was referring to the block of money in plastic that he'd taken from Boo's house, along with the twenty gees he'd grabbed from Drama's stash.

"Nah," Te'Qui shook his head. "That's all you, bro. We straight. But check this out, my nig. This will be our last time seeing each other. I don't wanna have shit to do witchu from now on. Don't call or text me for shit. I don't give a fuck what it's about, you feel me? If you slide by the crib, I'ma assume its 'cause you want smoke and I'ma try to knock yo' head off. You got that?"

T.J. stared at Te'Qui for a moment. Then, he busted up laughing at him, bowing his head and pounding his fist against the steering wheel like shit was hilarious. He brought his head back up and looked at Te'Qui, clapping his hands. "My nigga, you be acting like you the only gangsta in these streets.

You seen how I give it up. I don't give a fuck about nobody, including myself. If I truly felt that chu was a threat, I wouldn't hesitate to take you, yo' baby momma or yo' unborn seed out." he made his hand into the shape of a gun and pointed it at him. He then lowered his hand and said, "You good though, dawg. I prefer to do my thang solo. I never was one for the sidekick thang, so you good. I'm out." T.J. drove off and left Te'Qui behind in the street. "Ol' bitch-ass nigga, who the fuck do he think he is? I don't need that nigga! I've been putting in work by myself! Mothafucka better ask somebody!" T.J. glanced down at the floor on the passenger side and saw Te'Qui's cell phone. His forehead creased with lines as he quickly picked it up. He didn't need a code to unlock the device so all of Te'Qui's information was at his disposal. A wicked smile spread across T.J.'s face as an evil plan formed in his mind.

***

Drama stood before his full length body mirror modeling the white on white Armani suit he was dressed in. He turned from side to side as he adjusted his cufflinks. He was fresh to death for the night's occasion, which was an All White party at some big time record executive's mansion, in Beverly Hills. Drama stopped moving and took a real good look at his reflection, smoothing out the slight wrinkles in his suit. He looked like one million dollars in all one-hundred dollar bills, but there were a couple of accessories missing that would make his fit complete. Realizing what those accessories were, he snapped his fingers and walked over to the dresser. He pulled open his top dresser drawer and picked up a white bandana, tying it around his bald dome, Tupac Shakur style. Afterwards, he pushed the drawer shut and picked up a pair of shades.

The lenses of the shades were jet black and the arms of them were braided and gold. He slipped them bitchez on and then snapped on a matching bracelet, which was covered in diamonds. On that same wrist, he snapped on a Rolex watch which was flooded with diamonds also. He put a pinky ring on the pinky finger of that same hand that was dripping in ice. When it came to his other wrist he put on two Cuban link bracelets that were different in size and two gold and diamond rings. To top things off, he slipped on his hood famous gold chain which bared his name, Drama. Once the lights in the ceiling hit the piece, the diamonds in that mothafucka started dancing.

"Meka, you almost ready to go?" Drama called out to his date for the night as he scanned his collection of colognes posted together on the top of his dresser. Finding his Versace cologne, he picked it up and sprayed his neck and wrists. Still holding the bottle of the expensive ass cologne, he rubbed his wrists together and sat the bottle back down where he'd picked it up from.

Just then, Meka strolled into the bedroom in a white dress that looked exactly like the one that Marilyn Monroe wore. Meka was a shapely chick with huge tits and an enormous ass. She had an almond complexion and slanted eyes like a Korean. She wore her hair short and curly. There were pearls around her neck and wrist and she was toting a white leather hand bag.

Meka was a knock out; easily the most attractive woman that Drama had fucked with, which is why she was attending the mansion party with him.

"Am I ready? How about I let chu be the judge?" Meka smiled and opened her arms, spinning around in a circle like an ice skater. When she completed her three-hundred and sixty degree spin, her eyes landed on a smiling Drama. He approached her wrapping his arms around her and kissing her on the lips. Once he pulled back, she found him gazing deep into her light brown eyes. "Well?" she said, waiting to hear his response to her appearance.

"Oh, you sho' 'nough a certified dime, limme take another look at chu." He took her by the hand and slowly spun her around, taking a good look at her. He obliged her with his eyes as he bit down on his bottom lip, taking her in from head to toe. Meka definitely had it going on. She was all of that and a bag a chips. "Mmmmmm." He rubbed his hands together naughtily as he thought about all of the freaky shit he was going to do to her once they got back from the mansion party.

Right then, Drama's cellular rung and took his mind off of Meka. He picked his cell phone up from the dresser and looked at its screen. It was the chauffeur. He'd hired someone to drive him and his date to the party in the latest Maybach. At first he thought it was Boo's ass banging his line, trying to convince him to come chill with her and their son that night. He'd already told her that he was on company business, but he knew that she didn't give a fuck. The bitch was jealous and possessive and always wanted her way. He hated that shit about her.

Truthfully, Drama was tired of Boo. Sure she had some bomb ass pussy and a head game that was out of this world, but sex was all she had to offer a nigga. Boo was the typical hoodrat, as far as he was concerned. It didn't matter much to him that he had a kid with her. In Drama's mind it was fuck that little nigga and his momma. The only reason why Cordary was born in the first place was because Boo's trifling ass poked a hole in his condom before she'd put it on him the night they'd fucked. Boo had fucked around and told him that shit one night when they'd gotten drunk and high. The bitch was laughing about it like it was the funniest thing in the world and he wanted to strangle her ass. The only reason he didn't was because she told him about a lick she'd setup with T.J. once he'd come home. She aided Drama in jacking T.J. and he decided to keep fucking with her to see what else she may have to offer.

"Alright. We'll be out there in a second," Drama told the chauffeur before disconnecting the call and stashing the cellular inside of his suit.

"Who was that, baby?" Meka asked him.

"The driver; he's waiting for us out…" Drama's faced balled up and he clenched his teeth, clutching the left side of his chest. He stumbled backwards and Meka rushed to his side, catching him before he could fall to the floor.

"Baby, what's the matter?" Meka asked with a worried expression across her face.

"I'm-I'm okay. Just gotta lil' chest pain. I'll be fine though." He assured her as he stood upright and took a deep breath.

"You've been running the streets the past forty-eight hours. You haven't gotten an hour of sleep. That's not good for a man your age. You need to rest." She told him. "I'll tell you what, let's just blow off the party and-"

A frowned up Drama snatched away from her and said, "Fuck you mean a man my age? You tryna say I'm old?"

"No. I'm just saying that-"

He placed his finger against her lips. "As of now, you not saying a goddamn thang. As of now, we leaving this house to go to this mansion party in that expensive ass car parked outside my house. Is that understood?" he asked as he looked her dead in her eyes. She nodded yes. "Good. Now let's go."

Drama placed his hand at Meka's lower back and ushered her out of the bedroom.

***

The address that Boo had given T.J. had checked out. He found himself parked outside Drama's gated community waiting for him to come out for the past two hours.

"Here this old nigga go right now." T.J. said as he stared out of his night vision binoculars through the windshield. He'd just clocked Drama walking out of his house with Meka's fine ass. They were walking towards a Maybach which was parked curbside outside of the house. The chauffeur of the luxurious vehicle hopped out and jogged over to the opposite side of the car to open the back door.

Shits crazy! The nigga smashing my bitch is the uncle of Big Will, the CEO of Hood Rich records. Small world! But it's about to getta hell of a lot bigga once I squash this faggot-ass nigga!

T.J. grabbed his AK-47 with the pistol grip from off the backseat. He checked its banana clip to see if it was fully loaded. It was, so he reloaded it and cocked that bitch back. He then put a neoprene mask over his face and pulled the drawstrings of his hood, closing it around his head.

T.J. focused his attention back on the windshield and saw something that garnered his interest. He picked up his binoculars and looked through them. Through them he saw Drama lying on the ground outside of the Maybach with the chauffeur and Meka, who was on her cellular, looking worried at his side.

"Hello? Yes, it's my boyfriend! I think he's having a heart attack!" T.J. overheard Meka speaking into her cell phone.

"This old ass nigga having a goddamn heart attack!" Te'Qui slammed the binoculars to the floor. He then started punching on the dashboard, furiously. Having grown tired, he stopped and breathed heavily, staring out of the windshield. Right then, he heard the ambulance siren drawing closer and closer. Before he knew it, the emergency vehicle was speeding down the street and turning into the opening gates of the community. By this time there was a horde of people posted up outside. They stood out there watching as Drama was loaded inside of the ambulance and whisked away. "Fuck that! I ain't letting this bitch-ass nigga get away."

As soon as the ambulance made a right turn out of the gates of the mansion, T.J. fired up his G-ride and went after it. He sped up behind the ambulance, eventually pulling up beside it. T.J. let the front passenger window down and stuck his AK-47 out of it. As soon as the driver of the emergency vehicle saw the choppa, his eyeballs nearly popped out of his sockets and he swerved from out of the way of it. Stuck in his pose, still aiming his choppa at the driver, T.J. pulled the trigger. Fire spat out of the deadly end of the assault rifle, shattering the driver's window of the ambulance and splattering the driver's brain fragments against the windshield and dashboard. The ambulance swerved out of control, cutting through several lanes before slamming into a light post and curling it downward.

T.J. stopped the G-ride beside the ambulance and hopped out, running over to the ambulance. He snatched the driver's door of the ambulance open and found the driver slumped over into the passenger seat. After confirming his kill, he popped the double back doors open. The emergency vehicle's siren was still blaring as T.J. ran to the back of it. He opened the double doors of the ambulance and found the other E.M.T dazed and holding the side of his head. A terrified Meka was right beside him. Drama was stretched out on the gurney with an oxygen mask over his nose and mouth.

T.J. pointed his AK-47 at the E.M.T. When the E.M.T saw the hollow barrel of that act-right, AK-47, pointed in his face, his eyes bulged and he threw up his pink hands, begging for his life. "No, please, I-"

Blatat!

T.J. splattered the top of the E.M.T's dome, splashing his bloody, gooey flesh and brain fragments against the interior of the van. He then shot Meka in her mouth as she screamed and then her dome. She slumped against the inside of the ambulance. Climbing inside of the van, T.J. walked over to the E.M.T and sprayed his chest, dotting Drama's face and lower half with his blood. The old thug squeezed his eyelids shut and turned his head as the blood hit his face.

T.J. turned his attention to Drama after observing the work he'd just put in on the helpless E.M.T and Meka. "What's popping, Blood?" Drama didn't say a damn thang, he just stared up at T.J wondering if he was going to murder his ass or not. "You remember me, old head?" he asked him and pulled the neoprene mask from off his face, revealing his identity. "I got all the money and the work back y'all punk-asses jacked me for! But the way I see it, I ain't paid in full 'til yo' life is mine."

Drama mad dogged T.J. and took the oxygen mask from off his face, shouting out, "Fuck you! Kill me! Kill me, you bitch-ass nigga! I ain't scared to die!"

"I respect yo' G!" A scowling T.J. spayed that ass with automatic gunfire and made him do a quick dance. Drama's blood saturated his button-down shirt and some of it dotted the machinery and other stuff inside of the ambulance. "Hoe-ass nigga!" T.J. kicked him in his head and put the neoprene mask back on his face. He then took a few pictures of Drama's dead body with Te'Qui's cell phone and slid it inside of his pocket. Afterwards, he jumped out of the van and darted over to his getaway car. He fled from the murder scene and left the sound of Twelve's sirens filling the air behind him.

CHAPTER EIGHT

T.J. parked the G-ride used in Drama's murder on a residential block and wiped his fingerprints off of everything with a bandana. He grabbed his AK-47 from off the backseat and jumped out of the car, slamming the door shut behind him. He tossed the choppa into the gutter and stalked the streets until he found a car he liked. He came upon a burgundy Pontiac Grand Prix with sun burns on its rooftop and hood. T.J. pulled out his banga and looked up and down the street. When he didn't see anyone watching him, he busted out the driver's window with the butt of his gun. He then cleaned the windowsill of the jagged glass sticking up from where the window once was. Next, he reached inside of the Pontiac and opened it. Once he swept the broken glass from off the driver's seat, T.J. sat down and hotwired the vehicle. The car came to life and a smile came across his face. He slammed the door shut and pulled off, glancing back and forth between the windshield and the rearview mirror. He relaxed when he didn't see anyone watching him.

T.J. pulled out his cell phone and made a call.

"'Sup with it? We gon' have to bust that move a lil' sooner. You think you can get out tonight? Cool. I'll see you in a minute." T.J. disconnected the call and slid the cellular back into his pocket.

An evil genius is at work!

***

Te'Qui came through the door, shutting and locking it behind him. He made his way inside of the kitchen where he saw Kesha leaned over inside of the refrigerator, rummaging through it. He crept up on her while she was talking to whomever and smacked her on her ass.

"Aaaaah!" Kesha screamed startled, shooting her head up from out of the refrigerator. She looked to Te'Qui and smacked him on his arm a few times. She was wearing a Blu-Tooth headset and holding her cellular.

"You asshole, you scared the shit outta me!" Kesha said, wide eyed and breathing hard. His scaring her really got her heart working overtime.

Tranay Adams

"My bad, bae, I seen all that ass hangin' out the frig and couldn't help myself." He smiled and kissed her on the lips.

"Aye, my boo is here now, so I'ma let chu go girl. I'ma dip to the store. I'll holla at chu later, though. Alright now, bye," Kesha looked back inside of the refrigerator and grabbed a Pepsi, cracking it open. She tilted her head back a little as she took a drink from it.

"Who were you talkin' to, babe?" Te'Qui asked.

"Boy, you know that wasn't nobody, but Lisa's ass. I had to rush her off the phone. That hoe can talk her ass off." she bumped the refrigerator door shut with her hip.

"Where you off to?" He took the can of Pepsi from her and took a drink.

"Just to the store, I needa get out. I been cooped up in this house so long, I'm 'bouta go crazy."

"I feel you." he handed her the Pepsi back.

Kesha's eyes widen when she saw something on Te'Qui's shirt sleeve. "Babe, what happened to your arm? You're bleeding through your shirt sleeve."

Te'Qui looked to his sleeve and noticed he'd bled through the length of shirt he'd tied around his arm. This was the same arm he'd cut with the meat cleaver to create a diversion so that Cordary could escape T.J.'s wrath.

"Shit." Te'Qui said as he lifted the sleeve of his bloody shirt to look at the shirt tied around his arm. It was nearly soaked. "I'ma need stitches for this shit. I'm bleedin' like a bitch, bae."

"I'ma take care of you before I bounce from outta here." Kesha claimed, as she looked at the length of shir wrapped around his arm. Looking back up at him, she said, "I'm sure you got this as a result of fucking with that nigga T.J., right?" she looked at him like, *You need to leave that fucking psychopath alone.*

"Yep. That's exactly why I broke thangs off with that nigga tonight. We officially through."

"For real?"

"Yeah, I told his ass if I find 'em snoopin' around the crib, then I'ma knock his head off."

Kesha frowned up when he told her that. "You did?"

"Hell yeah."

"You sure you shoulda did that? I mean, I know my boo don't play but obviously that nigga doesn't either."

"I ain't wettin' that nigga."Te'Qui waved her off. "Blood act like he's the only gangsta in town. He bring any bullshit this way, I'm puttin' blood in his mouth. Show that ass how a real Eastside, Low Bottom nigga get down for his. You feel what I'm sayin'?"

"Sho' you right." she smiled as she caressed his cheek and kissed him. She just loved his thuggish ways. "I'ma run upstairs to get the first-aid kit so I can take care of that arm."

"Alright, momma," Te'Qui kissed her and smacked her on her ass again as she headed out of the kitchen. His eyes followed that bodacious ass of hers. She stopped at the kitchen's doorway, looked over her shoulders at him and made her chunky buttocks do a little dance. Smiling at him, she walked off to retrieve the first-aid kit from the upstairs bathroom.

When Kesha came back down stairs, she found Te'Qui getting dinner prepared.

"Boy, you can cook later, limme take care of your arm. Come on now." Kesha said, as she sat the yellow first-aid kit down on the kitchen table. She then grabbed Te'Qui by the hand and walked him over to the table, sitting him down in a chair. She pulled up a chair for herself and sat down, cleaning the cut in her man's arm. Afterwards, she stitched it up and wrapped it in an Ace Bandage. Having done all of this, she kissed his arm like a mother would her child's arm after a boo-boo. Looking up at him, she smiled and kissed him. Then, she placed all of the items she used back inside of the kit and closed it shut.

"Thank you, baby," Te'Qui told her as he held up his sleeve and looked at his arm.

"You welcome, my love." Kesha said as she rose from the chair with the first-aid kit. She kissed her man on the forehead and headed back upstairs.

Once Kesha had gone, Te'Qui went back to preparing dinner for that night. He was so engrossed in what he was doing that he didn't notice Kesha slip out of the house.

***

Club Vicious was popping like it always did on Saturday nights. Maybe even more since J. Cole and a host of other famous acts would be performing that night. There wasn't a shortage of beautiful women and fellas out on the dance floor having themselves a good old time. D.J Flip was on the turntables and he had the club rocking like a mothafucka. He was playing all of the hottest and latest hits. Mixing those shits with older cuts and then playing them solo. It was safe to say that the club was lit which was the reason why the line to get in was wrapped around the corner.

Ducked off behind the velvet rope of the V.I.P section was Big Will and Enzo. They were sipping champagne and taking in the scenery. They were surrounding by their most trusted goons. And every last one of them thug ass niggaz were packing something for the drama.

"Boy, you sho' know how to pick some talent. I'll give you that." Enzo told Big Will as he poured his champagne flute up again.

"Well, I'd hate to be the type of nigga to pat myself on the bat, but, uh," Big Will patted himself on the shoulder, smirking. He and Enzo busted up laughing. At the moment, J. Cole was exiting the stage and Killa Tay was coming up to perform his latest single which was blazing hot in the streets 'Act like you know'.

"Man, I'm glad I took a chance and invested in yo' vision. Pretty soon, a nigga gon' be able to get up outta these streets. As addictive as they are, they ain't worth spending a century behind bars for or windin' up getting killed in. Mothafuck that! I got big dreams and big plans to execute before I leave out this bitch. Ya feel me?"

"Fa sho'." he replied as he refilled his flute. After filling it to the brim, he sat the champagne bottle down on the table and turned to Enzo. "I'd like to propose a toast to the good life."

"To the good life," Enzo clinked flutes with Big Will and took a sip of the champagne.

Big Will and Enzo spent the rest of their night chopping it up and letting the thirsty bitchez trying to get at them entertain them. Having grown tired of the night life, they decided to take their leave early and hit up a Denny's, which was oddly enough, Enzo's favorite place to eat breakfast.

***

Big Will and Enzo stepped outside expecting their respective chauffeur driven bulletproof Suburbans to be curbside, but those bitchez weren't there. With furrowed brows the men looked around for their vehicles. Big Will was the first one to spot them. They were across the street inside of a lot you had to pay ten bucks to park in.

Big Will tapped Enzo and pointed across the street to their black on black, big body trucks. "There them shits go right there."

"Fuck them niggaz ain't where we told 'em to be? I'm puttin' my foot up Clyde's ass as soon as I see his mothafuckin' ass." Enzo swore with a scowl. He and Big Will then pulled out their cellulars and dialed up their individual chauffeurs. When the drivers didn't answer either one of them it seemed to piss them off further.

"Yo', what the fuck is up?" Big Will asked Enzo as he stashed his cell phone back inside of his suit.

"Who knows? Them two niggaz are probably asleep behind the wheel or sloppy drunk. Either way, ain't nobody walkin' away from this without havin' to have my shoe surgically removed from outta they ass! That's on my momma's grave." Enzo swore.

"Bet. Come on, Enzo, let's walk over there."

"Alright, y'all niggaz come on," Enzo motioned for his goons to follow him as he and Big Will headed over to the prepaid parking lot.

The gangstaz and their goons made their way across the street. Once Big Will reached the SUV he was driven to the club in, he found brain fragments and blood splattered against the driver's window, with a bullet hole surrounded by breakage in the glass. Big Will pulled open the driver's door and discovered his chauffeur, Glendale, dead with a gaping bloody hole in the side of his head.

"What the fuck?" Big Will's forehead wrinkled when he saw his chauffeur was dead as a mothafucka. He and his goons stepped back with shocked looks on their faces. Right after, they overheard Enzo holler out 'Oh shit' and they walked over to where he and his goons were. Once they reached them, they noticed that Enzo's chauffeur, Clyde, had suffered the same fate as Glendale.

"Damn, somebody done smoked Clyde's ass!" A shocked Enzo looked down at his driver's dead body as it hung halfway out of the truck.

"Nigga killed Glendale too, but who the fuck was it?" Big Will's forehead creased.

"I thought this might get chu niggaz' attention!" a manly voice called out from the night. Big Will, Enzo and all of their goons walked to the center of the parking lot and found a fat nigga wearing a hood over his head. Big Will and Enzo exchanged glances wondering who the fuck homeboy was in the all black attire with the hood over his head.

"Just who in the fuck are you, nigga?" Enzo asked.

With that question posed, the fat nigga slowly and theatrically pulled the hood from off his head and revealed his identity. It was T.J.

"I'm T.J., Blood. I just came here to drop a bit of info on you old niggaz." T.J. told them as he rubbed his hands together, looking between the larger than life street figures.

Enzo's eyelids narrowed as he stared at T.J. trying to recall his eyes. He imagined a bandana covering the lower half of T.J.'s face off and on, several times. That's when he realized T.J. was the nigga busting at him the night some fool tried to rob him in that very same parking lot that he was standing in.

"Wait a minute, I know this mothafucka!" Enzo announced once things clicked inside of his head. Big Will and everyone else looked at him with questioning expressions on their faces. "This the same fool that tried to rob me some time ago in this same fuckin' parkin' lot."

"That's right. I'm willing to tell you who that other man was with me, too." T.J. told him. He then looked to Big Will and said, "The same nigga smoked yo' uncle, the old head. Drama."

"Drama's dead? Bullshit!" Big Will pulled out his cell phone and hit up his uncle. He called that nigga three times but his jack kept going to voice mail. Having grown angry and frustrated, he put his cell phone back inside of his suit.

"I got proof. I can let chu see it. It's in my pocket." T.J. told him, waiting for him to give him the okay to pull out his proof. T.J. wasn't about to pull out Te'Qui's cellular and risk getting his ass smoked. Fuck that! He knew he had to handle the situation delicately.

Big Will nodded to T.J., letting him know it was okay for him to give him whatever he had in his possession.

T.J. pulled out the cell phone and tossed it over to Big Will. He watched as the big man's eyes flashed hurt and anger, seeing the flicks of Drama's dead body. Once he finished looking through the photos, Big Will looked up at T.J. with teary eyes and flaring nostrils. He blinked the tears back before he spoke again.

"If you got whoever cell this is, then that means you were there when they smashed unc. Am I right?" Big Will asked him.

T.J. put his hands up to let the big man know that he wasn't posing any threat to him. "Look, I thought we was going to rough the old nigga up 'cause he was fucking around with my nigga'z girl, Boo, the next thing I know, my homeboy was hopping out my ride with a goddamn choppa chopping yo' people down. I rolled with my nigga for a beat down, notta mothafucking 187. That's why I'm here now, tryna get immunity. You feel me? I'm not stupid, homie. I know how you and yo' man Enzo get down, y'all two of the biggest gangstaz in L.A. A nigga like me don't wan't them kinda problems."

"Fuck that, Blood! If you know who popped unc, then yo' ass better tell me now." Big Will demanded with a scowl as he pointed his finger at T.J.

"The only way I'm telling y'all jack shit is if you giving me immunity!" He looked at Big Will and Enzo waiting for their response.

"You laid that hit down with whoever killed my family, Blood. I know you did." Big Will barked back.

"Nah, you got me all wrong, my nigga. I was there when it went down, but I didn't pull the trigga." T.J. lied through his fucking teeth.

"You said you want immunity, right? That means a pass for your involvement." Enzo told T.J. "Alright. Well, I'm willin' to let chu getta pass, but chu gotta gift wrap ya man for me. I'm splashin' that nigga! I don't give a fuck! His life belongs to me!" he jabbed his chest with his finger with emphasis.

"And you, OG?" T.J. asked Big Will.

Big Will bowed his head and massaged the bridge of his nose. He took a deep breath and his shoulders hunched and fell. He knew he wasn't going to get the name of the mothafucka that popped Drama if he didn't give that fat fucka standing before him immunity, so he decided to give it to him. Looking back up at T.J., Big Will nodded and said, "Okay. You give up ya homeboy and you walk."

"Te'Qui." T.J. told him.

"Te'Qui? Why the fuck would Te'Qui want unc dead?" Big Will massaged his chin as he thought back to the tension between Drama and Te'Qui. When he recalled their run-ins, he understood why Te'Qui would want to split his relative's wig.

"Where do we find this cocksucka?" A frowned up Enzo inquired. He gritted and a vein bulged at his temple.

"I got his home address right here," T.J. pulled out a piece of paper from the pocket of his hoodie. Keeping an eye on the opposition, he walked over to a silver 600 Mercedes Benz and lifted one of its windshield wipers. He placed the piece of paper down on the windshield and laid the windshield wiper down on it. "So, we straight now, right? I'm free to go?"

"Fuck no! What chu thought this was?" Big Will smiled evilly and pulled out his gun. As soon as he pulled out his strap, Enzo and the rest of the goons pulled out their guns and pointed them at T.J. They were all ready to light that ass up once the word was given.

T.J. slowly lifted his hands up into the air as he looked around at all of the guns pointed at him. A wicked smile spread across his face and he said, "See, I knew yo' ol' bitch-ass was gon' pull some fuck-shit like this. That's why I took precautions."

"Precautions? Fuck is you talking about?" Big Will's forehead wrinkled.

T.J. whistled sharply. Instantly a bright red dot appeared on the left side of Big Will's chest. The big man and everyone else looked around wondering where a threat would approach, but they didn't see anyone. It wasn't until T.J. nodded to Big Will's chest that he looked down and saw the red dot. As soon as he did, a shocked expression crossed his face. When he looked back up, his eyes were as big as saucers and his mouth was hanging open.

"Y'all niggaz fallback," Big Will commanded and lowered his gun to his side. As soon as he took his gun off of T.J., his goons tucked their guns. The big man looked at Enzo and his crew, and they still had their bangaz pointed at T.J. "Enzo, tell yo' goons to tuck they shit, man. This fat mothafucka got me dead to rights." he tucked his gun on his waistline.

Enzo nodded and tucked his gun inside of his suit. He then addressed Booney and the rest of his goons. "Y'all niggaz tuck y'all straps, man."

With his command given, Enzo's niggaz put their bangaz away.

T.J. found himself being mad dogged by Big Will, Enzo and their goons. He could literally feel the heat of the intensity of their gazes. But he wasn't studying any of their asses; he didn't give a fuck about them staring him down. He knew their asses were in pocket just as long as his shooter had Big Will's ass marked for death, with that red dot.

"Y'all niggaz have a nice night," T.J., still smiling wickedly, threw the hood over his head and ran off into the night. Once he was out of Big Will and Enzo's goons' sight, the red dot disappeared from Big Will's chest. About a minute later, the squealing of tires could be heard as two cars sped away.

Big Will's face twisted with anger as he pulled out his cell phone and dialed someone up. He paced the parking lot ground as he listened to the phone ringing. While he was listening to the phone ring, Enzo and the goons were talking shit and swearing to get revenge.

"Yo', Berry, round up the platoon, it's on tonight, on blood gang!" Big Will swore into his cellular. He then snatched the piece of paper from off the windshield of the 600 Benz and looked at the address that T.J. had written on it. After memorizing the address on it, he balled the paper up and dropped it at his feet in a ball.

***

T.J. parked six houses down from Te'Qui's house. He kept his vehicle idling as he watched the block. A wicked smile spread across his lips when he looked into the side view mirror and saw two all-black vans coming up the street. He slid down in the driver's seat and pulled his hood over his head. He gripped his gun and looked out of the window. Right then, the vans drove past him. In the front passenger window of the first van, he saw the passenger pull a ski-mask over his head. In the front passenger window of the second van, he clocked the passenger, who was already masked up, picking an AK-47 up from off the floor.

"It's showtime," T.J. announced and picked up his cellular. Putting his fist to his mouth, he cleared his throat and hit up Te'Qui. As soon as Te'Qui picked up the call, he started in on him. "Fuck out the house, Blood, buncha masked up niggaz with choppaz 'bouta hit cho shit…"

Still on the jack with Te'Qui, T.J. watched as a dozen hittaz with AKs jumped out of the vans. They charged Te'Qui's home gripping their assault rifles.

Once T.J. wrapped up his conversation with Te'Qui, he tossed his cellular into the front passenger seat and busted a U-turn in the middle of the residential street. Adjusting his rearview mirror and looking into it, he saw one of the masked up niggaz attempting to kick down the front door of Te'Qui's house.

T.J. smiled devilishly as he ripped down the street.

***

Kesha came through the front door pulling the hood from off her head. She switched hands with whatever she was carrying wrapped up in a blanket when she shut the door behind her. She heard Te'Qui inside of the kitchen but she didn't want to bother him so she decided to head upstairs to their bedroom. She'd gotten about five feet from the first step, when he came out of the kitchen in a hurry. He was wearing an apron and carrying a pot and a wooden spoon stained with pasta sauce.

"Where you been, momma? Dressed in all black like you was out puttin' in work?" Te'Qui asked with furrowed brows, taking in his lady's attire.

"I, uh, umm, I was just browsing Target." Kesha told him.

"Oh, yeah, for what?"

"Oh, I was just looking for stuff to decorate the baby's room with."

"You shoulda told me, I woulda rolled out witchu."

"It's okay; we can just hit some stores tomorrow."

"Oh, fa sho'." Te'Qui noticed whatever she had wrapped up in a blanket, which made him curious as to what it was. "What chu got there?"

"This? A Japanese sword." she held up the blanket. "I was thinking about decorating our bedroom like a Dojo. You know, try a lil' something different. I'm getting kinda tired of looking at the same ol' decorations we got up now."

"Yeah, I feel you. I'm kinda tired of that shit too. It's played out." he claimed. "Look, I wanted you to taste this pasta I made from scratch and tell me what chu think."

"Mmmmm, babe, I love pasta." she licked her lips hungrily. "Limme try." she approached him as he got a nice helping of the pasta on his wooden spoon. He let her taste it and she shut her eyelids briefly, smiling and loving the taste. "Mmmm, babe, this is good. This is real good."

"Really?" Te'Qui smiled.

"Unh huh, yes." Kesha licked the little bit of pasta from off her lips.

"Well, I'm glad you like it, ma. 'Cause tonight we're havin' Italian." he kissed her lips and made his way back inside of the kitchen, tasting the pasta along the way.

"What's on the menu?"

"Ravioli and...." The cordless house phone rung and cut Te'Qui's conversation short. He walked over to the telephone which was hanging on the wall. He looked at the caller identification and saw T.J.'s number, which made him frown up.

"Who is it, bae?" Kesha asked with a furrowed forehead.

"T.J." Te'Qui said as he mad dogged the cordless on the wall.

The telephone continued to ring as Te'Qui and Kesha stared at it. Finally, Te'Qui took a breath and answered it, placing it to his ear.

"Fuck you want, nigga? What?" Worry spread over Te'Qui's face.

Kesha's forehead wrinkled hearing the concern in Te'Qui's voice. She leaned to the side to look inside of the kitchen. When she did, she saw Te'Qui sitting the pot of pasta on top of the stove and picking his gun up from the kitchen table top. Before she knew it, he was storming into the living room with his telephone glued to his ear and his banga down at his side. She watched as he peered through the blinds.

"Oh, shit!" Te'Qui said aloud, seeing the two vans of hittaz pull up outside of his house.

"Baby, what's wrong?" Kesha inquired, as she walked over to the window and peered outside of the blinds for herself. When she saw the vans parked in front of the house, her stomach dropped and her heart thudded. "Oh, my God!"

"Blood, come through the back of yo' house, I'ma park out in the alley and wait for you." Kesha overheard T.J. say to Te'Qui on the jack.

"Alright. I got Keesh. I'll be out there in a hot one." Te'Qui disconnected the call and tossed the cordless on the couch. He then turned to Kesha, putting his hand on her shoulder. "Bae, I need you to run upstairs and clean my safe out. The combo is 85-01-05. I'ma hold it down, down here. Now, hurry up." he kissed her on the forehead and took hold of the blanket in her hand. She looked at him like *What are you doing?* "Go on now, I got this. You gon' need both hands to carry that money down."

Reluctantly, Kesha released the blanket and hurried up the staircase.

Te'Qui looked inside of the blanket and saw that it was hiding a high-powered sniper rifle with a silencer attached to its barrel. His forehead creased with several lines wondering why his future wife was packing such a weapon, especially when she'd claimed to have gone window shopping earlier that night.

"Fuck is she doin' with this?" Te'Qui asked no one in particular. He then pushed that question to the back of his brain, and glanced through the blinds once again. His heart thudded seeing a dozen masked up hittaz with AKs spilling out of the vans. They separated in threes. Pairs of four went on either side of the house while the last four charged the short steps upon the front porch.

Bang, bang, bang, bang!

Te'Qui looked through the blinds and saw one of them niggaz trying to kick the door down. Hearing hurried footfalls coming from his right, he looked to find Kesha with two lumpy pillow cases coming down the staircase.

"Hit the backdoor! Go, go, go, go," Te'Qui waved the blanketed rifle towards the backdoor, signaling for Kesha to go to it. Kesha followed his instructions and he followed behind her, covering her ass in case them hittaz came through the door before they could clear the house.

Te'Qui stopped at Kesha's rear and turned to the front door. As he watched the front door, he pointed his gun at it and used his other hand to unwrap the sniper rifle. While he was doing this, Kesha was sitting her pillowcases down on the floor and unlocking the backdoor. By the time she'd finished unlocking the door, Te'Qui was pulling the rifle from out of the blanket. He lifted the rifle and pointed it at the front door, just as it swung open. He aimed the long assault rifle at the first mothafucka that crossed the threshold into his home and pulled the trigger.

Choot!

The man's forehead snapped back and his blood and brain fragments flew out of the back of his mask. He felt to the floor and the rest of the hittaz scrambled out of the way. When they saw Te'Qui and Kesha fleeing out of the backdoor, they opened fire with their AK-47s. Their bullets ripped through the cupboards and bottom cabinets, sending splinters flying everywhere.

Te'Qui and Kesha were ducked down and running when they came out of the backdoor of the house, bullets whizzing over their heads. They hurried down the short steps of the back porch, making tracks towards the double back gates, which were held together by an old rusty chain. Behind these gates was T.J. who had just hopped out of his car, two .9mm handguns at his sides.

B*locka!*

T.J. shot the chain that held the gates together and kicked them wide open. Seeing the hittaz pouring in from either side of the house, he pointed his twin bangaz at them, popping off crazily. The hittaz started dropping like flies, killing over in the grass.

"Come on, y'all! Come on!" T.J. called out, letting his handguns spit death.

"Get in the car!" Te'Qui told Kesha. Seeing that she was following his orders, he turned around and lifted both of his weapons. He joined in on the action with T.J., popping off his guns.

"Aaaaaah!" One of the hittaz hollered out and winced, having taken one in the chest.

"Gaaaahhh!" Another one of the hittaz took two in the neck.

Once Te'Qui had taken out two of the masked up men, he continued his sprint towards T.J.'s car. By this time, Kesha was jumping into the backseat and hollering for Te'Qui to hurry up. She'd spotted two more hittaz behind him and was afraid they'd kill him before they were able to get away.

T.J. had just made it back around to the driver's side of his vehicle when he clocked the hittaz that were on Te'Qui's ass. He pointed his twins at them and laid down some cover for his homeboy. The hittaz ducked down and returned fire. Bullets ripped through the side of T.J.'s car and shattered its tinted windows. T.J. and Kesha ducked to avoid the fire that the hittaz sent at them.

Seeing that his homeboy and his fiancée were in danger, Te'Qui whipped around to the threats at his back. He tucked his gun into his waistline and pointed the rifle at the propane tank which was located beneath a Black & Decker grill. Te'Qui squeezed his left eyelid shut and clenched his jaws. Once he had the sighting of his rifle lined up with the tank, he pulled the trigger.

Choot!

Ka-Boom! Boom!

The propane tank exploded and sent the hittaz flying across the backyard, on fire. They landed on the ground dead. Seconds later, their severed arms and legs crashed to the surface not too far behind them.

Te'Qui lowered the rifle at his side as he looked on at his handiwork, the golden orange flames of the fire illuminating him.

"Come on, Blood, we gotta go!" T.J. called out to Te'Qui. He'd just jumped behind the wheel of his car and slammed the door shut.

"Bae, come on!" Kesha called out of the back window to her man as well.

Te'Qui whipped out his handgun so it wouldn't be digging him in his groin. He then jumped into the front passenger seat and slammed the door shut behind him. Right after, T.J. was speeding down the trashy alley way. He looked up into the rearview and saw the raging fire in Te'Qui's back yard.

Twelve's sirens and fire truck sirens filled the air.

Tranay Adams

CHAPTER NINE

T.J. pulled into the back yard of a house that looked like it had seen better days. Once he killed the engine of his vehicle, he hopped out and slammed the door shut behind him. He went up the short steps that led to the back door of the old house which he opened with ease. Te'Qui and Kesha exchanged glances as they thought that T.J. must have been using the decrepit house for quite some time. They were right too. You see, ever since T.J. had been in the streets sticking shit up, he'd been using the house to count up the hauls from his various licks. The place had become sort of like a second home to him. Hell, he'd slept there quite a few times when he was down on his luck.

The backdoor of the house squeaked as T.J. pushed it open. He looked around and then stood aside, allowing Te'Qui and Keisha to enter. As soon as they crossed the threshold into the kitchen, they took in the scenery. The kitchen was dilapidated and decrepit. There was dust on its floors, walls and ceilings. There were also cobwebs high up in every corner, and spiders crawling on them. A couple of rats ran past the entrance of the kitchen which led into the living room. The living room was in the same shape as the kitchen. Only there were large holes in its floor. The holes were big enough to fit a human though. There was a big ass hole in the ceiling, too. In fact, there was a rusted pipe in that hole and it was dripping brown water.

"Hold on. You can't see mucha shit in here. Limme hit these lights," T.J. told the couple as they sat the pillowcases of dead presidents on the kitchen table. He then went around the kitchen lighting burned out wax candles, which left a golden orange light shining on everyone present.

"This yo' second home or some shit?" Te'Qui asked with furrowed brows.

"Hell naw! Sometimes I stash shit here 'til I get a chance to fence 'em, but that's it. A nigga can't keep hot shit where he lay his head at." T.J. told him.

Te'Qui nodded his understanding. He knew of mad niggaz that got popped with stolen goods in their house.

"Unh! Lil' dirty mothafucka!" T.J.'s face balled up as he stomped something with all his might, causing it to make a squished noise. As soon as Te'Qui and Keisha heard that squishing sound, their foreheads wrinkled and they looked down at T.J.'s sneaker. When he removed his sneaker from what he'd squashed they saw a fat ass rat lying on its side. The filthy fucker was lying in its own blood, twitching.

"Ewww," Keisha hooked her arm with Te'Qui's arm, disgusted by the sight of the dead rodent.

"Adios, amigo," T.J. kicked the dead rat out of the kitchen and into the living room, where it disappeared through one of the holes in the floor.

"Yo', good lookin' out on savin' me and wifey back there, my nigga." Te'Qui slapped hands with T.J., pulling him in and patting him on his back.

"Don't mention it. You my nigga. I'm down for you, like you down for me." T.J. told him.

"Fa sho'." Te'Qui replied.

"You okay, Kesha?" T.J.'s forehead creased as he looked to his homeboy's fiancée.

"Yeah, I'm good." A teary eyed Kesha lowered her head and sniffled. Right then, teardrops fell from her eyes and she wiped them away with the back of her hand.

Seeing that his woman was weeping brought great concern to Te'Qui. His forehead crinkled and he hugged her, rubbing her back soothingly.

"You okay, bae?" Te'Qui asked her.

"No. No, I'm not." Kesha spoke honestly this time, voice cracking with emotions. "I'm sorry. I'm so, so sorry, bae."

Te'Qui tilted Kesha's chin upward so she'd be looking him in his eyes. "Sorry about what, momma?" his brows wrinkled.

"This!" T.J. said to him.

When Te'Qui turned around and saw T.J. with one of his .9mms pointed at him, his eyes got big and his jaw dropped.

"Oh, shit, Kesha, move!" Te'Qui shoved Kesha away from him. He went to pull his banga from his waistline, but by then, T.J. was already shooting him. A bullet ripped through his gut and he threw his head back, wincing. He hit the carpeted floor and lay halfway out of the kitchen. He bawled in pain as T.J. approached him, shadow looming over him. He leaned down and pulled the banga from out of Te'Qui's waistline and slid it into his waistline.

T.J. stared down at Te'Qui as he continuously winced. He watched as he touched his wound and his fingers came away bloody.

"What the-what the fuck you shoot me for?" Te'Qui asked in a pained voice, wincing.

Tiaz Petty. Does that name ring a bell?" T.J. asked.

"Yeah, I know Tiaz. I told you about 'em, remember? He's dead now, so what the fuck does he have to do with this?"

"Meet his son, T.J. Tiaz Junior," he pointed his gun at his chest. "And his daughter, Kesha; my paternal twin." he pointed his banga at his sister who had tears cascading down her face.

When he revealed this, Te'Qui's eyes became as big as saucers and his mouth hung open. He was shocked. He couldn't believe the revelation that had been dropped on him, but he knew it had to have been true for things to have gotten to this point.

"You know, I started to just smoke yo' ass and get it over with, but baby sis convinced me to do otherwise. She told me about the money you had in yo' safe. She said you damn near hadda million dollas."

Te'Qui looked to Kesha with hurt in his eyes. Her disloyalty cut him deep. Kesha bowed her head. She knew she'd done some foul ass shit to him and she couldn't bear to look him in the face.

"See, I figured I coulda just tortured you to get chu to open that safe, but she told me you were way too fucking stubborn to do that. She said you'd die before you gave up one red cent of that money, and after kicking it witchu for a while, I had to agree."

Te'Qui looked to the mother of his unborn son, tears threatening to spill down his cheeks. "So, you never even loved a nigga? You been playin' me the entire time? Are you even pregnant?"

Kesha finally looked up at him with a shiny from crying. Shaking her head, she replied, "Baby, no. I really am in love witchu, and the baby growing inside of me is real. He or she is ours. I didn't..."

"She didn't really wanna go along with the plan, but I forced her to, three months before I got out. I realized who yo' punk-ass was once she sent me some pictures of ya'll while I was on lock. It had been years since the tragedy occurred but I'd never forget cho face...ever."

"Man, what the fuck are you talkin' about? I never met chu before the night you saved my ass in that parking lot across the street from Club Vicious." Te'Qui's forehead creased.

"Now, we met before that. You since you don't seem to remember, I'ma jog yo' memory. Just gimme a sec to slip into something a lil' bit mo' comfortable first, Crim." T.J. told him as he pulled an orange bandana from out of his back pocket and tied it around his head. He smiled mischievously at Te'Qui and pulled down his bottom lip, displaying what was tattooed on the inside of it: 7HCG4. This was 74 Hoover Criminal Gang. The same set that Scrappy and Tiaz pledged allegiance to. "Now, you didn't really think I wassa blood, now did you? Fuck nah! Like father, like son." He threw up his set. At this time, Kesha pulled out an orange bandana and tied it around her head, just like her brother did. She was in the same gang as the rest of her family.

"I'm sorry, baby." Kesha told Te'Qui as her eyes filled with fresh tears.

"Ain't shit to be sorry about, baby girl," T.J. turned to his sister and brushed the side of his hand against her cheek, affectionately. He then focused his hateful eyes on Te'Qui. "You see, this is an old fashion case of revenge. Yo' punk-ass uncle, Savon, smoked our pops, and yo' ass smoked our moms."

"Your moms? I popped yo-yo moms? W-when?" Te'Qui winced in pain as he held the wound in his gut. He was bleeding like a stuck pig and slicking the floor with blood.

"You wanna know when? Well, I'll tell you when..." T.J.'s eyes turned glassy as he went on to tell the story.

Scrappy pulled up into the driveway of her mother's home and hopped out of the car, slamming the door shut behind her. She ran to the curb and looked up and down the street. She waited until an oncoming vehicle drove by her before jogging across the street to her homeboy, Hittah's house. As she neared his yard, she clocked him on his front porch with a couple of the homies from their set. He'd just stuck a joint in his mouth and threw playful punches at one of their homies, who threw some playful punches back at him.

"Yo', Hittah, Hittah!" Scrappy called after him as she entered the yard and approached the steps.

"Hahahahahahahaha!" Hittah stopped playing around with his homeboy and stood upright, snatching the joint from out of his mouth. When it finally dawned on him that someone was calling after him, he turned around to his front lawn. His forehead creased with lines when his eyes landed on Scrappy. The first thing he noticed about her was the welt below her right eye and the blackish red blood dried at the corner of her mouth. He came to the conclusion that she'd gotten into a fight with someone, but with who? He didn't know. "What's happnin', Scrap? And what the fuck happened to yo' face, girl?" He pinched her chin between his thumb and finger and examined the damages to her face, carefully.

"That bitch Chevy. We threw hands today." Scrappy told him.

"Chevy? Who the fuck is that?" Hittah's brows crinkled, wondering who she was talking about.

"What up, Scrappy Doo?" one of the homies on the porch called out to her.

"What's the word, ma?" the other homie called out.

"Ain't shit. What's up, my niggaz?" Scrappy responded and threw up their hood. She then focused her attention back on Hittah. "Her brother, Savon, smoked Tiaz when they were locked up. I faded that high-yellow bitch at his execution today."

"Is that, right? They put his ass to sleep today?"

"Yeah." she nodded. "But I ain't through with her ass. Tonight I'm going after her and her punk-ass husband. That's why I'm here now. I need you to limme holda strap."

"Fa sho'. I got them all day. Follow me, homegirl." Hittah motioned for her to follow him as he headed up the steps upon the porch. He pulled the black iron door open and then the wooden door, crossing the threshold inside of his house. Scrappy

followed him down the corridor where they made a right into a bedroom. This was Hittah's bedroom. It consisted of a twin bed which was stationed against the wall. Its sheet was made up military style, with all of its corners folded and tucked neatly. He had a small flat screen television mounted on the wall, an end table at the center of the floor with all of his hygienic items on it and an army green footlocker at the foot of his bed. The bedroom was as clean as a whistle. There wasn't as much as a piece of lint on the floor.

With its limited furnishings and tidiness, Scrappy couldn't help noticing how much the bedroom resembled a prison cell which really didn't come to a surprise to her since Hittah had done a dime for a body in San Quentin. The way he carried himself and lived was proof that he was institutionalized. Hell, the nigga was still on prison time at that, getting up at five o'clock in the morning and shit.

Hittah shut and locked the door behind Scrappy as she stood where she was taking in the decor of his bedroom. He stuck his joint back inside of his mouth and motioned for her to follow him. They walked over to the closet where he opened its door and pulled the drawstring, restoring light to it. Hittah pushed the little clothing aside hanging on the rack and revealed a long back duffle bag on the floor. He grabbed the bag by its straps and carried it over to his bed, dropping it there. Afterwards, he took the joint out of his mouth and unzipped it. Staring down into the bag, he waved Scrappy over and took another pull from his joint. Still staring down into the bag, he narrowed his eyelids and blew out smoke, letting it waft around him.

"Gon' take a look. Get whatever piece of steel you want, homegirl." Hittah told her as he took a step back. While Scrappy busied herself pulling out different guns and aiming them across the room, he dipped his hand inside of the waste basket at the far corner of the bedroom. He came back up with an empty Mountain Dew can which he used to dump the ashes of his joint inside of. The rest of the time he watched Scrappy test out the guns inside of the bag, while continuing to smoke and dump ashes. "You fuckin' with that one?" he asked her of the long, chrome shotgun with the pistol grip she pointed at imaginary

targets around the bedroom. The satisfaction written across her face told him that she wanted the powerful weapon she held in her grasp.

"Yeah. I like this one." Scrappy lowered the shotgun at her side. Her eyes followed Hittah as he mashed out the ember of the joint and tucked it behind his ear. He then walked over to the closet where he got something from off of its top shelf. Once he finally came down with what he had retrieved, she noticed it was a big box of ammunition for the shotgun she'd picked out. He also grabbed another duffle bag from where it was hanging on a hook on the inside of the closet door.

"Look, Hittah," she started back up, watching him load the shotgun and shells inside of the extra duffle bag. "I'ma lil' short right now, but if you limme hold that shotty I'ma get right back at chu with that scrilla for...."

"Shhhhhhh." Hittah turned to her with his finger against his lips, hushing her. He then took her hand and placed the straps of the duffle bag inside of it and closed it up. "Homegirl, you don't owe me a thang. Tiaz was one of the few homies that made sho' my books was straight while I was up there in that cage. The least I can do is give his old lady the tools she needs to avenge his death. I would offer to roll out which chu, but knowing how you get down, I gotta feelin' you'd like to go on this mission alone. Am I right?" he grasped her shoulder and looked into her eyes. If she gave him the word, he was going to load up his thang and shed blood right alongside her. He had mad love for Tiaz, and considered him one of the realist niggaz to have ever picked up a flag.

"You right, homeboy. I gotta get at these folks alone." she looked at him, scowling.

Hittah presented her with a half smile and said, "That's what I thought. Gimme some love."

He opened his arms to her and she walked into him, embracing him. With that out of the way, he unlocked the door and pulled it open. They headed back out onto the front porch.

Scrappy stepped out of the house waving bye to the homies and switching hands with the duffle bag. Coming down the cement steps, she heard hurried footsteps at her right. When she looked she saw the smiling faces of her son and daughter. They'd gotten out of school about forty minutes ago.

"Heyyyyy, mommy!" Kesha called out to her mother and hugged her around the waist.

"Hey, pretty girl. How was school?" Scrappy rubbed her daughter's back and kissed her on top of her head.

"It was good." she replied.

"'Sup, momma?" T.J. greeted his mother with a hug as well. She ruffled the top of his close fade and kissed him on his cheek.

"How's momma's lil' man?" she asked with a smirk, rubbing the side of his face, affectionately.

"I'm straight." he replied. His brows furrowed seeing the welt under her eye. "Momma, what happened to yo' face? You got into a fight?"

Scrappy touched the welt under her eye and recalled that it was there. "Nah, I didn't have a fight. I tripped and fell."

"What's up, T.J. and lil' momma?" Hittah called out from the porch of his house where he was busy relighting his joint.

"Hey, uncle Hittah!" T.J. and Kesha responded in unison and waved at their street uncle, excitedly.

"Y'all come on, so we can cross the street." Scrappy nudged her son and daughter towards the curb so they could get ready to cross the street to her mother's home. Once an oncoming car had passed, Scrappy grabbed her daughter's hand and they jogged across the street, with her son following beside them.

Once Scrappy and her kids had crossed the street, they made it inside of her mother's yard and up the steps. She then knocked on the door and waited for her mother to answer. As she waited, she surveyed her surroundings. A moment later her mother, Ruth, unlocked the door and pulled it open.

"Yes?" Ruth frowned up as she took a pull from her Newport and blew out a cloud of smoke. She then dumped her ashes on the porch and sucked on the end of her cancer stick again, causing it to shrink in size. Ruth was an older, sassy black woman who stood a solid five-foot-eleven. Her dry, permed out, graying hair was pulled back in a small ass ponytail. There were black moles on either side of her face and at the back of her neck. She had a slight mustache and a caramel complexion. As

of now, she was wearing a big T-shirt with Winnie the Pooh on it, black sweatpants and house slippers which showed off her hard, ashy heels.

"Momma, I need you to watch the kids 'til I-" Scrappy began but her mother cut her off, rudely.

Ruth held up her meaty hand which stopped whatever Scrappy had to say to her right then. She took a healthy pull from her square and blew out another cloud of smoke. She then dropped what was left of her cigarette on the porch and mashed it out under her house slipper, leaving black ashes and embers on the surface. Afterwards, she looked up at her daughter and said, "Scrap, I'm not watchin' a damn thang 'til you kick in the money you already owe me for watchin' 'nem babies, so fork it over." She stuck out her hand and flexed her fingers.

"Momma, I ain't gotta dolla to my name right now. I'm not gon' have no money for a couple of days. I just need you to watch 'em for..."

"Unh unh," she shook her head. "Scrappy, you always late with my money for watchin' these kids. Now, I love 'em to death, but I love the roof over my head, the lights in my house and the A.C that keeps my big ass cool in this summa time heat. And do you know what I need to keep these here necessities and luxuries of mine? Money. I'm talkin' cold, hard, cash." she smacked the back of her hand into her palm for emphasis. She then placed her hand on the doorknob and said, "I need my money, Scrappy. Not tomorrow, or even the next day. I need all of mine right this minute. Now, do you have it?"

"No. But I can give it to you next-"

Scrappy was cut short as Ruth slammed the front door shut and locked it behind her.

"Ol' fat, flabby sloppy body, bitch," a scowling Scrappy said underneath her breath as she grabbed her daughter's hand and headed back down the steps, T.J. in tow. She was as hot as fish grease at her mother. When she first asked her to watch the kids when they got out of school so she could attend her cosmetology class (a class she missed that day to attend Savon's execution), she was surprised when she told her she'd have to pay her. You see, Scrappy's mother was too busy partying and

chasing men to take care of her when she was growing up. She gave her grandmother full custody of her so she could run the streets and do God only knew what. Scrappy felt like since her grandmother raised her that the least her mother could do was watch her kids seeing that she was trying to take her ass to school.

"Where are we going now, mommy?" Kesha asked her mother.

"We're gonna stop by the house for a second, baby." Scrappy informed her daughter.

Scrappy went home to get ready for the night's mission. She threw on a hoodie, gloves, black sunglasses and grabbed an orange bandana. She was going to fly her neighborhoods colors that night when she put in work. She knew Tiaz would be looking down at her and this would make him proud. Before she left out of the house, she kissed her fingers and touched them to the wallet size photo of her and Tiaz at prom which was situated at the corner of the nightstand's mirror. She then tapped her fist to her chest and headed into the living room of her house.

When Scrappy walked into the living room, she found T.J. and Kesha lounging on the couch watching cartoons. The illumination from the TV's screen shined on their young faces.

"Y'all come on, let's go." Scrappy told her children.

"Where are we going now?" T.J. sat up on the couch.

"I got some business I needa handle. Once I'm done, y'all can come back and watch all the cartoons you want." she told her children.

"Onna school night, ma?" he inquired.

"Yep, on a school night. You got my word, baby boy. Long as y'all promise mommy y'all gon' get up in the mornin'. We gotta deal?" she looked between the twins, anxiously awaiting their replies. They looked at each other smiling and nodding before they focused back on her. "Well, what do ya say?"

"You gotta deal, momma." T.J. approached his mother with his hand extended, to seal the deal with a handshake. Scrappy smiled as she shook her son's hand and then her daughter's hand. "Alright, now, let's go so momma can handle her business."

T.J. and Kesha grabbed their jackets and slipped them on, zipping them up and throwing on their hoods. They then followed their mother out of the house, pulling the front door shut behind them.

***

Scrappy sat slumped in the driver's seat as she watched Chevy and Faison's house. All of the lights were on so she was waiting until they went out before she hit their spot. As soon as the lights in the house were out, Scrappy slipped the black sunglasses onto her face and pulled her orange bandana over the lower half of her face. She then pulled her hood over her head and pulled its drawstrings, enclosing it around her head. Afterwards, she picked her shotgun up from the floor and racked it.

Scrappy looked into the backseat at T.J. and Kesha. They looked afraid and confused. "Y'all scoot down into the seat, momma will be right back." she kissed both children on their forehead. She went to hop out but Kesha grabbed her arm, halting her. "What's the matter, baby girl?" Scrappy saw the sadness in her daughter's eyes.

"I don't want chu to go, mommy. Can we just go home, please?" Kesha begged her mother, with tears threatening to spill down her cheeks.

"Yeah, momma, let's just go home." T.J. pleaded with his mother.

"We can't go yet. I have to set things right with these people, they're the ones that killed yo' daddy. They are the reason that you and yo' brother don't have a daddy anymore." Scrappy looked between her children. "They took 'em away from you, and I can't let 'em get away with it. You're daddy would turn over in his grave if he knew I did. You hear me?"

Scrappy used to fuck with Te'Qui back in the day. They were never together but they fooled around when neither of them were in a relationship. Scrappy winded up getting pregnant with the twins. She was going to get an abortion but Te'Qui talked her into keeping them. Through his life of crime he was able to afford to take care of her and his children. They made an agreement to co-parent without the baby momma/ baby daddy drama. Tiaz was a great father and Scrappy's best friend. So when she found out that he had been murdered while he was incarcerated she vowed to get revenge in his honor.

T.J. nodded and hugged his mother around her neck. Scrappy hugged her son with one arm and kissed him on the side of the head. She then focused her attention back on Kesha who had broken down crying. She pulled the little girl into her bosom, hugging her and her brother. She kissed them both on top of the heads. Once she broke their embrace, she looked them in their eyes.

"Now, y'all look," Scrappy started up again. "I'ma do what I gotta do in here and then we gon' leave. It won't take me long. And once I'm finish, we can order pizza. How about that?" she awaited her childrens' answers.

"Ma, can I get pepperoni and sausage on mine?" T.J. asked her, excitedly.

"Yes, baby boy. And how 'bout some ice cream to go with it?"

"Long as it's chocolate chip, count me in." he smiled.

"You got it, lil' man," Scrappy smiled behind her bandana and dapped up her son. She then ruffled his head playfully and looked to Kesha. "How about chu, lil' momma? What kinda pizza would you like?"

Kesha wiped her dripping eyes with the back of her fists, sniffling. She then looked up at her mother with a shiny wet face, saying, "Cheese-I'd like a cheese pizza, mommy. And Rainbow Sherbert ice cream."

"How many scoops, baby girl?" she held her chin up with her curled finger, as she looked into her saddened eyes.

"Two." Kesha held up two fingers.

"Two scoops it is." Scrappy assured her. She then hugged and kissed her kids. Next, she looked herself over in the rearview mirror to make sure she couldn't be identified under her disguise. Once she came to the conclusion that no one would be able to identify her, she grabbed her shotgun and hopped out of the car. She shut the driver's door quietly and held the shotgun low, like it was a hockey stick. Keeping her weapon low, she

looked back and forth over her shoulder to make sure there wasn't any nosy mothafuckaz out that could witness her handle her business.

Once Scrappy saw that the coast was clear, she entered Chevy's yard and hunched down. She made her way alongside the house until she entered the backyard. Once she made it upon the door of the back porch, she picked the lock and made her way inside as quietly as possible. The house was dark except for the light that the stove provided above. Still holding the shotgun low, she made her way past the stove, passing the living room and entering the hallway. Scrappy heard shower water running, so she pushed the bathroom door opened quietly. When she did, she met the heat from the steam of the shower and saw a woman's silhouette behind the shower curtain, as she washed up.

Scrappy pulled her bandana down from the lower half of her face so that Chevy could see exactly who it was giving her the business. She then crept over to the tub and snatched the shower curtain back. A startled Chevy whipped around. Her hair was slicked back and her naked body was shiny with wetness. Her eyes nearly leaped out of her head and her mouth hung open, seeing the woman she'd threw hands with at Savon's execution.

Scrappy's face balled up with animosity. Lifting her shotgun, she took a step back from the bathtub and said, "Remember me, bitch? This is for Tiaz!"

Bloom!

The first blast smacked Chevy up against the tiled wall, splattering her blood against it. The back of her head and body deflected off the wall, but a second blast forced her back up against it. She slid down in the tub dead, leaving a bloody smear behind her on the wall. The hot shower water continued to run, washing off some of the blood smeared on the wall.

Scrappy observed her handiwork for a moment before coming out of the bathroom. As she was stepping out into the hallway, the door of the master bedroom was opening and Faison was coming out with a fat ass .357 Magnum revolver. Once he saw Scrappy with the shotgun, he knew what time it was so he tried to blow her head off.

Blam! Blam! Blam!

Scrappy pulled her head back inside of the bathroom, narrowly missing getting her head knocked off. She stuck her shotgun out of the doorway and around the corner, blasting. A lucky shot caught Faizon in the chest. His eyes became as big as golf balls and his mouth open. He looked down and saw blood pouring out of his chest. Once he croaked in pain, Scrappy knew she'd gotten him.

With Faison at her mercy, Scrappy decided that now was the best time to capitalize off of the situation. She racked her shotgun and swung out into the hallway, pulling the trigger. The report from the powerful weapon was loud and dangerous.

"Aaaah!" Faison hollered out in agony, feeling fire rip through his chest again as he was propelled backwards. He fell against the side of the doorway and fired his revlver at Scrappy, missing her. Sliding down to the carpeted floor, Faison fired off one more shot before dropping the hand holding the .357 beside him. His head fell back against the doorway. His eyes were stretched wide open and his jaw was slack. He was dead.

Scrappy approached Faison cautiously and placed two fingers to his neck, checking his pulse. As soon as she confirmed that he was dead, she heard the other bedroom door creak open. Swiftly, Scrappy turned around ready to send some hot shit through a nigga'z chest. She lowered her shotgun once she saw a young Te'Qui standing in the other bedroom's doorway. She felt sorry for him when his eyes landed on his slain father. She could see the heartbreak and tears building in his eyes. Instantly, the grief written across his face changed to one of bitterness and hatred. His nose scrunched up and he balled his hands into fists. Acknowledging the hostility in his face, Scrappy braced the stock of the shotgun against her shoulder and aimed the weapon's barrel at the youth's chest. Her mind played tricks on her as she hesitated to pull the trigger, seeing Te'Qui morph back and forth between her children.

Realizing that she couldn't bring herself to take the life of a child, Scrappy lowered her shotgun at her side and pulled the bandana up over the lower half of her face. She then rushed into the living room, through the kitchen and out of the back door.

She jumped down into the lawn of the backyard and ran along the side of the house. Having cleared the yard, she ran across the street towards her car. Reaching the curb, she deposited the shotgun inside of the gutter and reached for the door handle of her vehicle.

Blam!

Scrappy's chest exploded and her blood splattered against the driver's window. T.J. and Kesha's eyes grew big and their mouths formed O's. They couldn't believe their innocent eyes. Their mother had been popped in front of them. They observed their mother whip around to where the shot had come from, only to get popped in the chest two more times. Her blood dotted the side of her car and she dropped to the sidewalk. As soon as she did, she revealed Te'Qui standing behind her. His eyebrows were slanted and he was biting down on his bottom lip. His father's .357 Magnum revolver was pointed at Scrappy's car, as its barrel wafted with smoke.

Te'Qui lowered the .357 and stood beside Scrappy, looking down at her. Horror was etched across her face as she stared up at him, accusingly. She tried to say something to him, but she only managed to choke and gag on her own blood.

"Mommyyyyyy!" Kesha called out to her mother. She and T.J. jumped out of the car and rushed to Scrappy's side. They stood on either side of her and held her bloody hands. Scrappy smiled weakly for them, but she ended up coughing up blood. T.J. and Kesha's faces were slicked wet from crying. They'd lost their father, and now they were losing their mother. "Mommy, please dont die, please don't leave us. We love you."

"You can't die, momma. We love you so much. What would we do without you?" T.J. asked as he used his blood stained hand to wipe away his dripping tears. He sniffled and more tears seemed to flood his cheeks.

"It's-it's okay, mommy's babies, I'm going on to a better place," Scrappy claimed. "I'm going to heaven."

"Is that the same place that daddy went to?" Kesha asked innocently. When Tiaz was murdered in jail, Scrappy had told her and her brother that he died and went to heaven. That

heaven was a beautiful place. And only the specialist of people went there.

"Y-yes, baby. That's-that's-," Scrappy winced as she coughed up more blood. "That's where daddy is, and I'm going to be with 'em. And if you're-you're good down here, then-then you and your brother can come there with us, too."

By this time, T.J. and Kesha were sobbing hard, scared to death that they were going to lose their mother.

Twelve's sirens filled the air, but Te'Qui hadn't budged. He stood there holding his banga and watching Scrappy spend her last moments with her children.

"You promise, mommy?" Kesha asked her mother.

Scrappy placed her bloody hand against the side of her daughter's face and smiled weakly. "Yes, baby girl, I promise."

"I don't want chu to die, momma. I want chu to live forever and ever. Please, don't go." T.J. whimpered. His mother looked to him and rubbed the side of her face, leaving a bloody hand impression behind. She smiled at him as well.

"I'm sorry, baby boy..." Scrappy eyes rolled to their whites and her head dropped to the pavement. She expelled her last breath through her wide open mouth and her body went still.

"Momma? Momma?" T.J. shook his mother harder and harder, trying to get her to respond but it was already too late. She was gone.

"Mommy, wake up! Wake up, please!" Kesha shook her mother alongside her brother, but she wasn't moving.

At this time, Twelve was pulling up back to back. The red and blue flashing lights of their vehicles illuminated Te'Qui, T.J. and Kesha. The doors of the police cars popped open and the cops hopped out, drawing their guns on Te'Qui. They ordered him to throw down his revolver and he obliged. Afterwards, one of the cops moved in to handcuff him. Te'Qui was placed into the back of one of the police cars. He watched as the coroners came and took Scrappy's body away. He looked to her children and found T.J. mad dogging him, tears streaming down his cheeks. His eyebrows were arched and his nostrils were flaring.

"I'm gonna kill you, you hear me? Huh, do you fucking hear me? You're dead! You're fucking dead!" T.J. hollered out to

Te'Qui. He tried to run over to him but the cops restrained him. "Limme go, limme the fuck go, you bastards!" he struggled to break free from the police officers' arms, but their hold was like steel. Eventually, T.J. got tired of trying to fight the cops off and went limp in their arms. He broke down sobbing and crying, teardrops splashing on the street.

"It's going to be okay, son. It's going to be okay." One of the police officers assured him.

"So, this is what this is all about, huh? Some get-back for me poppin' yo' moms when the bitch peeled my momma and my daddy? Nigga, fuck you and her! I'll spit on that hoe's grave!" Te'Qui spat at T.J.'s feet, still holding his wound. His entire hand was bloody now. He was sweating profusely and had turned pale.

T.J. looked at him smiling devilishly, resembling Satan. "I feel you, now feel this!" He pointed his gun at Te'Qui's forehead as he mad dogged him, waiting for his fate to be sealed.

Choot!

T.J.'s eyes bulged and his mouth dropped open. A surprised look spread across his face, and he slowly turned around. He was shocked to see Kesha standing behind him holding the sniper's rifle which was wafting with smoke, having been fired.

"I'm sorry, T.J., but I can't let you kill 'em. I love 'em." Kesha said apologetically as tears cascaded down her face. Her brother scowled at her and went to shoot her, but she shot him again. The bullet slammed into him, lifting him off his feet. He crashed to the floor and his gun went up into the air, dropping to the surface.

Kesha lowered the sniper's rifle and pulled Te'Qui upon his feet.

"Uhhh!" Te'Qui winced from his wound. Holding his gut, he walked over to T.J. He took the keys to his car out of his pocket and put it in his pocket. He then took the gun off of T.J.'s waistline and picked up the one he'd dropped. When he stood up from picking up the gun, he looked down at his deceased homeboy's face. T.J.'s eyes were bugged and his mouth was ajar. He was clearly dead from the expression on his face.

Kesha broke down weeping having looked down at T.J.'s face. Her shoulders rocked and she bowed her head, big teardrops fell from her eyes and splashed on the floor. Te'Qui limped over to her and threw one of his arms over her shoulders, consoling her as best as he could. He kissed the top of her head and rubbed her back soothingly.

"Come on, ma, let's get outta here." Te'Qui told her.

Still weeping, Kesha looked up into Te'Qui's eyes, tears constantly spilling down her cheeks. "I'm sorry, bae. I never meant to hurt chu, I…"

"Shhhhh. Right now isn't the time; we gotta get that money and get outta here."

"Okay." she nodded.

"Come on." he nudged her towards the kitchen with one of his guns.

Te'Qui and Kesha made their way into the kitchen. He hoisted a duffle bag over his shoulder and she hoisted one over her shoulder. As soon as they turned around, they found a deranged T.J. charging at them. He had a large splinter in his hand, and it was cocked back in a stabbing motion.

"I'm gonna kill you, you fucking whore!" T.J. screamed at the top of his lungs.

Te'Qui stepped in front of Kesha and pointed both of his guns at him. He popped his toys off back to back.

Blocka! Blocka! Blocka! Bloc! Bloc! Bloc! Blocka! Blocka! Bloc! Bloc!

T.J. dropped his splinter to the floor as he was hit with a barrage of bullets. His head bobbed and he danced on his feet, moving backwards. He took one last step back and went flying through an enormous hole in the floor of the living room.

"Aaaaaah!" T.J. hollered out in freefall. "Uhhh!"

Te'Qui and Kesha walked over to the enormous hole in the floor. They peeked over into it and saw T.J. impaled on some rusty pipes sticking from out of the floor. His eyes were as big as golf balls and blood was pouring out of his mouth. Holding on to the rusted pipes sticking from out of his torso, he looked down at them. His head then fell back and his arms and legs stiffened. He was without a shadow of a doubt dead.

Te'Qui, still looking down at T.J., took a deep breath. He then tucked his bangaz into the front of his Dickies and grabbed Kesha by her hand, leading her out of the decrepit house.

Te'Qui and Kesha walked down the short flight of steps of the back porch. Te'Qui popped the trunk and they dumped their duffle bags inside of the trunk, slamming it shut afterwards. They went to climb inside of the vehicle, but a sharp whistle at their rear drew their attention. They looked and found Big Will with a long ass, black shotgun.

"Fuck you think you going, lil' nigga?" Big Will asked, with hatred plastered on his face.

Instantly, Te'Qui stepped in front of Kesha and pulled out his bangaz again. When he heard someone jump down behind him. He glanced over his shoulder. He found Enzo standing to his feet after having climbed over the fence. He was clutching a shotgun too, except his was long and chrome.

"Yeah, fuck you think yo' young ass going?" Enzo said off of Big Will.

"What's y'all beef, Blood?" Te'Qui asked Big Will. He figured that Enzo must have figured out that he was the one trying to rob him that night at Club Vicious, but he didn't know how he found out.

"Yo' bitch-ass tried to rob me. And don't try to deny it either 'cause yo' lil' fat-ass homeboy dimed you out." Enzo mad dogged him.

Once Enzo had finished speaking, Big Will spoke up. "You killed unc, Blood. You killed Drama. That's family. And nobody touches my mothafuckin' family."

"I didn't touch Drama, but I can't say I hadn't planned too. I suppose T.J., my fat-ass homeboy, told you otherwise though. Am I right?"

Big Will mad dogged Te'Qui hard as fuck, but he didn't say anything though. A single tear slid down his cheek and his nostrils flared. That was enough to let Te'Qui that the answer to his question was yes.

"Well, I can already see there ain't no way I can talk my way outta this shit. We gon' have to get it poppin', am I right?"

Te'Qui looked back and forth between Big Will and Enzo, to see what they'd have to say.

"You mothafucking right," Enzo assured him.

"Cool. Big Will, you already know a young nigga with the shits."

"Gotsa to tip my hat to ya, I do respect yo' gangsta." Big Will conceded with a nod.

"As I do yours," Te'Qui replied. "Check this out, my girl's preggo, let her walk. Y'all let my boo walk and we can get into some gangsta shit."

"She can bounce." Big Will said, stepping aside so Kesha could walk past him.

Chick-chick!

Enzo racked his shotgun and pointed it at Kesha, saying, "Nah, fuck that! The bitch stays put! She rides wit 'em so she can die wit 'em. Fuck 'em both!" keeping his eyes on the couple, Enzo spat on the ground.

"I wasn't going no where no way, bitch-ass nigga!" Kesha mad dogged Enzo, standing back to back with Te'Qui. "Like you said, I ride for my man," she pointed her sniper rifle at Enzo. "We can get it poppin' right here and right now."

"Bae, fuck are you doin'? I can probably get Big Will to let chu walk." Te'Qui said to her in a hushed tone, wincing. His eyes were on Big Will, but he was speaking to Kesha.

"Fuck these niggaz, bae. If it go down, then it go down." she spoke fearlessly. "At least this way, if we die, you and the baby and I will all be together in heaven." Uneven tears rolled down Kesha's cheeks and she took one hand off her rifle to wipe them away.

"I love you, ma." Te'Qui told her.

"I love you even more." Kesha proclaimed.

"Shall we?" Big Will asked of the showdown.

"Yes, we shall." Te'Qui replied.

And with the question having been answered, an ghetto orchestra played.

Bloom! Bloom! Bloom! Blocka! Blocka! Blocka! Bloc! Bloc! Choot! Choot! Choot! Blocka! Bloc! Bloc! Choot! Choot! Bloc!

A cloud of gunsmoke loomed in the air. Seconds later, bodies hit the dirt, leaving Te'Qui and Kesha standing victorious.

Kesha looked ahead to find Enzo lying on the ground, still gripping his shotgun, dead. She looked down at her duffle bag and it had thirty small holes from shotgun pellets. The rounds from Enzo's powerful weapon struck the duffle bag, shielding her. To be sure she hadn't been hit; Kesha patted herself down for wounds, discovering that she was okay.

"I'm okay, I'm okay." Kesha said surprised. She had been sure she was going to end up shot or dead. "Bae, I got 'em, I got his ass." she turned to Te'Qui. He was still on his feet, but Big Will was lying on his back, dead. His shotgun was lying above his head on the ground.

"I got Big Will, too." Te'Qui said with pain in his voice. When Kesha grabbed his arm, she saw his blood pelting the dirt.

"Oh, my God, you're bleeding!" Kesha said in a panic.

"Awww, fuck, nigga, shot me," he groaned and touched the side of his face, fingers coming away bloody. He dropped to the dirt on his knees and fell on his side, ending up on his back.

Te'Qui lay on the ground with a bloody face and torso. The side of his face was singed and there were several small holes in it from buckshots.

"That mothafucka shot me, baby." he lifted his head from off the ground and looked down at his body. At this time, Kesha was lifting up his shirt to examine his wounds. His torso was singed, bloody and had small holes in it from the buckshots. "Awww, shit, Keesh, this is it! This is it for me, ma! I'm done, I'm done."

"No, no, no, don't say that! You're not gonna die, you're not gonna die!" Kesha cupped Te'Qui's face and looked into his eye. He was blinking his eyelids, struggling to keep his eyes open. His bloody hands held her wrists as he tried to meet her gaze. "Look at me; you look at me, gotdammit! You're not gonna die! Repeat after me, I'm not gonna die! Say it, I'm not gonna die!"

"I'm not-I'm not gonna..." Te'Qui's eyes rolled around and she smacked him to gain his attention. His eyes looked to her, struggling to hold her gaze. "I'm not gonna die-I'm not gonna die."

"Yes, yes, yes, baby. That's it, that's it." Kesha looked up at the sky, hearing Twelve's sirens filling the air. She knew that the law would be there soon and she didn't want to be anywhere in the area with all of those dead bodies lying around.

Kesha fished through Te'Qui's pockets and got out the car's keys. She ran over to the car and unlocked the door, pulling the backdoor open. She then ran over to Te'Qui, grabbing him under his arms and pulling him towards the vehicle. He was pretty much dead weight so she was struggling as she dragged him. On top of that, beads of sweat had formed on her forehead and ran down her face. It took some effort, but she managed to get him into the backseat. Once she slammed the door shut, she jumped in behind the wheel and backed out. Next, she shifted the car into drive and floored it. The car crashed through the double gates, and made a right into the alley.

Kesha ripped down the trashy ass alleyway, looking back and forth between the windshield and Te'Qui. His bloody hands were lying on his waistline and he was staring up at the ceiling, eyes hooded. Seeing him like that scared the shit out of Kesha. To her, he looked like he was dead, lying face up inside of a coffin.

"Come on. Come on, baby. You gotta stay with me now. Stay with me," Kesha, still looking back and forth between her lover and the windshield, grabbed Te'Qui's hand. She held it firmly, as she drove through the alley. Looking ahead, she saw several police cars race past her line of vision, red and blue lights flashing.

"Bury me..." Te'Qui said just above a whisper, loosening his grip on Kesha's hand.

"Hold on, baby. I'm finna bust a turn from outta here," Kesha told him. Reaching the end of the alley, she made a left turn and sped down the block. She glanced into her rearview mirror and saw the rear ends and flashing lights of the police cars that had passed her when she was speeding down the alley. "Okay, baby. Now, what were you saying?" she glanced into the backseat at him; his eyelids were nearly shut.

"Bury me-bury me a," he spoke in a whisper this time, sounding very weak.

"No, no, no. I will not bury you! You can't die, bae! You cannot leave me and your child in this world alone." she cried, fresh tears coating her cheeks. "You hear me? You cannot do this to me, to us."

"When I die...make sure you bury me a g. Bury me a g, bury me a mothafuckin'g."

The only things that could be heard then were the blaring police sirens and Kesha's sobs.

"Te'Quiii, Te'Quiiii, Te'Quiiiii, wake up, baby! Please, wake up! Te'Quiiiii!" Kesha's bone chilling screams ripped through the air.

Staring up at the ceiling of the car, Te'Qui was confronted by a big bright florescent light. The ray of light was so strong it could blind your average man, but Te'Qui was staring into it without so much as batting an eye. He saw himself running towards his loved one, Chevy, Faison, Baby Wicked, etc. They were all standing in a gorgeous green, grassy field with beautiful blooming daisies surrounding them. The flowers and grass moved having been disturbed by the cool occasional breeze of the warm weather. The sun was shining at his loved ones back as well. They were all wearing smiles across their faces. They looked happy too; far happier than they did when they were alive.

Seeing his loved ones receding before his eyes, and the brightness of the sun growing brighter and brighter, Te'Qui started running harder and faster. In fact, he was running so hard that he could hear his heart pounding in his ears and his husky breathing. Worry stretched across his face and water pooled in his eyes. He feared this would be his last time to reunite with his family and friends. That if he didn't take advantage of this opportunity that he'd never see them again, ever. That thought terrified him.

"Haa! Haa! Haa! Haa! Haa! Haa! Haa!" Te'Qui huffed and puffed as he ran, tears sliding down his cheeks as he desperately tried to touch his relatives with his outstretched hand. "Wait, wait, don't leave me! I need you! All of you!"

Te'Qui's loved ones grew smaller and smaller, and the sun grew even brighter. It wasn't long before his relatives and loved ones disappeared before his eyes and the sun over shadowed him. Te'Qui stopped running and looked up at the sun. He placed his hand above his eyebrows and stared up at the sun, looking through narrowed eyelids.

"Noooooo! Nooooo! I don't wanna go yet! I don't wanna..." Te'Qui screamed and screamed, which caused veins to bulge at his temples and neck. He wailed long and loud, tears continuously sliding down his cheeks and dripping off of his chin. "Noooooooooo! Noooooooooo!"

The blinding rays of the sun eventually swallowed up Te'Qui as he screamed at the top of his lungs. Shorty thereafter, the sun gradually receded and the wails of a baby flooded the hospital room.

"Waa! Waa! Waa! Waa! Waa! Waa!" a bloody, slimy baby hollered and hollered as he was pulled from between Kesha's chubby legs. The doctor holding him with his latex gloved hands, turned around to Te'Qui, who was standing off to the side. He was dressed up just like the doctor was. He had on what looked like a bonnet, surgical mask, apron and gloves. He nipped the umbilical cord and handed the scissors to one of the nurses. He then walked over to the sink with the doctor holding his son, where he washed him off. While he was busy doing this, Kesha was being cleaned. Once the baby had been washed and rinsed, he was dressed in a red beanie with Outlaws in black stitching. He was then wrapped up firmly in a blanket and placed into Te'Qui's arms. The young gangsta looked down into his son's face, smiling. It was nine months later, and he had survived his gunshots wounds. The side of his face was scarred badly from the hot pellets of Big Will's shotgun and his stomach had also been marred. Still, by the grace of God, he was alive and well.

"Hey, lil' man, how you doin', huh? How you doin'?" Te'Qui asked as he tickled his son's chin. The little guy had the perfect combinations of his parents' features. He wasn't anything short of beautiful.

Te'Qui passed the baby to Kesha. She stared down at her bundle of joy, smiling. She was sweaty and her hair was matted on her face.

"Hey, baby boy, happy birthday. Happy birthday…" A crease formed on her forehead and she looked up at Te'Qui. She realized that they hadn't come up with a name for their new born son yet.

Te'Qui held Kesha's gaze as he thought of a name for their son. Once a name came to mind, a smirk formed at the corner of his lips before he replied. "We'll name 'em Brice. That was Baby Wicked's government name."

Kesha smiled and said, "Brice. I like that name. Brice it is." She kissed baby Brice and brushed her nose up against his, lovingly. Te'Qui put his arm around Kesha and kissed his son's forehead. He then kissed Kesha.

And they went on to live happily ever after.

To Be Continued…
Bury Me a G 5
Coming Soon

Submission Guideline

Submit the first three chapters of your completed manuscript to ldpsubmissions@gmail.com, subject line: Your book's title. The manuscript must be in a .doc file and sent as an attachment. Document should be in Times New Roman, double spaced and in size 12 font. Also, provide your synopsis and full contact information. If sending multiple submissions, they must each be in a separate email.

Have a story but no way to send it electronically? You can still submit to LDP/Ca$h Presents. Send in the first three chapters, written or typed, of your completed manuscript to:

LDP: Submissions Dept
Po Box 870494
Mesquite, Tx 75187

DO NOT send original manuscript. Must be a duplicate.

Provide your synopsis and a cover letter containing your full contact information.

Thanks for considering LDP and Ca$h Presents.

<u>Coming Soon from Lock Down Publications/Ca$h Presents</u>

BOW DOWN TO MY GANGSTA

By **Ca$h**

TORN BETWEEN TWO

By **Coffee**

BLOOD STAINS OF A SHOTTA **III**

By **Jamaica**

STEADY MOBBIN **III**

By **Marcellus Allen**

BLOOD OF A BOSS **V**

By **Askari**

LOYAL TO THE GAME **IV**

LIFE OF SIN II

By **T.J. & Jelissa**

A DOPEBOY'S PRAYER **II**

By **Eddie "Wolf" Lee**

IF LOVING YOU IS WRONG… **III**

LOVE ME EVEN WHEN IT HURTS **II**

By **Jelissa**

TRUE SAVAGE **VII**

By **Chris Green**

BLAST FOR ME **III**

A BRONX TALE III

DUFFLE BAG CARTEL

By **Ghost**

ADDICTIED TO THE DRAMA **III**

By **Jamila Mathis**

Tranay Adams

LIPSTICK KILLAH **III**

WHAT BAD BITCHES DO **III**

KILL ZONE **II**

By **Aryanna**

THE COST OF LOYALTY **II**

By **Kweli**

SHE FELL IN LOVE WITH A REAL ONE **II**

By **Tamara Butler**

RENEGADE BOYS **III**

By **Meesha**

CORRUPTED BY A GANGSTA **IV**

By **Destiny Skai**

A GANGSTER'S CODE **III**

By **J-Blunt**

KING OF NEW YORK IV

RISE TO POWER II

By **T.J. Edwards**

GORILLAS IN THE BAY II

De'Kari

THE STREETS ARE CALLING II

Duquie Wilson

KINGPIN KILLAZ III

Hood Rich

STEADY MOBBIN' **III**

Marcellus Allen

SINS OF A HUSTLA II

ASAD

TRIGGADALE II

Elijah R. Freeman

MARRIED TO A BOSS 2…

By Destiny Skai & Chris Green

KINGS OF THE GAME II

Playa Ray

<u>**Available Now**</u>

<u>RESTRAINING ORDER</u> **I & II**

By **CA$H & Coffee**

<u>LOVE KNOWS NO BOUNDARIES</u> **I II & III**

By **Coffee**

<u>RAISED AS A GOON I, II, III & IV</u>

<u>BRED BY THE SLUMS I, II, III</u>

<u>BLAST FOR ME I & II</u>

<u>ROTTEN TO THE CORE I III</u>

<u>A BRONX TALE I, II</u>

By **Ghost**

<u>LAY IT DOWN</u> **I & II**

<u>LAST OF A DYING BREED</u>

<u>BLOOD STAINS OF A SHOTTA I & II</u>

By **Jamaica**

<u>LOYAL TO THE GAME</u>

<u>LOYAL TO THE GAME II</u>

<u>LOYAL TO THE GAME III</u>

<u>LIFE OF SIN</u>

By **TJ & Jelissa**

<u>BLOODY COMMAS I & II</u>

Tranay Adams

SKI MASK CARTEL I II & III

KING OF NEW YORK I II,III

RISE TO POWER

By **T.J. Edwards**

IF LOVING HIM IS WRONG...I & II

LOVE ME EVEN WHEN IT HURTS

By **Jelissa**

WHEN THE STREETS CLAP BACK I & II III

By **Jibril Williams**

A DISTINGUISHED THUG STOLE MY HEART I II & III

LOVE SHOULDN'T HURT I II III

RENEGADE BOYS I & II

By **Meesha**

A GANGSTER'S CODE I & II

By **J-Blunt**

PUSH IT TO THE LIMIT

By **Bre' Hayes**

BLOOD OF A BOSS **I, II, III & IV**

By **Askari**

THE STREETS BLEED MURDER **I, II & III**

THE HEART OF A GANGSTA I II& III

By **Jerry Jackson**

CUM FOR ME

CUM FOR ME 2

CUM FOR ME 3

CUM FOR ME 4

An **LDP Erotica Collaboration**

Bury Me a G 4

BRIDE OF A HUSTLA **I II & II**
THE FETTI GIRLS **I, II& III**
CORRUPTED BY A GANGSTA I, II & III
By **Destiny Skai**
WHEN A GOOD GIRL GOES BAD
By **Adrienne**
A GANGSTER'S REVENGE **I II III & IV**
THE BOSS MAN'S DAUGHTERS
THE BOSS MAN'S DAUGHTERS II
THE BOSSMAN'S DAUGHTERS III
THE BOSSMAN'S DAUGHTERS IV
THE BOSS MAN'S DAUGHTERS **V**
A SAVAGE LOVE **I & II**
BAE BELONGS TO ME
A HUSTLER'S DECEIT I, II
WHAT BAD BITCHES DO I, II
By **Aryanna**
A KINGPIN'S AMBITON
A KINGPIN'S AMBITION **II**
I MURDER FOR THE DOUGH
By **Ambitious**
TRUE SAVAGE
TRUE SAVAGE II
TRUE SAVAGE **III**
TRUE SAVAGE **IV**
TRUE SAVAGE **V**
TRUE SAVAGE **VI**
By **Chris Green**

A DOPEBOY'S PRAYER

By **Eddie "Wolf" Lee**

THE KING CARTEL **I, II & III**

By **Frank Gresham**

THESE NIGGAS AIN'T LOYAL **I, II & III**

By **Nikki Tee**

GANGSTA SHYT **I II &III**

By **CATO**

THE ULTIMATE BETRAYAL

By **Phoenix**

BOSS'N UP **I , II & III**

By **Royal Nicole**

I LOVE YOU TO DEATH

By Destiny J

I RIDE FOR MY HITTA

I STILL RIDE FOR MY HITTA

By **Misty Holt**

LOVE & CHASIN' PAPER

By **Qay Crockett**

TO DIE IN VAIN

SINS OF A HUSTLA

By **ASAD**

BROOKLYN HUSTLAZ

By **Boogsy Morina**

BROOKLYN ON LOCK I & II

By **Sonovia**

GANGSTA CITY

By **Teddy Duke**

A DRUG KING AND HIS DIAMOND I & II III

A DOPEMAN'S RICHES

HER MAN, MINE'S TOO I, II

CASH MONEY HO'S

By Nicole Goosby

TRAPHOUSE KING **I II & III**

KINGPIN KILLAZ

By **Hood Rich**

LIPSTICK KILLAH **I, II**

CRIME OF PASSION I & II

By **Mimi**

STEADY MOBBN' **I, II**

By **Marcellus Allen**

WHO SHOT YA **I, II**

Renta

GORILLAZ IN THE BAY

DE'KARI

TRIGGADALE

Elijah R. Freeman

GOD BLESS THE TRAPPERS I, II, III

THESE SCANDALOUS STREETS I, II, III

FEAR MY GANGSTA I, II, III

THESE STREETS DON'T LOVE NOBODY I, II

BURY ME A G I, II, III, IV, V

Tranay Adams

THE STREETS ARE CALLING

Duquie Wilson

MARRIED TO A BOSS...

Tranay Adams

By Destiny Skai & Chris Green

KINGS OF THE GAME II

Playa Ray

BOOKS BY LDP'S CEO, CA$H

TRUST IN NO MAN

TRUST IN NO MAN 2

TRUST IN NO MAN 3

BONDED BY BLOOD

SHORTY GOT A THUG

THUGS CRY

THUGS CRY 2

THUGS CRY 3

TRUST NO BITCH

TRUST NO BITCH 2

TRUST NO BITCH 3

TIL MY CASKET DROPS

RESTRAINING ORDER

RESTRAINING ORDER 2

IN LOVE WITH A CONVICT

Coming Soon

BONDED BY BLOOD 2

BOW DOWN TO MY GANGSTA

Tranay Adams